Alluring Darkness

ALSO BY RAVEN WOOD

To see the most recently updated list of books by Raven Wood, please visit: www.authorravenwood.com

CONTENT WARNINGS

Alluring Darkness is a bully romance intended for mature readers. It contains violence and graphic sexual content. If you have specific triggers, you can find the full list of content warnings at: www.authorravenwood.com/content-warnings

ALLURING DARKNESS

RAVEN WOOD

ISBN 978-91-988025-4-2 (paperback)
ISBN 978-91-988025-3-5 (ebook)

Cover design by Krafigs Design

www.authorravenwood.com

For everyone who sees a completely unhinged book boyfriend who is practically a walking red flag, and thinks: "Ohh red is my favorite color!"

This one is for you.

1

RAINA

Apparently, I'm not emotionally stable enough to be an assassin. They say that I'm too short-tempered, lack restraint, and that I'm downright unhinged. Given that I poisoned my seventh-grade chemistry teacher for not recognizing my genius, I'm inclined to agree.

That was one of the times when I was glad that my father was a hitman. When I came home and proudly told them what I had done, he went back there and covered it up so that it just looked like a tragic accident instead. But after that, my parents decided that I was ill-suited to follow in my father's footsteps to attend Blackwater University and become a contract killer. So the burden of upholding our family's great legacy has fallen solely on my brother's shoulders.

And as I look down at his bruised and unconscious body, I can't decide whether I want to kill the person who did this to him or kill *him* for not telling me that he was in danger.

"I don't understand," my mother says, tearing her gaze from Connor and turning it to the nurse standing next to the bed.

"Mrs. Smith—" she begins.

"Do not *Mrs. Smith* me," Mom snaps. Her pale green eyes flash with anger as she stabs a hand towards where Connor is lying sedated. "How could this have happened? This is a school for *hitmen*! People whose entire skillset involves hurting others. Surely there must be rules preventing the students from murdering *each other* before their education here is done!"

An apologetic look drifts across the nurse's freckled face. "Well, yes, of course there are. But—"

"Then how come my son is lying here, looking like he was beaten within an inch of his life? We're lucky that nothing is broken! His whole future could have been destroyed. So what, in God's name, happened?"

"Well, he, uhm..." She clears her throat and glances around the rest of the university's hospital wing, as if she's afraid to be overheard. Then her worried brown eyes shift back to us. "According to witnesses, your son almost shot Eli Hunter during a training exercise."

My mom goes unnaturally pale. Narrowing my eyes, I frown at her since I don't understand what caused the reaction. But the nurse keeps speaking.

"So we suspect that this was payback for that," she finishes.

"Then why hasn't anyone done anything about it?" I ask, scowling at her.

Uncertainty swirls in her eyes, and she looks at me as if she doesn't even understand the question. "Because it's Eli Hunter."

"What does that even mean? Who the hell is Eli Hunter?"

Both the nurse and my mom whip their gazes around as if they're afraid that someone heard my outburst. Then Mom slides hard eyes to me and shakes her head.

"Raina," she says, her voice full of quiet admonishment. "Enough."

With great effort, I bite my tongue to stop my angry retort. Crossing my arms, I settle for a scowl instead.

Since my parents decided nine years ago that I shouldn't become an assassin, they have kept me firmly out of that world. I know that my father's side of the family has been hitmen for generations and that our family is one of the great ones, or we were before my dad died at least, but that's practically all I know about this bloody world of theirs.

"Is there any risk of… continued targeting?" Mom asks, shooting a pointed look towards Connor's battered body.

The nurse gives her a helpless look that I think was supposed to be sympathetic. "Unfortunately, yes. According to rumors, the Hunter brothers have been overheard saying that they will make your son's life a living hell this entire year."

Mom runs a hand over her face and then through her blond hair. "God help us." Desperation floods her features as she looks back at the nurse again. "This is his senior year. He needs to do well. *We* need him to do well, otherwise…"

She trails off.

Deciding that I've heard enough, I spin on my heel and stalk right out of the hospital wing.

"Raina!" Mom calls after me.

But I don't stop. And she doesn't go after me. She thinks that I'm being emotionally unstable again and that I'm storming out to throw an angry tantrum. Technically, I know that I *am* a bit unhinged. But sometimes I just wish that people would stop assuming that I never think anything through.

Even though I don't understand everything about this

world and this university, I understand enough to know what I need to do now.

Following the signs, I make my way out of the hospital wing and through the academy's administrative building until I reach the admission's office. Undecorated concrete walls stare me down as I pass through the corridors.

As opposed to other elite universities, this one wasn't built to be beautiful. It was built to be practical. Isolated on a stretch of flat grasslands, it's far enough away from the nearest town that no one will hear the gunshots that no doubt always echo from this sprawling complex of buildings. There is also a forest and a lake close by, which I assume are used for various training exercises. But I don't know for certain, since Connor's explanations of what exactly he studies here have always been very vague.

I push open the metal door that is labeled as the admission's office. It's a small space. Only one person is sitting behind a desk in front of me. A woman, who looks to be in her forties, with brown hair and blue eyes. Light shines in from the windows behind, painting her athletic body with sharp contrasts.

"Hello," she says. There is a slight frown on her face as she looks at me. "Can I help you?"

"Yes. I would like to enroll in Blackwater University."

A surprised laugh escapes her throat.

I just continue staring at her.

When she realizes that I'm dead serious, she clears her throat and then folds her hands on her desk before giving me a patient look. "I'm afraid that's impossible. The semester started three weeks ago, and you need to submit an application before that."

I reach into the bag slung over my shoulder. Her hand

immediately shoots down to something just underneath the desk. Surprise flickers through me when I realize that she most likely reached for a gun. Does she really think that I'm going to pull out a gun from my bag and shoot her because she denied my request? But then again, this is a school for hitmen, after all.

Holding her gaze with amused eyes, I pull out my wallet instead. She relaxes and returns her hand to the desk. While fishing out my ID, I close the distance between us and then place the card in front of her.

"I'm Harvey Smith's daughter," I announce. "I'm a legacy student, which means that you can't refuse me."

Surprise flashes across her face, and she raises her eyebrows while looking between me and the ID card. Then she gives me a slow nod. "One second while I verify that."

I shrug while she presumably opens some kind of file on her computer to check that the information from my ID matches whatever their registers say. The fact that I'm even physically present in this room right now already means that I've been vetted and cleared to walk through the front gates, but I suppose she has to check again anyway.

"Alright, everything seems to be in order," she says eventually. She gives me a little smile as she looks up from her computer and hands my card back. "I've registered you in the database now, and I will inform the instructors shortly, so you can start tomorrow."

"Great."

"As for the housing situation..." She grimaces apologetically. "Legacy students usually get first pick of the freestanding houses. However, since the semester has already started, all of those are already occupied. The best I can do is a dorm room."

"That's fine."

The clacking of her keyboard fills the silence as she does something else on her computer for another minute. I let my gaze drift towards the window where the parking lot is visible. It holds a mix of incredibly expensive cars and really shitty ones that look like they belong in a scrapyard. A testament to the fact that far from all aspiring hitmen come from money.

I'm snapped back to the present by the noise of a printer whirring. Sliding my gaze back to the woman before me, I watch as she takes the papers that came out of the printer and then puts a black keycard on top of the pile before handing it all to me.

"Alright, we're all set," she says while I take the bundle. "That's the keycard to your dorm and the various training areas. And I've also printed out your schedule and a map and any other information you might need."

"Thank you," I say as I stuff the papers and keycard into my bag. Then I flick another glance towards the window. "Which car belongs to Eli Hunter?"

She blinks at me, clearly stunned by my question. "Why?"

"I've heard that he's not very… forgiving. So I want to make sure that I don't park next to him and accidentally scratch his paint when I open my car door."

"Oh." Understanding floods her face. She pushes up from her desk and moves over to the window. "You see those four black Range Rovers over there?"

I walk up so that I'm standing next to her. Sweeping my gaze over the parking lot, I find the incredibly expensive-looking cars that she's pointing at. "Yes."

"Those belong to the Hunters. From left to right, they belong to Eli, Rico, Kaden, and Jace."

Since I'm all out of self-restraint for the day, I roll my eyes at the ridiculousness of it all. Of course all four of them drive fucking Range Rovers.

But instead of commenting on that, I thank the very helpful woman and make my way out of her office. I glance at my phone, but my mom still hasn't tried to call me, so I just slide it back into my bag and set course for the parking lot.

Warm September winds whirl between the gray concrete buildings and tug at my hair as I stride out of the door and across the pavement. Since it's only ten o'clock in the morning, the students are presumably all busy with their various classes. And that means that the parking lot is completely deserted.

I pull my keys out of my bag and twirl them in my hand as I stroll straight towards Eli's car. Bright sunlight shines down from the clear blue sky, making the light reflect against the gleaming black surface.

With a wicked grin on my lips, I stop on the driver's side of his spotless Range Rover and crouch down.

And then I use my keys to carve *Small Dick Energy* into the side of his car.

2

ELI

There's a mass of people standing around my car by the time my brothers and I reach the parking lot. I narrow my eyes in suspicion. There are lots of fancy cars here, and even though it is the latest model, it's not like my Range Rover is anything remarkable. Not to mention that there are three identical ones parked right next to it.

It sounds as though some of the people are laughing. Or maybe gasping. But it's hard to tell because of the strong winds that whoosh across the pavement.

On my left, Kaden and Jace are still arguing about who actually won the informal marksman competition they decided to have this afternoon. But on my right, Rico slides his dark eyes towards me.

"What's going on?" he asks, keeping his voice low.

"I'm not sure," I reply without taking my eyes off the crowd.

One of them turns around, and his eyes go wide as he spots us. His mouth moves. The others snap their gazes to us.

Then they all scatter like fucking cockroaches.

Now, Jace and Kaden at last notice that something is going on. They cease arguing to whip their heads around, looking at the people sprinting away.

"What the fuck?" Jace very eloquently declares.

Kaden looks to me. "Eli?"

Since I don't know what's going on either, I say nothing as we close the final distance to our cars. I study my car as I pass by the other three. It looks fine.

Then I round the back of it and come up on the driver's side.

I stop.

For a moment, I can't comprehend what I'm seeing.

My brothers come to a halt next to me as well, their eyes also locked on the doors before us.

I blink. Slowly.

Someone has keyed my car.

And not just keyed it. Someone has carved the words *Small Dick Energy* in massive letters across both the driver's side door and the back door.

Then Jace erupts into laughter, and reality comes rushing back to me. While he's doubled over, gasping for breath between waves of laughter, I whip my head around in search of the people who were standing around my car less than a minute ago.

My eyes land on the guy who was the first to spot us. He has just made it to his car and is frantically trying to get inside and start it. Rico and Kaden follow my gaze. I jerk my chin.

Both of them take off towards the car. I start towards it as well while Jace jerks his head up and straightens. Raking a hand through his dark brown curls, he blinks as if trying to figure out why we all left.

"Aw shit," he says. "Right."

He sprints past me right as the guy gets his car started. Panic pulses across the guy's whole face as he swerves his car out of the parking space. But he doesn't make it more than ten feet before Jace leaps into the way and slams his palms down on the hood of the car. It screeches to a halt before it can mow him down.

The guy reaches for the door handle, but before he can grab it, Rico yanks the door open. Terror washes over the guy's features, and he tries to scramble over to the passenger side, only to find Kaden pulling open the door and sliding into that seat. I stalk the final bit to the driver's side and stop next to Rico.

"It wasn't me," the guy blurts out, his terrified eyes darting between the four of us. "It wasn't me. I swear to God, it wasn't me."

I cock my head. "Really?"

"Yes. Yes. I swear it."

"Then who?"

He swallows. "I don't know. We all found it like that when we got here."

"Sounds very convenient," Jace calls from where he's still bracing his hands on the hood of the car. With a devilish grin on his face, he shoves down a couple of times, rocking the car. "Don't you think?"

"Want me to drag him out of there and break his knees?" Rico asks casually, as if inquiring whether I want a cup of coffee.

The guy jerks back and tries to scoot over to the other seat before he remembers that Kaden is currently occupying it. Kaden flashes him one of his signature psychopath smiles.

Raw desperation bleeds into the guy's voice as he begs, "Please. Please, I swear I didn't do this." A light flares up behind his eyes, and he presses out his next words so quickly that he almost trips over them. "You can check the security cameras! Then you'll see that it wasn't me."

Hope shines in his eyes now. I want to grind it underneath my heel until there is nothing left but fear, but the man has a point. If he had been stupid enough to actually do it, he wouldn't have told us to check the footage. And I really do want to know who is suicidal enough to do something as foolish as to key my car.

"Kaden," I begin.

Our captive stiffens.

I hold his gaze in silence for a few seconds before finishing with, "Check his driver's license."

Without question, Kaden reaches over the console and slides his hand into the guy's jacket pocket. He flinches but doesn't resist. Kaden fishes out a brown leather wallet and then flips it open and pulls out the driver's license. After memorizing the details on it, he gives me a nod and then tosses both the wallet and the card into the guy's lap.

"You'd better hope you're telling the truth," I announce. "Or we'll be paying you a little visit later."

"I am," he blurts out while scrambling to pick up his wallet and driver's license before they can fall to the floor. "I swear I am."

Without bothering to reply, I jerk my chin and start back towards the academy's administrative building with Rico next to me. Jace drums his hands on the hood of the car a few times while Kaden climbs out and throws the door shut behind him. Then they fall in on my other side.

The moment we're gone, the guy floors it and speeds out of the parking lot.

"Aw, I wish you would've let me beat him up," Jace

complains as we make our way towards where the people in charge of security have their offices.

"If he is the one who keyed my car, I'll let you do more than that," I promise him.

He throws his fist into the air in an excited gesture. "Yes!"

While we walk, I can feel Rico watching me from the corner of his eye. He always does that. Watches me. Trying to figure out if whatever thing that just happened is what finally sends me off the deep end. And I get it. I understand why he worries. But frankly, after what I went through when I was younger, it's ridiculous to think that someone keying my car is what will at last make my mind snap completely. Though to be fair, I know that what I went through is the reason why he worries. But still. I just wish he would stop feeling so guilty about it. None of it was his fault, after all.

The door to the security office vibrates as I pound my fist on the metal.

A moment later, it's opened by a man wearing a bulletproof vest over a tight black shirt. He gives the four of us a quick once-over before inclining his head in respect.

"What can I do for you?" he asks.

"We need to see the security footage from the parking lot," I reply.

He nods and then opens the door wider before motioning for us to step inside. We follow him to the screens that take up half of the wall. They show most parts of the academy. I flick my gaze over all the screens, reconfirming what our father told us about the blind spots before we even set foot on this campus.

"From when?" the guard asks as he pulls up a program on one of the computers.

"This afternoon," I reply.

It takes a couple of minutes for him to speed through the video until we find what we're looking for.

"Stop," I say once I see a lone figure crouch next to my car. "Go back."

He rewinds it and then plays it again. This time at normal speed.

A young woman who looks to be around our age walks out the doors and into the parking lot. She has straight black hair that falls down almost all the way to her waist, and bangs that cover her forehead. The camera is too far away to reveal much of her facial features, but the way she walks tells me more than her face probably could.

She doesn't sneak up to my car. She strolls. Fucking *strolls* up to it while casually twirling a set of keys in her hand. No fear. No hesitation. I stare in utter disbelief as she crouches down by my car and starts carving into it.

Next to me, Rico and Kaden are watching with raised eyebrows as well.

Jace, on the other hand, chuckles and throws an elbow into my ribs. "One of your fucks? Damn, bro, you must've really left her unsatisfied."

"No," I say.

No, I would most definitely remember fucking someone like this. Confusion swirls through my chest as I watch her straighten again once she's done. Based on how she looks next to my car, she's about average height for a woman. But that's not what caused the confusion inside me.

I narrow my eyes as I study her body.

She looks… soft. Sure, she has a rather slim body. But she also has thighs and hips and tits, which admittedly make her pretty hot, but she doesn't look nearly athletic enough to be a student here.

"Who is she?" I ask.

My brothers shrug.

By the desk, the security guard flips through some papers. "We got word from the admission's office that a new student would be starting. I think that's her, but I can't find her name right now."

A new student, huh? At least that would explain why she looks so soft and unathletic. But it sure as hell doesn't explain why she would stroll into the parking lot and carve *Small Dick Energy* into the side of my car her first day on campus.

"Alright," Kaden says with a shrug. "We'll just catch her before school tomorrow then."

I nod in confirmation, but I still can't take my eyes off the screen. With stunned disbelief still pulsing inside me, I watch as the girl flicks her long black hair back behind her shoulder and then saunters away.

But just before she disappears from view, she looks right up at the security camera.

And smiles.

I blink.

Who the hell is this girl?

3

RAINA

Only the faint murmur of nurses talking in another room disturbs the silence. Sitting on a chair next to Connor's bed, I watch the way his chest slowly rises and falls as he sleeps. Then I shift my gaze up to his bruised face.

He looks nothing like me. Dad passed on his straight black hair to both of us, but apart from that, no one would ever guess that we're siblings. Connor got Dad's gray eyes and unremarkable features. It's not an ugly face. Nor a beautiful one. It's completely bland. The kind of face that people forget the second it's gone. In other words, the perfect face for an assassin. Our grandfather had the same kind of features. And his father before him too. It's part of what made the Smith family such a legendary house of hitmen. At least before everything went to hell.

Tilting my head back, I stare up at the gray concrete ceiling and heave a deep sigh.

We used to be rich. And I mean *filthy* rich. We used to have wealth on par with what the Hunter family must have, who can apparently afford to buy four of the latest model Range Rovers for their sons without issue. I still remember the extravagant gifts that Dad would always bring home to Mom after he had completed some high-profile job or other.

But that fortune is gone now.

And so is Dad.

Because of one fucking mistake.

I don't know all the details, since at that point, my parents had been keeping me away from that world for years. But Mom told me that Dad had been hired by the Morelli mafia family to take out some politician. Apparently, Dad made some kind of mistake and everything went to hell. People died, including Dad. Money was lost. And it created one hell of a mess for the guy who had hired Dad for the job.

The next thing I knew, a man in an expensive black suit came to our house with a bunch of documents. I still remember the way Mom's hand trembled when she signed away almost our entire fortune to him as repayment for the damage caused. It settled the score with the Morelli family, but it left our family on the brink of ruin. Both financially and socially.

And since our parents had declared me too unhinged to become a good assassin, the entire burden of restoring Dad's legacy and our family name in the eyes of the underworld, as well as saving us from financial ruin, has fallen solely on Connor's shoulders.

Sadness and guilt twist my heart as I look at my brother's face again. He never speaks of it or shows it, but I know the immense pressure he's under right now. And I have never been able to do anything to help him. But that is about to change.

"Raina?"

I startle at the sound of Connor's voice. Shaking off the melancholy that had fallen over me, I blink and then flash my brother a smile. "What's up, Con?"

He huffs out a laugh, but it's quickly cut off as he winces and wraps a hand around his ribs. Pain stabs into my heart at the sight of it, but I keep it firmly off my features because I know that he would hate the pity.

"What are you doing here?" he asks once he has eased back onto the pillows again.

I frown at him as if that's the stupidest question ever. "I'm memorizing the color and pattern of your bruises so that I can paint it later. What else would I be doing?"

Another baffled laugh almost erupts from his chest, but he manages to stifle it this time. Shooting me a mock scowl, he says, "Stop trying to make me laugh when you know that my ribs are bruised, you sadist."

I just flash him a wicked grin.

Shaking his head, he huffs out an amused breath.

For a while, we just sit like that. In comfortable silence. Outside the door, two nurses walk past while discussing some other patient who, from the sounds of it, accidentally burned his eyebrows off during a chemistry class. I almost scoff at that. What kind of idiot doesn't know how to handle dangerous chemicals properly?

"What are you really doing here?" Connor asks at last, breaking the silence in our room.

"Checking on you." Seriousness descends over me as I hold his gaze while slowly shaking my head. "What the hell happened, Con?"

The fluffy white pillow lets out a huff as he drops his head back against it heavily while heaving a deep sigh. "I don't know."

"They told me you almost shot someone called Eli Hunter, and that he's really not the kind of guy you take a potshot at."

"I didn't!" The words tear out of him with surprising force, and anger flickers in his gray eyes. "I didn't aim for him. I swear, someone must have somehow sabotaged my rifle. I checked it before we went out on the exercise. But then there was like a five-minute window where we all had to listen to the instructors. Someone must have messed with it then."

Worry washes over me, and I frown. "Who?"

"I don't know. But I need to find out so that I can prove it to the Hunters. Otherwise, they're going to keep coming at me all year. And I can't graduate as one of the top three if I have those fucking psychos coming after me all the time."

Another wave of sorrow crashes over me. I can hear the strain in his voice. Can hear the panic and fear he feels when he thinks that he might not be able to graduate at the top and restore our family's honor.

As if he realizes that I noticed all that, he quickly wipes all traces of emotion from his face and instead gives me a reassuring smile. "Don't worry about me, Raina. I've got this covered. Just go home and focus on your own studies. The world needs more skilled chemistry teachers."

It's true that I'm a skilled chemist. The teacher part, on the other hand, I'm not so sure about. But my parents decided that it was the best career path for me, so I took their advice and applied to the chemistry teacher program at our local university. Apparently, teaching high school students bleeds the patience and emotional stability out of every teacher, so my parents figured that it would be the best place for me to blend in. No one would notice that I'm a bit crazy since all teachers lose their shit after a few years on the job.

"Sure," is all I reply since I have no plans on returning to that university. But Connor doesn't need to know that yet. "Just... be careful, Con."

"You too."

He doesn't promise that he will be careful. He never does. And neither do I. But neither of us comment on it, because we both know that any such promise would be a lie. He's training to become a hitman, and I'm, well... me.

After gently patting his arm, I stand up from the chair and make my way out of the hospital wing. As I follow the corridors and stairs away from the administrative building and towards the actual university part of the building complex, I can't help but feel a sense of dread.

I might be a shitty teacher, but I'm an even worse assassin. I'm not athletic. I can't run for miles or pull myself up using only my arm muscles. I don't know anything about how to blend into crowds or camouflage myself in different types of environments. My knowledge of knives only extends to chopping ingredients for food, and I've never even held a gun.

When I left my dorm to head to Connor's room, the entire university had been empty because it was so early in the morning. But now, a mass of students fills the hallways. And as I sweep my gaze over their faces, that awful sense of dread washes over me again.

I am so fucking out of my depth here.

I am going to fail every single class.

And I don't like failing. I don't like feeling clueless and stupid. But Connor has been shouldering our family's burden alone for far too long. Now, it's time for me to help him.

I can't restore our father's legacy. I can't be a top-rated

assassin. But I can make sure that Eli Hunter's wrath is solely focused on *me* so that Connor can finish his senior year without interference.

Straightening my spine, I draw in a bracing breath.

And then I walk into my first class.

4

ELI

People cast nervous glances at us as they pass us on the way to the doors, as if they're all trying to figure out if we're here for them or not. With our arms crossed, we stand side by side a few steps from the doors, watching the crowd that streams past and searching for the suicidal girl who keyed my car yesterday. No luck so far.

Morning sunlight slants across the horizon, turning the fields around us a pale orange and glinting in the windows of the cars in the parking lot. I slide my gaze to the three Range Rovers a short distance away. Mine is being fixed today, so I had to ride with Rico this morning.

Another wave of incredulity washes over me as I think back on what I saw on that footage yesterday. Our family is untouchable. We're one of the most feared families in this entire state. My father is a legendary hitman, as are all of my uncles. And we're connected, both financially and by blood, to the Morelli family. The one mafia family that almost everyone at this entire university dreams of landing a permanent contract with. No one messes with us.

Sure, there are some rival families who would love to take us down a peg or two so that they can rise to the top, but none of them have enough members on this campus to challenge us right now.

So who the hell is the absolute maniac who decided to carve *Small Dick Energy* into the side of my car?

"How did you sleep?"

I blink, yanked out of my thoughts by Rico's sudden question. Flicking my gaze around the area, I notice that the crowd has started to thin out, so no one is close enough to hear us.

I slide my gaze to Rico, and immediately wish that I hadn't. That usual hint of concern is present in his brown eyes. I want to snap at him that I'm fine, but I manage to restrain myself. His concern is justified, after all.

"As usual," I reply.

Which means, barely at all. For the past nine years, ever since it happened, I've barely slept. Jace often jokes that it's why I'm so volatile. The problem is that I think he might be partly right.

Rico hears the quiet dismissal in my tone, and thankfully drops the subject.

We stand there for another couple of minutes while some stragglers hurry from their cars and jog into the building to avoid being late. I scowl at the now empty parking lot. Still no sign of the girl.

"Maybe she finally realized whose car she keyed," Kaden says from next to me. He runs a hand over his jaw while sweeping his gaze over the parking lot. "And was too scared to show her face here now."

"Damn straight," Jace fills in, a devilish grin on his face.

"Maybe," I say, but there's no conviction in my voice.

There was something so incredibly deliberate about the way she did it. The way she just strolled up to my car without hesitation. The way she smiled at the security camera afterwards. I'm having serious trouble believing that she didn't know whose car it was.

Next to me, Kaden glances down at his watch. "If she was coming, she would've been here by now. Classes have already started."

Rico grunts in agreement.

Uncrossing my arms, I straighten and shelve this problem for now. I will figure out who she is, and I will find her. And then she will pay.

"Alright," I say. "Let's get going."

We leave the parking lot behind and stride into the building before splitting up. Blackwater University has a three-year education system, and we're all in different years. Well, everyone except Rico and Kaden.

Jace is on his first year since he's only twenty, and I'm on my senior year since I'm the oldest. Both Rico and Kaden are twenty-one, and started at Blackwater at the same time, so both of them are on their second year.

I run my gaze over Rico again before he and Kaden disappear down another hallway. Technically, Rico isn't my brother. He's my cousin. His mom is my dad's sister. Or she was, before she and her husband were killed. Rico became a part of our family after that. But even before that blood-soaked night, I have always considered Rico my brother.

The door to the lecture hall creaks slightly on its hinges as I pull it open. Some of the first-years closest to the door turn to look when I step across the threshold, but they quickly snap their gazes back to the slightly raised dais at the front of the room. The instructor, a stern-looking woman in her fifties, slides her gaze to me. But she doesn't comment on my tardiness. Because of our connection to the Morelli family, even the staff at Blackwater takes great care not to cross us.

I level a hard stare on the student in the closest aisle seat, and she quickly scrambles out of it and moves farther in. Sliding into the now empty seat, I slouch against the backrest and roll my neck.

This is my least favorite class. It's basically nothing more than a long information session that I skipped when I was a freshman because I was bored out of my mind. But dear old Dad ordered me to finish it this semester because, and I quote, *none of my sons will be known as slackers and lazy dropouts.*

I almost let out a huff of laughter at the thought. If only he knew the shit that Jace gets up to.

Lounging in my seat, I sweep a lazy glance over the first-years in the rows ahead of me.

A jolt shoots through me.

My heart thuds in excitement, and I sit up straight, as my eyes land on a girl halfway across the room. She has long black hair and thick bangs. And a very soft-looking body.

It's her.

Shifting my position slightly, I lean to the left so that I can study her better.

Fuck, she's gorgeous. Not only does she have a perfectly soft and curvy body that just begs to be broken, but her face is also stunning. Pale green eyes and luscious lips. It's the kind of face that draws the eye of every man in the room.

I drum my fingers on my thigh as I continue studying her. Once again, I can't figure out what the hell she's doing here. With a face like that, she won't be a very effective assassin. But then again, not all hitmen need to be anonymous. Our family is proof of that. Half of the people in this state know exactly what we are, and they still die every time one of us is sent out on a mission.

Sliding my phone out of my pocket, I send a quick message to our group chat, telling my brothers that I found her and where to meet me after class is over.

Normally, I can barely manage to get through these lectures. But now, it's fucking excruciating. All I want to do is to just drag her out of this room and confront her right this second. But I force myself to remain in my seat.

I want her to feel safe right now. To feel like she has gotten away with it. Because it will make her fear so much sweeter when I corner her later and exact my vengeance.

She tried to humiliate me by keying those words into my car for everyone to see, so I will return the favor and do something that will make her feel small and weak and utterly humiliated. And since she wrote *Small Dick Energy*, I know exactly how to do it.

Payback really is a bitch.

5

RAINA

I could feel someone's eyes burning holes in my head all throughout the lecture. But I didn't want to give him the satisfaction of turning around to look, so I kept my gaze on the professor the whole time. When she at last dismissed us, I quickly swept my gaze over the people rising to their feet and gathering their things, but I couldn't see anyone looking in my direction. But now, as I walk towards the front doors and the canteen, I keep my eyes and ears open. He's here. I know he is.

Warm September winds whirl between the buildings. Since the heat of summer hasn't broken yet, I'm wearing a short black skirt and a simple green t-shirt. The skirt flutters slightly around my thighs as I walk down the steps and then turn in the direction of the canteen.

One second, there's a mass of people ahead of me, moving and talking.

The next, they all part like the damn Red Sea.

Trailing to a halt, I raise my eyebrows at the man now blocking my path.

He's tall, at least a head taller than me, which means that I have to crane my neck to see his face. And what a face it is. Sharp cheekbones and a strong jaw. Eyes the color of burnt gold that glitter in the morning sunlight. Black hair perfectly styled. And a scar that cuts through his left eyebrow and ends at the top of his cheek.

My heart flips. He looks like a fucking warrior god.

I flick a quick glance down his body, and my core throbs in response. Even through the fabric of the tight black shirt he's wearing, I can see the contours of his lethal muscles. And I can't help but wonder what it would feel like to have that body trapping me against a bed.

Based on how everyone immediately moves out of the way for him, I already know who this is. This is Eli Hunter. But damn, I didn't expect him to be this fucking hot.

"Do you know who I am?" he says. It's phrased like a question, but it sounds more like a command.

Adopting my most casual expression, I give him a nonchalant once-over. "Should I?"

His jaw tightens slightly. "Normally, when someone doesn't even know who they're addressing, it buys them a scrap of mercy. But ignorance is not an excuse in this line of work, so I figure I should teach you that lesson now and save you some trouble down the line."

"Yeah…" I drawl. "I'm still waiting for a name."

"You carved *Small Dick Energy* into the side of my car yesterday."

"Oh, you're Eli Hunter!"

"So you do know who I am?"

I shrug.

A sharp glint flickers in his eyes. For a moment, we just stand there, watching each other. The other students have all moved past, which means that we're the only ones left on the edge of the parking lot now.

Then Eli jerks his chin. "Get in the car."

Following his gaze, I notice with no small amount of smugness that there are only *three* Range Rovers parked a short distance behind him now. I slide my gaze back to him.

"No," I reply simply.

He narrows his eyes, and a lethal note creeps into his voice as he says, "It wasn't a request."

"Well, it sure as hell couldn't have been an order, so then I don't know what it was."

"You can either get into the car willingly… or I can make you."

I snort. "You and what army?"

Somewhere behind me on the left, the front doors are opened. Eli shifts his gaze to them, and a vicious smirk curls his lips.

Then he slides his gaze back to me. "This army."

A surge sweeps through me as three guys with brown eyes and the same dangerous expressions on their faces show up. They take up position on my other sides, boxing me in completely. I flick an assessing glance over them.

The one on my right has straight black hair, just like Eli, and he's twirling a knife in his hand with expert movements. There's a sadistic gleam in his eyes that sends an uncharacteristic shiver down my spine.

Both the guy on my left and the one behind me have dark brown hair that curls a little. The man behind me looks composed and neat, while the one on the left, the youngest looking, has that messy and yet effortless just-rolled-out-of-bed look.

I glance over their bodies. They're all built similarly to Eli. Tall, toned, and with an impressive array of lethal muscles.

Crap. Eli brought all of his brothers to confront me as well? This was not quite the way I had imagined things were going to play out. But oh well. Attack is the best defense.

Raising my eyebrows, I let out a mocking laugh while spinning my hand in the air to indicate all of them. "Did you all practice this little routine, or what?"

A very brief hint of surprise flickers in Eli's eyes before he hides it again. He had clearly expected me to be afraid. Not to mock them.

"This her?" Just-rolled-out-of-bed guy asks.

Eli keeps his eyes on me as he replies, "Yes."

"Damn. She's kind of hot."

"Jace," Eli says, a warning note to his voice.

Jace raises his hands in mock surrender before drawing a hand through his messy curls and shrugging. "Just saying."

"Kaden," Eli says, sliding his gaze to the neat-looking guy with straight black hair. "Get her in the car." Then he turns to the composed curly-haired one behind me. "Rico. Keys."

Metallic clinking fills the silence as Rico tosses his car keys to Eli. Catching them in one hand, he turns around and starts towards the Range Rovers.

Kaden's dark eyes are locked on me as he spins his knife one last time before he slides it back into his thigh holster. I glance down at it. There are several more blades there.

With my eyebrows raised, I let out a disbelieving laugh as he starts advancing on me. "If you're planning to force me into a car, you really shouldn't have put that knife away."

Eli just keeps walking towards the car, but his three brothers laugh mockingly.

"Ballsy," Jace comments while dragging an assessing look up and down my body. "I'll give her that."

"You—"

He lunges. I whip around to face him and raise my arms to defend myself. But it was just a trap. The moment my back is turned, Kaden closes the distance between us and grabs me from behind. With one hand around my throat, he uses his other to force my arm up my back.

"Asshole," I mutter as he uses his grip on me to move us towards the car.

He twists my arm higher up, drawing an involuntary whimper from my lips. Around us, Jace and Rico chuckle.

Up ahead, Eli unlocks Rico's car and gets into the driver's seat. I keep my mouth shut as I'm dragged up to the car as well. Jace throws open one of the back doors before Kaden shoves me inside. Then Jace plops into the seat next to mine. I try to scoot over to the other one, but before I can get far, Kaden slides inside, leaving me trapped between them.

As soon as Rico has gotten into the passenger seat, Eli speeds the car out of the lot and down the road. I glance towards the street that will take us to the residential area where all the dorms and houses are located. It's technically close enough to walk, or at least bike, which is what I do, but most students still drive their cars to campus.

But once we reach the crossroads, Eli turns in the other direction.

"Uh, where are we going?" I ask as he drives us down a deserted road.

"Somewhere with less security cameras," Jace replies, a broad grin on his face.

"Fewer."

He frowns at me. "What?"

"*Fewer* security cameras."

For a moment, he only stares at me in disbelief. Deadly silence thrums around me, but I swear I can hear Eli snort softly from the front seat.

"Are you for real?" Jace blurts out at last. Looking up at his brothers, he follows it up with, "Is she for real?"

They just shrug.

Jace turns his attention back to me. "Listen..." With a frown on his face, he yet again shifts his gaze to his brothers. "Wait, what's her name again?"

Only silence answers him.

To be honest, I am a bit offended that they haven't even bothered to learn my name.

"Raina," I fill in once it becomes apparent that they truly don't know it. Flashing him a sweet smile, I add, "Nice to meet you."

"I..." Confusion swirls in his eyes as he trails off.

But before he can figure out what he had been about to say, Eli pulls off the road and stops the car on a dirt patch on the side of it. Without saying a word, he throws open his door and stalks out. Rico does the same. Since I'm stuck between two walls of muscle, I just sit there in the middle of the backseat until Jace at last gathers his wits and opens his door. I watch him climb out but make no move to follow him.

"You either climb out on your own," Kaden says from behind me. "Or I shove you out. Either one is fine with me."

Blowing out an annoyed sigh, I get out of the car and straighten next to it. Apart from us and the car, there are only yellowing fields around us. I can still make out the university across the flat stretch of land, but it's far enough away that no one can see us. Or hear my screams, I suppose.

A thud sounds as Kaden slams the car door shut. Since he

climbed out behind me instead of using his own door, I have to move away from the car so that he won't mow me down.

Winds rush across the fields, making them sway around us.

All four Hunters just stand there around me, staring me down. I know that they're doing this to intimidate me. Bringing me to a deserted spot where I'm alone, outnumbered, and hopelessly outmatched... It's Intimidation Tactics 101.

But little do they know that I'm not intimidated by violence. Since I've seen so much of it from a very young age, it doesn't scare me. In fact, it's usually the opposite. I know that it's fucked up, but oftentimes, violence turns me on. And especially if the guy inflicting it is as hot as Eli Hunter is.

So instead of cowering before these clueless men, I spread my arms wide and turn in a circle to motion at the area around us while I let out a derisive laugh. "Seriously? A dirt patch on the side of a deserted road? Could you be any more cliché?"

None of them take the bait. The only one who does anything is Jace, and he just flicks a quick glance at Eli. But when Eli only continues staring me down, Jace shifts his attention back to me as well.

"I will give you one chance to explain," Eli begins, his dark voice wrapping around my body like a silk sheet. A sheet that's about to be used to strangle me. "For your sake, I suggest you take it."

Crossing my arms, I just raise my eyebrows. "I'm still waiting for a question."

"Why did you carve *Small Dick Energy* into the side of my car yesterday?"

"Why do you think?"

When he only continues holding my gaze with those unforgiving eyes, I scoff and roll my eyes.

Uncrossing my arms again, I stab a hand towards the car a few strides away. "You drive a Range Rover." I shoot a pointed look down at his crotch before flashing him a vicious smirk. "Anyone who drives a car like that is clearly compensating for something."

His eyes dance. With mirth or malice, I can't tell. And he lets out a cold huff of amusement. "Would you like to test that theory?" Before I can answer, he shifts his gaze to his brothers. "Get her on her knees."

My knees hit the dirt hard as Kaden kicks at the back of my legs. I yank my arms forward to brace myself on the ground, but Rico quickly grabs my wrists and pulls them behind me again.

I raise my head right as the sound of a zipper being pulled down cuts through the air. On my knees, I watch as Eli pulls his cock out of his black jeans.

And man was I wrong about the size of his cock.

But before I can say anything, he bends down and wraps a hand around my throat. He holds me trapped like that for a few seconds. When he finally speaks, every word pulses with threats.

"I hope you have dental insurance." His eyes sear into mine. "Because if I feel your teeth, you're going to need implants in your whole mouth. Do you understand?"

Saying nothing, I just hold his gaze.

"Answer," he growls.

My clit throbs at the sheer command in his voice. "Yes."

"Good. Now, open your mouth."

While still holding his gaze, I do as he says. He releases his grip on my throat and instead slides his hand into my hair.

I'm pretty sure he meant what he said, so I shift my lips so that he can't feel my teeth when he pushes his cock into my mouth. A small smile of approval drifts across his face as he looks down at me.

He draws his other hand through my hair as well before gripping it on both sides, holding my head in place.

Then he fucks my mouth.

Dominantly. Brutally.

I'm not giving him a blowjob.

He is *fucking* my mouth.

It's all I can do to make sure my teeth don't scrape against his skin as he thrusts in and out while gripping my hair hard. My gag reflexes are triggered over and over again as his cock hits the back of my mouth. Then he starts going deeper. Pushing into my throat. I try to breathe through my nose while he fucks my throat savagely.

Then he stops.

With his cock still inside.

I choke repeatedly, my gag reflexes uselessly trying to push his massive length out of my throat. An involuntary tear leaks from the corner of my eye. Eli shifts one hand down to it, wiping it away with his thumb and smudging some of my mascara.

"Why are you choking?" Eli taunts, his dick still buried deep in my throat. His dark golden eyes glitter as he smirks at me. "I thought you said my cock was small?"

I choke again, and my body instinctively tries to pull away. But several pairs of strong hands keep me firmly in place on my knees.

My clit throbs. And I know that it's wrong as hell, but I don't care, because I'm so fucking turned on right now. Turned on by the dominance and the brutality of it all. And by the sheer power that Eli Hunter holds over me in that moment.

At last, Eli pulls out.

I gasp in a breath and double over as he finally releases his grip on my hair too. But Rico is still trapping my arms behind my back, so I can't brace myself on the ground. Instead, I just drag in deep breaths while bent over.

Then I look back up again.

And grin.

Eli blinks at me, the only evidence of his surprise. He's still standing there right in front of me, his hard cock just inches from my face. Holding his gaze, I shift my grin into a sly smile.

Next to him, Jace is staring at me with a confused frown on his face. "Are you... fucking turned on right now?"

And since I have absolutely no impulse control whatsoever, I lean forward and plant a kiss right on the crown of Eli's cock. It's nothing more than a quick peck, but he jerks back and stares at me with stunned eyes.

For a moment, everything is dead silent.

Then Jace bursts into laughter. Shaking his head at me, he presses out, "You're fucking crazy!"

If he only knew how many people have called me crazy over the years. Granted, they're probably right. But still. Even lunatics can get tired of hearing how insane they are.

But Eli isn't looking at me like I'm crazy.

Instead, he's staring at me with an expression that I can't read at all.

6

ELI

Glancing up into the rearview mirror, I study Raina where she sits in the backseat between Kaden and Jace as I drive us back to campus. She's leaned back, alternating between drumming her fingers on her thighs and flexing them beside her, and she's humming. Fucking *humming*. She has got to be the strangest girl I've ever met.

After turning onto the final street, I cast another glance at her gorgeous face. At those sparkly green eyes. At the slight traces of smudged make-up underneath her long lashes. My cock stirs at just the memory of how her luscious lips felt around it.

Another wave of confusion and incredulity washes over me.

She's not scared now, and she wasn't scared back then. It makes no sense. Because of who we are, and who are family is connected to, everyone is fucking terrified of us. Normal people out in the neighborhoods. The other students. The instructors. Everyone. But not her. And I can't figure out why.

I almost miss the final turn into the parking lot because I'm so wrapped up in the mystery that is Raina. From the passenger seat, Rico casts me a glance from the corner of his eye when I yank on the steering wheel and practically skid his car in through the gates. Thankfully, though, he doesn't comment.

In the back, Raina just keeps humming along to music that isn't there.

Part of me wants to crack her skull wide open just so that I can see what the fuck is actually in there. My still semi-hard cock, on the other hand, wants to know what it would be like to fuck that soft body of hers.

But mostly, I just want to break her. I want to keep pushing her to see just how much she can take. And what happens when she finally snaps.

I flex my fingers before squeezing the steering wheel hard.

Fucking hell, I've only known this damn woman for less than half an hour, and I'm already becoming obsessed with her.

I park the car in the same spot as before. It's still empty, just like I knew it would be. The one next to it is empty as well, as if everyone was expecting my Range Rover to appear at some point today too.

After turning the ignition off, I toss the keys to Rico and say, "Give us a minute."

In the mirror, I can see Jace grinning and wiggling his eyebrows at me. Kaden and Rico just exit the car without comment. A second later, Jace does too.

Three thuds sound as they close the doors behind them.

I remain where I am, my head facing forwards, but I meet Raina's eyes in the rearview mirror. She just raises her eyebrows expectantly.

"You got off easy today," I inform her. "Normally, if someone had keyed my car, I would've broken every one of their fingers. But since it's apparently your first day on campus, I decided to show you a little mercy."

A soft chuckle escapes her lips. "Did you now?"

"Yes. But this was a one-time act of mercy. So if you ever try to mess with me again, if you even so much as look at me with disrespect in those defiant eyes of yours, I will show you exactly what I do to people who cross me."

Silence falls over the car for a while, thick and heavy, while we just hold each other's gaze.

Then she bursts out laughing. I blink, watching through the mirror as she makes a show of wiping tears of laughter from her eyes.

"Oh my God," she presses out between fits of laughter. "You really do practice these threatening speeches and dramatic entrances beforehand, don't you?" Dragging in a deep breath, she sits up straight again and raises her eyebrows. "Tell me, do they ever work?"

For a few seconds, I can't think of a single thing to say. In the past five years, I don't think I've met a single person who wasn't afraid, or at least a bit nervous, in my presence. And to have that shattered by someone like *her* is so fucking jarring that I don't know how to react.

Turning around in my seat, I meet her gaze head on for the first time since we got into the car. Rage roars through me, because I suddenly feel embarrassed by how easily she managed to throw me off my game.

"Let's get something straight," I grind out between gritted teeth. "If I wanted to, I could crush you underneath my heel without even breaking a sweat. This is the only warning you get. Bow down, and *stay* down, or you won't like what happens next."

She holds my gaze with narrowed eyes, but doesn't say anything.

I jerk my chin towards the door. "Now, get out before I change my mind."

Fabric rustles as she slides over the backseat and towards the door behind me. I turn so that I'm facing forwards again, and reach for the handle as well.

Cold steel presses against my throat.

"Let's get something straight," Raina mimics.

On instinct, I move to get the blade away.

But before I can so much as lift a hand, she pushes it harder across my throat and tuts, "Ah, ah, ah."

Fury and incredulity flash through me, but I stop moving. Glancing down, I study the knife. And the fury is replaced by utter shock. The blade is one of Kaden's. Did she fucking pickpocket Kaden right here in the car with all four of us around her?

"Now, let's get something straight," Raina repeats in a mockingly sweet voice as she leans forward.

With the knife still positioned across my throat, she moves until her lips are right next to my ear. When she speaks, her warm breath caresses my skin, making blood pulse to my cock again.

"If you ever force me into a car again, I will put you on your back and watch as you choke on your own lungs." Meeting my gaze in the rearview mirror, she flashes me a smile laced with insanity. "Clear?"

Before I can answer, she yanks the blade away from my throat and tosses it onto the passenger seat beside me. Then she briskly opens the door and saunters away.

I'm left sitting there, staring between her and the knife.

Her long black hair swings across her back and her skirt swishes around her thighs as she strides towards the canteen building. Raking a hand through my hair, I shake my head at her retreating back.

What the fuck is wrong with this girl?

7

RAINA

Soft murmuring fills the massive building. While pretending to listen to the conversation at my table, I scan the space around me. Tall bookshelves line the walls and form several aisles across the floor too. Between them, in the open spaces, are tables where people sit and work alone or in pairs and groups.

To be honest, I didn't expect there to even be a library at Blackwater University. I thought this career path was mostly just a physical one. But apparently, being a hitman is more than just stabbing people with the pointy end of a blade. As it turns out, you also need to know things like science and math and psychology so that you can plan advances, trajectories, escape routes, how people will react to different situations, and other stuff like that.

I sweep my gaze over the various tables again. No sign of Eli. I've seen his little brother Jace from time to time, since he takes some of the same classes as me. But ever since I put a blade to his neck in that car, I haven't had any more run-ins with the infamous Eli Hunter.

Worry gnaws at my bones. I need to keep his wrath focused on me so that he will forget about Connor. Maybe I need to do something else to draw his attention?

"Raina, are you even listening?"

Giving my head a quick shake, I snap out of my musings and quickly return my attention to the people at the table. There are three of them. They're all first-years, just like me. Though I suspect that every one of them is a year younger than me since they all most likely started at twenty when they were supposed to.

Magda, the girl who spoke, is a thin girl with hair so blond it's almost white, and there is a no-nonsense air about her. Next to her is Gabriel, looking like a true all-American boy-next-door with his blond hair, blue eyes, and easy smile. The last one is Paulo, a dark-haired guy with sharp eyes, who I haven't been able to get a proper read on.

"No, sorry, I spaced out a bit," I reply, flashing Magda an apologetic smile. Before she can bring the conversation back on track, I steer it towards a topic I really need to know more about. "I heard that there's a guy called Connor Smith in the senior class, and that he's apparently one of the top students, but I haven't seen him around."

The three of them exchange a glance.

"He's probably still in the hospital wing," Paulo says carefully.

I raise my eyebrows as if this is news to me. "Why?"

"Eli Hunter and his brothers gave him the beating of a lifetime."

"Connor is that unlikeable, huh?"

"No, I wouldn't say that."

"So he just knows how to make enemies then?"

Gabriel chuckles. "Are you kidding? Half of the senior

class are jealous of him for being so fucking good at everything."

My mind churns as I turn that over in my head. So, a lot of people are jealous of Connor? But the question is, who is jealous enough to sabotage his rifle in order to bring down Eli's wrath on him?

"Apparently, he's Harvey Smith's son," Paulo says, lowering his voice conspiratorially.

Gabriel raises his eyebrows. "*The* Harvey Smith?"

"Yes."

"Hey," Magda interrupts, leveling her pale gaze on me. "Isn't your last name Smith too? Don't tell me you're also—"

"Harvey Smith's spawn?" I fill in, and then snort as if that's ridiculous. "Oh, I wish. But no, I'm just one of the millions of normal Smiths in this country."

It's better if no one knows who I really am. Because if it becomes known that Connor is my brother, then Eli might realize that I'm purposely drawing his attention away from Con and towards me instead.

"That reminds me," a new voice says.

I turn to my left to find a girl with an incredible resting bitch face lean over from the table next to us. I don't know her name, but I'm pretty sure she's in our year too.

"You're that new girl who transferred in like five days ago right?" Resting Bitch Face continues.

"Yeah?" I reply.

"What are you even doing here? I've been watching you in all of our classes this week, and you're fucking terrible."

A flash of irritation shoots through me. I know that she's right, of course. I am fucking terrible. At everything. Well, except for chemistry. But that class hasn't started yet. So all I do now is to walk into training hall after training hall and fail at everything we're supposed to do. And it's already grating on my nerves, so I sure as hell don't need this girl to rub it in my face.

"And I don't mean just because you started three weeks after us," she continues. "Your basic skills are so far below average that you'll never catch up to the rest of us. So why even bother coming here at all?"

Adopting a lazy expression, I give her a nonchalant shrug. "Because I was bored."

"Bored?"

"Yes."

When I offer no further explanation, she shakes her head at me. "You're fucking crazy."

I narrowly prevent myself from grabbing the nearest book and hurling it straight into her stupid face. Instead, I let a psychotic grin curl my lips. "I know."

She jerks back and blinks at me.

Before she can recover, I turn to my table companions. "Excuse me, I have somewhere else to be."

"Uhm, yeah, sure," Gabriel manages to press out.

The others just watch me as I push my chair away from the table and then stride towards the doors. Leaving the library behind, I instead set course for the chemistry lab.

Deep down, I know that I should have stayed. I need to find out who tampered with Connor's rifle, and that means that I need to continue stealthily interrogating people. But I can't do that when all I can think about is what color that girl's face would be if I just happened to slip some poison into her drink one day.

I need to clear my head, and the best place for that has always been a chemistry lab. So I will mix some poison for

Resting Bitch Face in order to calm down, and then I can decide whether I'm going to actually use it on her or not.

My head is still spinning with annoyance and questions and plans as I round the next corner.

And slam straight into someone's chest.

A hiss sounds as he sucks in a breath of pain between his teeth.

The collision sent me stumbling a step back, and when I finally right myself and look up, I'm met with Connor's still bruised face.

His gray eyes go wide as they lock on me. "Raina?"

I didn't expect him to be up and about quite this fast, so for a few seconds, I just stare at him while I'm trying to figure out how to play this. Since I still haven't figured it out, all I manage to say is, "Hey, Con."

Confusion washes over his features. Then he flicks a quick glance up and down the corridor, as if he's worried that someone might see me. Grabbing me by the shoulder, he pulls me into an empty office and then closes the door. I'm thankful for the extra seconds to formulate a plan.

There is no way that I can tell Connor what I'm really doing here. He might think I'm crazy and odd, but I know that he's very protective of me. So if he finds out that I'm here to be a shield for him against Eli's wrath, he will do everything in his power to make sure that doesn't happen. I'm pretty sure he would even go so far as to tell Eli what I'm doing. And we can't have that.

So I decide to play to his insecurities. He is carrying our family's entire burden on his shoulders, and I know that he is secretly worried that he won't be able to do it. That he will fail and let us down. Let Dad down. And if I hit him there, he will miss even the most obvious clues in his anger and hurt. I know that it's cruel. But it's the only way I can protect him.

"What are you doing here?" Connor asks, eyes wide with confusion, once we're out of sight.

While blocking out the guilt twisting inside me, I frown at him and shake my head as if the answer to that should have been obvious. "Studying."

"Studying? What do you mean, *studying*?"

"At Blackwater University. I've enrolled as a student."

He jerks back, completely baffled. "What? Why?"

"Because someone needed to step up and try to save our family from ruin."

He looks like I've just slapped him across the face. Pain stabs through my heart at the hurt that flashes in his eyes.

"You think I'm not good enough?"

Since I don't trust myself to speak, I just shrug.

Anger joins the terrible hurt in his eyes. "So, what? You think you can just... take my place? That you can just magically fix everything? I've spent *years* working for this, Raina!"

"Yeah, well, since you've clearly made enough enemies to land you in the hospital wing instead of focusing on your classes, I think we need a backup."

"You?"

"Me."

"You're delusional. You're not even trained for this, Raina. You won't be helping our reputation. All you will be doing is further tarnishing it, because you don't know a single thing about this world!"

"Then don't tell them that I'm your sister. Tell them that you have no fucking clue who I am. But I'm not leaving."

"Fine," he snaps. "That's exactly what I'll do."

Good. Because I can't have him accidentally blowing my cover with Eli.

For a few seconds, the two of us just stare each other down. My heart is breaking at the sight of that anger and pain in Connor's eyes when he looks at me. But I swallow down the lump in my throat while trying to convince myself that this is for the best.

"You know, I always thought you were different," Connor begins, that awful hurt lacing his voice. "That you actually... understood." Anger creeps into his tone again as he flicks a dismissive glance up and down my body. "But I guess not. Good luck, Raina."

Before I can compose myself enough to respond, he yanks the door open and stalks out. It vibrates in its frame as he slams it shut behind him.

Tears threaten to spill from my eyes. I blink them back with great effort and instead draw in a deep breath to steady myself.

It's better that he's angry.

At least then, he will stay out of harm's way.

8

ELI

Keeping my distance from Raina is harder than I anticipated. All I want to do is to launch attack after attack, chipping away at her defenses until she is reduced to a trembling ball of fear, begging me for mercy. But to do that, I have to build up anticipation.

She can't possibly think that I would let her little stunt in the car slide, so she'll know that I will be coming for revenge. And sometimes, waiting for the other shoe to drop is worse than the act itself. So I have been keeping my distance, leaving her to constantly have to look over her shoulder. And building her fear and paranoia. Soon, it will be time to strike.

Chatter comes from the open doors to the canteen up ahead. I roll my shoulders back, trying to dispense the restless energy inside me. It works poorly. I really need to find someone to take that out on.

"Your grandfather called yesterday, by the way," I say, casting a glance at Rico from the corner of my eye.

While we continue towards the canteen, he raises his eyebrows and turns to face me. "He did?"

"Yeah. I talked to Dad this morning, and he mentioned it."

"Huh. What did he want?"

"A report on your progress."

Rico snorts and rolls his eyes. "Of course he did. I swear, I love the guy, but damn he can be so fucking bossy."

"Well, there's a good reason for that," Jace comments from my other side as we enter the packed canteen.

"Still, that doesn't—" Rico begins before being cut off.

"Hey, isn't that Connor?" Kaden interrupts.

We all turn and follow his gaze.

Sure enough, Connor Smith is stalking out the doors on the other side of the room. I only have time to see the back of his head and half of his jaw before he disappears from the canteen, but it's enough to confirm that he is still sporting an impressive number of bruises.

A grin spreads across my lips.

Some of my best work, that. Lots of pain but nothing permanently damaged. Which means that I can do it again soon.

"So, he's out of bed, huh?" Jace says, running a hand over his jaw. Then his eager eyes find mine. "Should we...?"

"I think we have a more pressing problem," Rico replies before I can say anything.

He jerks his chin towards our table, and we all tear our gazes from the doorway where Connor disappeared and look at the empty metal table and the six chairs around it.

Except, it's not empty.

Surprise flashes through me.

There, seated in one of the chairs in the very middle, is Raina. She has a tray of food in front of her and she's eating calmly as if she doesn't have a care in the world. I scan the tables around her. A few people flinch and snap their gazes back to their own plates, as if they're worried that I might take out my anger on them for not making sure our table was clear.

To be fair, I am tempted. I had planned to give Raina a bit more time to worry before I struck, but who am I to pass up an opportunity to punish her if she just delivers herself to me like this on a silver platter?

Tense silence spreads through the large room as the four of us prowl up to Raina. She doesn't even bother looking up from her food. Instead, she simply cuts a piece of salmon and pops it in her mouth.

Only once we're standing right in front of her on the other side of the table does she deign to look up and meet our gazes. After swallowing the bite of food, she arches a dark brow at me. "Can I help you with something?"

Instead of answering, I just hold her gaze while Kaden and Rico pull out the chairs on her left and right, and sit down. Jace takes a seat opposite her.

"There are other tables, you know," she says, flicking her wrist to motion at the empty ones scattered around the room. Then she shrugs. "But if you're that desperate for my company, then by all means, join me."

The silence in the room is now so prominent that I can almost feel it pulsing against my eardrums. Everyone seems to be holding their breath, waiting to see how this will play out.

I study Raina. But I can't get a read on her, so I'm not sure if she's challenging me on purpose, or if she truly didn't know that this is our table. Given what she did in the car, my money is on the former. But I still decide to inform her, hoping to see the color drain from her face in fear as she realizes her mistake.

"This is our table," I tell her.

"Your table?" She snorts and rolls her eyes. "What is this? High school?"

Okay, so she's definitely doing this on purpose.

All around us, people are staring. Waiting to see what I will do. I know exactly what I *want* to do. But I'm not sure if it's the best move. On one hand, there are a lot of people here, and I can't let them see her disrespect go unpunished. But at the same time, there are a lot of people here, which means that there are a lot of witnesses.

"Leave," I grind out between gritted teeth while trying to keep a tight hold on my restraint.

A small smirk plays at the corner of her lips as she holds my gaze. It sends a spike of alarm through me. Because for a moment, I swear that those perceptive green eyes of hers can see straight through all my bullshit and read exactly what is going on inside my head.

But all she says is a simple, "No."

"I'm—" I begin, but she blows out a frustrated sigh and cuts me off.

"I swear, it's like you only have two braincells left and they're both fighting for third place."

The cafeteria sucks in a collective gasp.

And for a while, all I can do is stare at her.

Then my restraint at last snaps.

Raina shoots up from her seat as I advance on her, but my brothers stand up as well and block her path before she can slink away. Rounding the table, I grab her arm and drag her towards the table's short side. She growls curses at me, but she's no match for my strength.

Positioning her hips against the edge of the table, I plant my palm between her shoulder blades and shove her face down over the table.

"Hold her," I tell my brothers.

Jace and Kaden immediately place their hands on her wrists, holding her arms stretched out before her and trapped against the table, while Rico locks his fingers around the back of her neck. She tries to yank against their grip, but all she can do is to wiggle her ass.

I stare at that ass, that perfect ass hidden by a black skirt, as I slide my leather belt out of my pants. It produces a snap as I pull it out sharply and then fold it across the middle.

Raina's gaze darts towards the sound, and her eyes go wide with shock as she sees the belt in my hands.

"Don't you dare," she warns.

Moving up beside her, I efficiently push her short black skirt up to her waist and then pull her panties halfway down her thighs. Then I whip her bare ass with the belt.

Raina gasps. And so do the people around us.

I whip the belt again. It produces a snapping sound as it connects.

"Act like a brat..." I begin.

Snap.

"And I'll spank you like a brat."

Snap.

She yanks futilely against my brothers' hold on her. When that doesn't work, she grits her teeth and presses her forehead down hard against the table. I spank her with the belt again. And again. Until at last, a whimper spills from her lips.

A shuddering breath whooshes out of her afterwards, as if she knows that she has just lost. She wiggles her ass, as if trying to relieve the pain. My cock stirs at the sight of her now pink skin.

I watch her freshly spanked ass while I slide my belt back into my pants. Then I move so that I'm standing right behind her. Another small whimper escapes her when I press my body harder against her sensitive skin. I glance at Rico, and he immediately takes his hand away from her neck and steps back.

Bracing one hand on the tabletop, I lean forward over her body and grab her long black hair. She tries to pull her wrists free again, but Jace and Kaden keep her firmly trapped. Winding her hair around my hand, I keep going until it's tight enough that I can pull her head up from the table. I grind my thighs against her ass, and watch as she bites back another whimper.

With my hand in her hair, forcing her to crane her head back like that, I lean down farther over her and place my lips next to her ear. "You have no idea who you're playing against, princess. Better wave the white flag now while I'm still willing to accept your unconditional surrender."

She laughs. It's not a scared sound. It's smug and full of challenge.

"Playing?" she says, that mocking tone back in her voice. "Oh we haven't even started playing yet."

"Is that so?"

"Yes."

I let out a dark chuckle, and it sends a shiver through her body. "Then why are you bent over a table with your ass freshly spanked for everyone to see?"

I expect her to blush in embarrassment. Or maybe growl a curse. But only a sharp smile curls her lips.

"Because you and I are just getting started."

9

RAINA

My skin was so tender that I was barely able to sit through the entire class I had after Eli's attempt to humiliate me in the canteen. But thankfully, that damn bastard had at least allowed me to pull my panties back up on my own. Because if he had been the one to do it, he would have felt how fucking wet I was.

The way his entire body exuded power, the way he held that belt, the way he ground himself against my ass and pulled on my hair afterwards... My heart is pounding just thinking about it. But I didn't want him to know that, because then he would probably have commented on it loudly enough for the whole canteen to hear, and that would have been more humiliating than the actual spanking.

I roll my shoulders back as I get into position on the padded mat.

At least the discomfort is long gone now. And thank fuck for that because today is my first lesson in hand-to-hand combat, and I suck at that as it is without adding aching ass cheeks into the mix.

I'm paired up with Magda, which is both a blessing and a curse. She's so damn fast that I can't even begin to block her moves. But at least she doesn't have enough brute strength to break my bones when her strikes land. So there is that, I suppose.

Leaping back, I desperately try to avoid the swift kick she throws at my hip. I manage to dodge it by a mere inch. But when I land, I'm so off balance that I can't block her right hand. It slams into the side of my ribs, making me stumble to the right.

"Keep up," she snaps.

Massaging my ribs, I straighten again while growling, "I'm trying."

"You're screwing me over. If I can't practice against someone who knows what she's doing, then I will fall behind."

"I know. I'm sorry. Look, I—"

The door to the sparring room is yanked open. A ripple goes through the room as Eli Hunter saunters across the threshold. My heart flips in my chest.

Our instructor, Mr. Hansen, turns towards the disturbance and opens his mouth as if to tell the intruder to get the hell out. Then his sharp eyes land on Eli, and all traces of anger disappear from his stern features in a flash. He is in his mid-forties. Tall and muscular, and with a scar across his jaw. I have come to understand that the Hunters hold some kind of sway on this campus, but it is still baffling to see a man like Mr. Hansen check his tone around a student half his age.

"Hunter," he says in a neutral tone. "I'm in the middle of class."

"I can see that," Eli answers.

His golden-brown eyes scan the crowd until they land on me. My heart skips a beat again when a sly smile curls his lips.

"I heard that you have a student who started three weeks after everyone else," Eli says to Mr. Hansen, but his eyes remain locked on mine.

Clothes rustle as everyone turns to look at me. I keep my chin up and a nonchalant expression on my face, but my pulse is now thrumming in my ears.

"So I thought I might help her catch up by instructing her personally," Eli continues. At last, he breaks eye contact and shifts his attention back to Mr. Hansen before finishing with, "Since you have so many other students who need your attention, and no patience for people who don't even know their foot from their elbow."

The other students chuckle. My cheeks heat, but I'm hoping it's not visible in the bright light from the fluorescents in the concrete ceiling.

I already have a feeling that Mr. Hansen doesn't like me very much, and that is confirmed by the contempt on his face as he casts a glance at me.

Then he lifts his broad shoulders in a shrug and flicks his wrist at Eli. "Knock yourself out." His gaze finds my sparring partner. "Magda, pair up with Jessica instead."

"Yes, sir," she says, and quickly hurries away.

"The rest of you, enough dawdling! Get back to work."

The other students leap to obey his order. Sparring matches start back up, and the sound of punches and kicks striking flesh once more echoes between the gray concrete walls.

From across the room, Eli locks eyes with me again and flashes me a smile tinged with insanity. Then he starts towards me. I have to suppress the primal urge to back away as my pulse hammers and dread washes over me. Shit. This is going to be humiliating.

Eli advances on me until he is standing only two strides away. Amusement glitters in his eyes as he slowly drags his gaze up and down my body. "How's your ass?"

Instead of answering, I shoot a pointed look at the spot where I pressed a knife a few days ago, and then raise my eyebrows. "How's your throat?"

Holding my gaze, he smirks and casually adjusts his cock through his pants. "How's *your* throat?"

Since I don't have a comeback for that, I just cross my arms and glare back at him instead. He huffs out a satisfied chuckle.

"You know how to surrender, right?" he says.

"I'm afraid the word is not in my vocabulary."

He snorts. "Cute."

I narrowly prevent myself from jerking backwards when he abruptly takes a step towards me. Grabbing my wrist, he easily pulls it away from my chest and instead moves it towards his hip.

"In a sparring match, when your opponent has you so hopelessly pinned that you can't save yourself, you submit." Using his grip on my wrist, he moves my hand so that my palm touches his hip twice. "By tapping out."

"I knew that," I mutter.

"Good." A wicked grin spreads across his lips. "Because you're going to practice that move a lot this afternoon."

Before I can retort, he releases my wrist and steps back again. I rub my thumb over the spot where his fingers were locked a few seconds ago.

"Square up," he commands.

Biting back a snarky reply, I raise my hands into the

position that Mr. Hansen showed me about half an hour ago. Or at least, I hope so. Eli frowns at me but doesn't comment.

Then he strikes.

I don't even have time to blink in surprise. I expected him to… I don't know. Say something first? But he doesn't. He just flashes forward and slams a fist into the side of my ribs.

Pain pulses through my ribcage as it lands, and I suck in a gasp as I stumble sideways. Eli moves again. This time, I at least try to yank my arms into position to block it. But his hit lands anyway.

He backs me across the floor, getting strike after strike in. But the more of his punches that land, the more I realize something incredibly surprising. The hits don't hurt as much as I expected them to. And given Eli's impressive physique, there is only one explanation for that. He is pulling his punches.

The realization stuns me so much that I blurt it out without thinking. "You're pulling your punches."

"Well… I don't want you to break too quickly." A smirk ghosts across his lips. "I like playing with my food."

He trails to a halt.

My chest heaves from exertion, but he isn't even breathing heavily. In fact, he looks completely unaffected as he rakes his gaze over my already exhausted body. I flick a glance over his shoulder.

He has backed me so far across the floor that we've ended up on the other side of the sparring hall. Mr. Hansen and my classmates are still training, and even if they had been able to hear us from all the way over here, none of them are paying us any mind.

"You clearly suck at using your fists," Eli says.

I bristle at the comment, but he is right, of course, so I just glare back at him in silence.

"Try kicking me instead," he says when I don't take the bait.

Narrowing my eyes in suspicion, I try to figure out what he is planning. But actually landing a kick on him and wiping that smug expression off his features would be so damn satisfying that I can't resist the temptation to try.

In the hope of catching him off guard, I quickly shift my weight and slam my foot towards his hip.

His hand immediately shoots down towards it.

Shock crackles through me as he locks his fingers around my ankle. Holding my leg trapped up in the air like that, he flashes me a smile that sends ice skittering down my spine. Then he moves.

He walks a few steps to the side, using his grip on my ankle to pull me with him. Since my leg is up in the air, it forces me to hop after him on one foot. He moves again. And again.

Embarrassment sears my cheeks. I can *feel* the heat radiating from them, so I can only imagine how red they must be.

With a vicious smirk on his lips, Eli pulls on my leg again, forcing me to jump after him while I flail my arms to keep my balance.

For some reason, this is more mortifying than being spanked in the middle of a packed cafeteria. And based on the look in that damn bastard's eyes, he knows it.

"Want to tap out?" he taunts.

I grit my teeth and try to yank my ankle away from his hand, but his grip only tightens. Then he starts to move faster, forcing me to frantically hop after him.

"Fine," I snap at last.

But before I can so much as shift my hand towards my thigh, he pulls on my leg. Hard. It makes me lose my balance and sends me toppling backwards.

Air explodes from my lungs as I hit the padded mat back first. I raise a hand towards my chest while I try to suck in a deep breath.

Eli kicks my hand aside. It slams into the mat again while he crouches down over me. I have barely managed to get air back into my lungs when he presses his knee against my chest, pinning me to the floor and restricting my breathing again.

"Go ahead then," he says, locking smug eyes on me. "Tap out."

For a few seconds, I just glare back at him. He shifts more of his body weight to the knee on top of my chest. I bare my teeth at him but then move my palm to the padded mat beside me and tap twice.

Eli lets out a satisfied chuckle.

Taking his knee off my chest, he straightens and brushes off his hands. I leap to my feet while his back is halfway turned and aim my fist straight at his side.

He whips around. I'm one inch away from landing a strike when he wraps his fingers around my wrist and stops it.

My stomach lurches as he uses my momentum to somehow flip me over and send me slamming down on the mat again. This time on my stomach. I try to gasp in a breath while Eli settles his weight on my ass and twists my still trapped hand up my back.

"Trying to strike when your opponent's back is turned?" he says from above me. "Sneaky. But not very honorable."

"What the fuck do you know about honor?" I growl.

He pushes my hand higher up. Pain ripples through my

arm at the unnatural angle, and I have to grit my teeth to bite back a whimper.

"I never said that *I* care about honor," he muses. "But I do love having yet another excuse to punish you." I can hear the fucking smirk in his voice as he commands, "Submit."

I just clench my jaw harder. He shifts his weight on my ass, making his cock grind against it. If it's by accident or by design is unclear, but it sends a flash of electricity through my body that is distracting enough that I momentarily forget that he is trying to hurt me, not fuck me.

He forces my hand farther up. A whimper rips from my throat. It feels like my arm is going to snap in half.

"Submit," he orders again in a voice pulsing with command.

If he actually decides to break my arm, I will be in real trouble, so I yank my hand up and frantically tap it against the mat next to me.

He stops pushing my hand upwards but doesn't release me. Instead, he leans down closer to my ear and whispers, "Good girl."

A shudder courses through my body.

Given the victorious laugh that spills from his lips, he probably thinks it was a shudder of fear. Oh, if he only knew…

At last releasing my hand, he stands up again, leaving me lying on the ground. I slowly push to my knees and roll my aching shoulder. Then I get to my feet as well.

Eli is standing there, two steps away, watching me like a predator. I flick a quick glance towards Mr. Hansen and the others. They're still sparring, and no one is even bothering to look in our direction.

"Oh, they can't save you, princess." Raising a hand, he

twitches two fingers at me. "Come on then. Try again."

And since I can't let him think that he has won, I do exactly that.

Again and again, I come at him and try to get at least one kick or punch through.

But every time, I end up on the floor with no other choice but to tap out. He reads my moves every single time, and reacts so quickly that I can barely see the attack coming before I'm on my back again. Anger flickers through me as he yet again demonstrates just how outclassed I am against him. There has to be something I can do to throw him off his game.

Air explodes from my lungs once more as I slam into the mat yet again. Before I can so much as lift my head, Eli is there.

Straddling my hips, he grabs both of my wrists and moves them so that he can pin my hands underneath his knees. I kick my legs and buck my hips, trying to get him off me. But it's no use. I try to yank my hands away, but he just puts more of his body weight onto my palms, keeping them firmly pinned to the ground.

"It must be so frustrating," he says, a taunting note to his voice. "Being this weak and helpless."

"I'm not helpless," I growl while still trying to somehow get my hands out from underneath his knees.

"Oh really? Would you like me to demonstrate just how helpless you are against someone like me?"

Before I can reply, he leans forward and wraps his hand around my throat. While bracing the other against the ground next to my head, he tightens his fingers around my neck until he's cutting off all of my air.

I struggle to get him off me, but it only makes me grind my pussy against his cock where he straddles me. That, combined with the feeling of his powerful body pinning me to the ground and the sheer dominance pulsing from him as he chokes me, sends lightning crackling through me.

He must have misread the shudder that racks my frame, because he just smirks and says, "Yeah, I know. With your hands pinned like this, you can't even tap out."

His eyes stay locked on mine as he tightens his grip just a little more. My lungs scream for oxygen.

"Do you know what you do when you can't tap out?" He raises his other hand and brushes my bangs aside, his fingers sending sparkles dancing over my skin. "You beg."

Since there is nothing I can do to break his grip, I just lie there, looking up at him while he holds my life in the palm of his hand.

"I will allow you to breathe again in a few seconds. I suggest you use the opportunity to beg me for mercy."

Air rushes back into my lungs as he relaxes his grip on my throat. I cough and drag in desperate breaths until my starved lungs are full again. But I have to admit that the bastard at least knows how to choke someone properly, because my neck doesn't even hurt from his grip.

For about half a minute, I just lie there underneath him, sucking in deep breaths. He keeps his hand resting over my throat. He's not squeezing, but it's a solid weight meant to remind me that he is still in control here.

Once my breathing has evened out, Eli arches his eyebrow expectantly. "Well then, princess. What do you say?"

"Choke me harder, Daddy."

Utter shock pulses across his features, and he jerks back in stunned surprise. It's enough to take his knee off my right hand for a second. I use that second well.

Yanking my hand up, I slam my fist into his jaw.

10

ELI

The auditorium is packed with people, but my eyes are locked on the dark-haired girl sitting halfway to the stage. She is leaning slightly sideways in her seat, speaking to a blond guy next to her, and she hasn't looked in my direction even once. I flex my fingers and try to suppress the urge to go find a sniper rifle and shoot that blond guy in the back of the head.

"If you could quiet down, please," Professor Lawson says, her voice barely carrying over the noise even though she is speaking into a microphone. "We're ready to start."

The people in the closest rows immediately stop talking, but the ones higher up have clearly not heard her because they continue chatting in their seats.

"SHUT IT!" Mr. Hansen bellows.

He is standing two strides away from the mic, but his loud voice still hits it. Several people wince as the grating sound of electronic feedback cuts through the room.

Deadly silence falls over the massive hall.

"Ah, uhm, thank you," Professor Lawson says to Mr.

Hansen. She gives him a small smile, to which he responds with an uncharacteristically self-conscious nod, before she turns her attention back to the students of Blackwater University. "Those of you who are on your second or third year already know what this is about."

A ripple of anticipation washes through the room.

"In a few weeks, it's time for the annual tournament," she announces.

Some of the seniors let out whoops of excitement.

"Yes, quite exciting indeed." She smiles. "Now, I'm sure that all of you first-years are wondering what this is all about." After pausing for a second, she asks, "How many of you have read *The Hunger Games*?"

A tiny minority of people raise their hands. Raina is not among them. Narrowing my eyes, I study the back of her head. I wonder what kind of books she read while growing up. Perhaps something like *How to Be an Unpredictable Force of Nature*.

I still haven't gotten over what she did in that sparring hall the other day. *Choke me harder, Daddy*. Fucking hell, I did not see that one coming. I've never met anyone who surprises me, and challenges me, the way she does.

"Well, that was a truly depressing number," Professor Lawson remarks. Drawing a hand through her brown curls, she sighs. "Okay, how many of you have at least seen the movie, then?"

A lot more hands are raised this time. Raina's among them.

"Great," Professor Lawson says, sounding a bit more cheerful. "This tournament is kind of like that. Except in teams."

Silence descends on the massive room as the first-years glance at one another.

"We're gonna kill each other?" a guy calls from somewhere to my left.

"No." She waves her hands. "No actual killing. But apart from that, anything goes." After a brief pause, she tilts her head to the side and adds, "Well, not anything. We do prefer to keep any permanent injuries to a minimum."

Tension ripples through the first-years while the rest of us lean back in our seats with grins on our faces. I continue watching the back of Raina's head while Professor Lawson explains that each team will start at a different place outside the forest and that the objective is to kill the target at the center while also avoiding or incapacitating the other teams. It's impossible to tell what she's thinking, though.

"Normally, there are teams of four," Professor Lawson continues. "But this year, there will be teams of five."

Surprise flashes across the faces of several people around me. My brothers all frown, and Rico glances towards me.

"There will be at least one person from each year on every team," she continues. "And you will find out the teams today."

Paper rustles as her assistant scurries over and hands her a stack of documents. Then she begins reading out the teams. Lounging in my seat, I wait with a smile on my face until she gets to my team.

"Next up, we have Eli Hunter."

The people closest to us sneak a few quick glances. They all know that my team is never selected randomly. It always consists of the people that I want on it.

"Rico Hunter," she continues reading from her paper. "Kaden Hunter. Jace Hunter."

My brothers all turn towards me and grin.

"And Raina Smith," she finishes.

Surprise flashes in my brothers' eyes, and some people gasp closer to where Raina sits.

"Seriously?" Jace hisses while the professor continues on with the next team.

I just shoot him a sideways glance.

On my other side, Rico leans closer and speaks in a soft voice. "Are you sure about this, Eli? She's the weakest person on this entire campus."

"I know," I reply.

"Then why the hell is she on our team," Jace mutters. "This is my first time. I want us to fucking crush it."

I slide my gaze to Kaden, waiting to see if he's going to protest too. But he just sits there, watching me with calm dark eyes and waiting for me to explain my reasoning.

"All four of us are here this year," I say, looking each one of them in the eye. "We all know that the four of us can carry this entire tournament on our own."

A smug grin spreads across Jace's mouth. Rico tips his head to the side, as if conceding the point. I look at Kaden, who nods.

"So there is no reason to worry," I continue. "I made sure that Raina is on our team because we deserve to have some fun along the way."

Now, Kaden smiles too. It's the sadistic one full of quiet anticipation that he so often wears.

"In two weeks, team training is starting," I say. "Which means that the four of us and Raina will have entire afternoons together. And do you know what that means?"

Kaden's smile widens while Jace rubs his hands together. Rico just lets out an amused huff.

"That means that we will have all the time and privacy in the world..." I match their grins. "To torment her."

11

RAINA

Everyone around me shoots me sympathetic looks. Frowning, I glance between them while the people in the auditorium slowly start getting to their feet.

"What?" I ask.

Magda draws in a breath and shrugs. "Well, it was nice knowing you."

"What does that mean?"

From my other side, Gabriel gives me an apologetic look. "It's just… the Hunters are insane."

"Yeah, but I'm on the same team as them." With the frown still on my face, I shake my head a couple of times to show that I really don't understand their reasoning. "Shouldn't that mean I'm in the safest position possible?"

"No offense," Magda begins in a tone that makes it clear that she doesn't actually care one bit if I'm offended or not. "But you're the weakest person here."

"Ouch," I mutter, but then shrug. "But okay, what does that have to do with anything?"

"Everyone knows that the Hunters can influence the

instructors so that they get the people they want. Why do you think all four of them are on the same team?"

"Not to mention that it's usually four people per team," Gabriel adds. "And now it's suddenly five."

"So?" I prompt.

"So they *wanted you* on their team," Gabriel says. "And given who they are, do you really think they did that to help you?"

"No," I admit.

Magda snorts and shoots me a pointed look. "That's what you get for calling Eli Hunter stupid in front of an entire cafeteria full of people."

"Well, to be fair, I also carved *Small Dick Energy* into his car."

Paulo, who had been quietly drinking from his water bottle, sprays water across the seat in front of him before he manages to slap a hand in front of his mouth. Thankfully, the person who was sitting in that seat has already moved away. But some other students nearby turn to look at us.

"You did *what?*" Magda blurts out while Paulo fights to swallow down the rest of the water in his mouth.

All three of them gape at me. I just shrug in reply.

"Girl, you're crazy," Paulo says, shaking his head at me. Then he steals a quick glance over his shoulder. "Don't take this the wrong way, but I'm starting to think that maybe being seen with you isn't such a good idea."

Both confusion and annoyance ripple through me. I really don't understand the power dynamics in this place. Everyone here is training to be an assassin. They're *all* dangerous. So why does the Hunter family hold so much sway? I get that there are four of them while most people are here on their own, or with just one sibling. But still. It doesn't explain why they have the power to influence the teachers too.

Not for the first time, I curse my parents for their decision to keep me completely separate from this world. Even if they decided that I was unfit to be an assassin, they should have at least told me things. After all, no matter what they want for my future, I'm still Harvey Smith's daughter. Being kept in the dark is more dangerous for me than learning about all the messed-up shit that goes on in this world.

"I did that like a week and a half ago," I reply to Paulo's comment. "And they've already taken revenge for that, so I don't think you need to worry." The padded seat flips back up into the backrest as I get to my feet. "But I was leaving anyway."

"Oh, come on," Gabriel protests. "You don't have to leave."

Paulo drags a hand through his dark hair and flashes me a sheepish smile. "I'm sorry. I didn't mean it like that."

"It's alright," I assure them, and wave my hand. "I was actually planning to leave because there are some people I need to talk to. Now that everyone is here, can you point out the strongest people in the senior year? Apart from Eli and Connor, I mean."

Surprise blows across their faces, but I think they feel bad about Paulo's comment, because they just point out the five other students who are fighting for a spot in the top three. I thank them and promise them that I'll see them later. Then I start towards the first guy.

Apparently, my plan to keep Eli's attention on me is working like a charm. Everyone else is acting like I've just received a death sentence, but being put on Eli's team is the best thing that could have happened because it means that it will be easier for me to mess with him. Connor needs to perform well during that tournament, and if I'm on the Hunters' team, I can make sure that they actually leave him alone so that he can shine without their interference.

One part of my plan is on track. Now, I just need to figure out who tampered with his rifle so that we can hand that person over to Eli instead and get Connor completely off the hook. But to do that, I need to know who has the most to gain from Connor's downfall. And the people highest on that list of suspects are the other students fighting for the top three spots.

Soft murmuring fills the high-ceilinged auditorium as all the students discuss the team selection and the upcoming tournament. Some of them look to be searching for their team members while others appear to just be talking with their friends.

The senior I'm approaching is standing with two other guys who look to be his friends rather than his new team members. Or maybe both. I can't tell since I don't know their names or remember any of the other teams.

My pulse flutters nervously as I approach them. I have no idea how to just walk up to a group of guys and strike up a conversation. But I need to do this.

To protect Connor, I need to make this work.

12

ELI

I'm just about to turn towards the door when I notice Raina leaving her seat and striding straight through the crowd. Trailing to a halt, I narrow my eyes as I track her movements.

Surprise flits through me when she walks right up to Thomas O'Connell and his two friends. He's one of the best hitmen in my year, so what the hell does Raina think she's doing talking to him?

"You coming?" Kaden asks from where he has stopped and turned back to me a few strides away.

Without taking my eyes off Raina, I reply, "Meet me outside."

There is a slight pause. Then he says, "Alright."

From the corner of my eye, I can see my brothers head towards the door. But I keep my full attention on Raina.

She's talking to Thomas and his friends now. I can't hear what they're saying from up here, but the expressions on their faces quickly went from surprised and befuddled to satisfied and interested once Raina started speaking.

They chuckle at something she says, and she tosses her hair back and places a hand on Thomas's arm.

A flash of rage roars through me.

The crowd parts before me as I stalk down the steps towards them.

Does she really think that she can just do whatever she wants? That she can bat her eyelashes at anyone and everyone? No. She is not even allowed to breathe without my permission.

She doesn't get to have friends or partners. She doesn't even get to have casual fuck buddies. She's not allowed to have anyone. Only me. Unless I say otherwise, she will only ever know my touch, my voice, my body, as I do whatever the hell I want with her.

Thomas spots me as I advance on them. But Raina has her back to me, so she just continues talking to the other two guys.

"Hunter?" Thomas says it both like a greeting and a question.

"Leave," I order.

Raina whirls around at the sound of my voice while Thomas dips his chin in acknowledgement. He and his two friends immediately start to retreat.

After shooting me a scorching glare, Raina spins back to them and waves her hands. "No, wait, you don't have to leave. I still haven't—"

Her words are cut off by a yelp as I grab her and throw her over my shoulder.

For a few seconds, she just lies there on my shoulder as I start towards the door, as if she can't believe what's happening. Then reality apparently snaps back to her.

"What the hell do you think you're doing?" She kicks her

legs and pounds her hands into my back. "Put me down, you fucking neanderthal!"

People around us turn to look as I continue towards the door, but no one is stupid enough to try to intervene.

Raina keeps struggling to get free, but I easily hold her in place with an arm over her back.

"You fucking asshole," she growls with impressive menace while she continues squirming on my shoulder. "I swear to God, I am going to—"

I slap her ass. Hard.

She sucks in a gasp. Stunned silence follows it. Then she snaps, "You bastard! Stop—"

"Stop acting like a brat," I cut her off as I stride into an empty room on the other side of the corridor. "And I'll stop spanking you like one."

A truly vicious string of curses answers me while I kick the door shut behind us. Then I move over to the wall and set Raina down.

She immediately tries to move aside. I slap my palm against the wall next to her head, blocking her way with my arm. Trapped between me and the wall, she drags her eyes to my face.

I almost start slightly at the rage burning in those green eyes of hers.

"You had no right!" she screams, and gives my chest a hard shove that does absolutely nothing to push me back. "You had no right to interrupt our conversation like that!"

For a moment, I'm too stunned to reply.

For the first time since I met her, she looks genuinely angry. And not just angry. She looks *furious*.

She didn't even look mad when I fucked her throat on the side of the road or after I spanked her ass in the middle of the canteen or when I humiliated her in the sparring room.

But now, because I scared off some guys she was talking to, she looks ready to tear my throat out. Why? Why would that be such a big deal to her?

Pushing aside the confusion for now, I raise my eyebrows and reply, "No right, huh?"

"Yes!" She shoves at my chest again. "But apparently, you're too stupid to—"

I yank up my other hand and lock it around her throat. Taking a step closer, I press farther into her space. Her tits brush against my body as her chest heaves with anger. It sends sparks of electricity shooting through me and makes blood rush to my cock.

"Watch your mouth, princess," I warn, leaning down so close that I'm almost breathing the words against her lips.

"Or what?" she retorts, glaring up at me.

"Or I might gag you." I stroke my thumb over the side of her neck. "Or decide to fill your throat with something else."

She shudders, either at my words or at my touch, and something flickers in her eyes. But I don't think it's anger.

"Would you like that, princess?" I push.

She bites the inside of her cheek, but only continues glaring up at me in silence.

"Which one?" I shift my hand so that I can draw my thumb over her bottom lip instead. "For me to shove my cock down your throat again? Or for me to force a massive ball gag into your mouth and secure it behind your head with a lock that only I have the key to, so that you can't speak unless I allow it?"

Another shudder courses through her body, and her eyes shutter briefly.

I smirk. "Or both?"

She draws in a shaky breath.

My cock aches. Fuck, I shouldn't have spoken all that out loud. Because now, doing both of those things, and more, to her perfect body is all I can think of.

Her chest heaves, and she stares back at me with eyes that burn with a whole host of emotions. Then she drags in a deep breath, and a wicked smile slides across her lips instead.

"Try it," she taunts. "And I'll kill you in your sleep."

A huff of amusement escapes my chest. I shift my hand back down to her throat and give it a firm squeeze. "Threats, huh? You just watched me send one of the best hitmen in the entire senior year scurrying away with his tail between his legs after just one word from me, and you think threats is your best course of action here?"

"Yes, why is that?"

"Why is what?"

"Why is it that everyone backs away when you so much as glance in their direction?" She shakes her head, and genuine confusion swirls in her eyes. "It makes no sense. Everyone here is training to be an assassin. So why is everyone so damned scared of you?"

I raise my eyebrows in surprise. "You don't know?"

"No."

Releasing her throat, I take a step back and cock my head as I study her. "How can you not know?"

A hint of annoyance and embarrassment flickers across her features as she crosses her arms defensively and glances to the side. "My family didn't want me to become a hitman. So I'm... not exactly familiar with all the politics in this world."

For a few seconds, I just watch her in silence. Is this the reason why she doesn't fear me like everyone else? Not because she somehow sees through all of my bullshit and doesn't care that I'm violent and volatile. But simply because she doesn't *know*.

Disappointment blows through me.

Once she understands how this world works, she will probably start acting like everyone else and stop challenging me the way she does.

A heavy weight settles in my stomach.

But if that's the case, then I need to know, so I block out all of those feelings of disappointment and instead ask her a question that I know she will say yes to.

"Would you like me to show you?"

13

RAINA

Eli strides up to the driver seat of his now once again spotless Range Rover. I branch off, heading for the passenger's side door. I've barely gotten the door open when a hand appears on it, shoving it closed again.

"Cute," Rico says with a snort. Then he jerks his chin towards the door behind instead. "In the back."

I scowl back at him in annoyance for a second, but then roll my eyes and release the handle. Kaden is standing next to the now open door to the backseat, twirling a knife in his hand.

Even though he isn't even looking at the blade, he doesn't miss a single spin as he raises his other hand and motions towards the open door. "After you."

Not bothering to say anything, I just stalk past him and slide into the car. Before I can even sit down properly, the other door is yanked open and Jace flops into the seat next to me.

From the passenger's seat ahead, Rico turns around and frowns at him. "Where did you get the bat?"

Jace slams the door shut behind him and leans back in his seat. He's holding a baseball bat in his right hand, resting it against his shoulder. "It was just lying there on the field, so I picked it up."

Rico chuckles and shakes his head while turning back to face the windshield. "Of course you did, Golden."

Sitting up straight, Jace levels the bat at Rico and uses it to threateningly tap the side of his seat. "Stop calling me that."

"If that bat leaves so much as a single smudge on my seats, I'll beat your ass to kingdom come," Eli warns, locking eyes with Jace in the rearview mirror.

On my right, Kaden snickers as he gets in and pulls the door shut. "Did he bring his dirty toys into the car again?"

"Oh the irony of you trying to give me shit about dirty toys," Jace retorts, and cuts him a pointed look.

Based on the sly smile that curls Kaden's mouth, I'm pretty sure they're not talking about frisbees and footballs.

"If you're done bickering," Eli interrupts. "Put your fucking seatbelts on."

Surprise flickers through me.

"That means you too, princess," Eli says, meeting my gaze in the mirror.

After four clicks have sounded, he nods and pulls out of the parking lot. I watch the fields flow past the window as he drives us away from Blackwater and towards the nearest city. The late afternoon sun casts orange and golden streaks across the land.

Tearing my gaze from the view, I shift my attention back to the people around me. Both Kaden and Jace are sitting with their legs spread wide in that typical arrogant male way, leaving me having to press my knees together. Jace is absentmindedly drumming his fingers on the bat's handle while he stares out the window. On my right, Kaden does the same, except he is twirling a knife in his hand instead.

My gaze drops down to the other blades peeking out of his thigh holster. Shifting my weight discreetly, I move my hand towards it. Then I pause for a few seconds. Once I'm sure that none of them are looking at me, I gently slide one of the knives from its sheath.

A hand shoots down and locks around my wrist. I suck in a startled hiss.

The others turn to look at me while Kaden raises my trapped hand. Golden sunlight gleams against the blade I'm still holding.

"I was wondering if you'd try that again," Kaden says, flashing me a sharp smile.

I try to yank my hand out of his grip. But when it doesn't work, I just let a nonchalant expression settle on my features instead. "You were expecting it?"

"Fool me once..."

Eli is keeping his attention on the road, but he steals a glance at me in the mirror. The rest of his brothers are watching me with eyes full of anticipation, as if they can't wait to see how this plays out.

"How did you do it?" Kaden demands. "The first time. How did you manage to steal it without me noticing?"

Because I'm a chemist. I have incredibly steady hands and gentle fingers from spending the past decade handling dangerous chemicals. But I want to keep that information to myself for now, so I decide on a different answer.

Holding his hard stare, I reply, "Because maybe I'm not quite as worthless as everyone here seems to think."

From the rearview mirror, I can feel Eli's gaze burning holes in the side of my head. But I keep my eyes on Kaden.

"I will only say this once," he begins, slowly, enunciating every word clearly. "No one touches my blades."

With his hand still locked around my wrist, he forces my arm back, moving the knife in my palm closer to my own throat. I try to stop him. It doesn't work. I even wrap my other hand around his wrist, using that to try to halt his movements as well. But it's like fighting the tide. And I can't just drop the blade because it will land right in my lap if I do.

Cold steel kisses my skin as Kaden positions the knife underneath my chin.

"Understood?" he demands, his eyes so cold that I almost get frostbite just holding his gaze.

I try to move both his and my hand away again, but when it doesn't work, I force myself to press out, "Yes."

He doesn't release my wrist. Just continues staring me down.

"The same goes for you," Eli suddenly says. "If you stain my seats with her blood, I will make you clean it up by hand."

Jace chuckles.

It breaks the dangerous tension in a flash. Kaden releases my wrist and plucks his knife from my grip before sliding it back in its sheath. Then he draws a hand through his straight black hair and flashes me a smug smile.

Blowing out a long breath, I shake my head and then settle back into my seat.

The rest of the car ride passes without any more death threats.

A slight frown creases my brows as Eli drives us to a residential area. Fancy houses and immaculate gardens line both sides of the wide street. I watch them as Eli begins to slow down.

"Pick a house," he says.

"What do you mean?"

"Just point to any house."

Since I have no idea where he's going with this, I just point to a random house halfway down the street. Eli pulls up next to it. It's white, with trimmed hedges around the small lawn and a white stone path leading up to the pale wooden door.

Eli rolls down the window next to Kaden a fraction, and then he turns to me. "Stay in the car."

"And do what?" I ask, befuddled.

"Watch. Listen. And I'll show you exactly what kind of power our family possesses."

Before I can answer, the four of them get out of the car and close the doors behind them. I scoot across the backseat until I'm sitting next to the window Eli cracked open.

My pulse flutters.

I half expect them to stalk up to the house and kill the people inside, but they don't. In fact, they don't really do anything. I watch with furrowed brows as the four of them position themselves by the side of the car.

Eli and Rico, who are in the middle, just casually lean back against the car while crossing their arms. On either side of them, Kaden and Jace do the same, except Kaden is nonchalantly twirling a knife in his hand and Jace is resting the bat against his shoulder.

For about a minute, nothing happens.

Sunset is close now, turning the sky dark red and purple at the horizon. The lights are on in the house, which means that someone must be home.

The confusion inside me grows as they just stand there, watching the white house.

Then the front door is cracked open. I lean closer to the window as a couple in their mid-thirties cross the threshold and move out onto the patch of white stone in front of the house. They leave the door open behind them, and yellow light from the hallway spills out onto the stones.

Fear pulses on their faces as both the man and the woman stop a few steps from the door. Then they drop to their knees. Eli and his brothers just remain standing by the car, doing nothing.

"Please," the man calls. "There must be some kind of mistake."

None of them reply.

The man motions towards their still open front door. "Take whatever you want. We won't fight back. So just... please don't hurt us."

The Hunters just keep watching them in silence.

Heat spreads through my core. The complete control they have over this couple, without even uttering a single word or moving one muscle, is making my heart pound and my clit throb.

"We'll do whatever you want," the woman calls, desperation lacing her voice. "But we *have* paid our dues for this month. I swear. Please, call Mr. Morelli."

Eli slides his phone out of his pocket and then moves his thumb as if he's calling someone. But from this angle, I can see that the screen is black. He holds it to his ear.

After pretending to listen to the nonexistent person on the other end of the line, he puts the phone back into his pocket and says, "You're fine."

Both of them drag in a shuddering breath of relief. But they stay on their knees, as if waiting for permission.

Eli jerks his chin. "Go back inside."

My clit aches with dark desire as I watch the couple hurry back inside while thanking the Hunters repeatedly. I shift my weight, pressing my thighs together. Jesus Christ, power like this is so fucking hot.

I scoot back to the middle of the seat as the Hunters return to the car. No one says anything as they get in and put their seatbelts on. After rolling up the window again, Eli does a U-turn and then drives back out of the neighborhood.

Only when we're back on the big road have I gathered my thoughts enough to shake my head and ask, "What just happened?"

"The first thing you need to know is that there are two types of assassin families," Eli says while keeping his eyes on the road. "There are the ones who are completely anonymous. The ones who look like just an average American family that no one ever suspects."

Like *my* family. But I can't tell him that, so I just nod instead.

"And then there are families like ours," he continues. "The ones who everyone fears because they all know that we are killers for hire."

"But if everyone knows that you're hitmen, why don't they just report you to the police?"

"Because they all know that we are the Morelli family's closest allies and most trusted assassins."

Even if they hadn't forced my mom to sign away our fortune as payment for Dad's screw-up, I would have known who the Morelli family is. Everyone does. They're Italian mafia. In fact, they're the largest, and most dangerous, mafia family in this entire state.

I flick a quick glance over the four brothers, once again noting their dark hair and brown eyes and olive complexion.

"You're related to them?" I say. It's half statement, half question.

"Yes," he replies. "Our mother is a Morelli."

"I see." My mind is working hard to process all of this information, but I need to know more so I keep pushing. "But even so, if people know that you commit murder, why hasn't anyone called the police on you?"

"Someone tried that once." Eli meets my gaze in the mirror. "What do you think happened to them?"

On my left, Jace scoffs and adjusts the bat on his shoulder. "Besides, do you really think we're stupid enough to leave any actual proof?"

"We also have half the police force in our pocket," Rico adds nonchalantly from the front seat.

"I see," I repeat.

A smirk spreads across Eli's lips as he meets my gaze in the rearview mirror again. "So that's why they all bend over and take it in the ass like a little bitch." Cruel amusement flickers in his eyes. "Because then we let them live."

I snort and roll my eyes at him.

Outside the windows, the sun has now set and darkness spreads across the fields. Only the streetlights along the road break up the gloomy landscape around us.

We drive in silence the rest of the way while I process this information.

Deep down, I know that I probably should be terrified right now. Eli has just told me that his family is related to the Italian mafia family that rules this state with an iron fist. That they kill anyone who dares to oppose them and that they have the police on their payroll, which means that they also get away with their murders. And I'm currently alone with all four of them in a car.

They could just take me to the woods right now and put a bullet in the back of my head, and no one would ever know. But for some reason, I just can't bring myself to be scared.

I'm not sure if it's because I don't think they would actually kill me, or if the way I grew up has just made me so used to death that my sense of self-preservation is somehow simply broken.

"People say that you're crazy." I can feel his brothers stiffen around me, but I keep my eyes on Eli in the mirror as he pulls into the now deserted parking lot outside the school. "Are you?"

His eyes find mine. "People say that you're crazy too. Are you?"

"Maybe." I flash him a grin tinged with insanity. "Let's just say that there's a reason why my family didn't want me to be a hitman."

He lets out a huff that sounds like half surprise, half amusement as he parks his car next to Rico's. Their cars are the only ones left in the lot. Well, except for my bike, which is locked to the rack closer to the doors.

Instead of replying, he just unbuckles his seatbelt and gets out of the car. His brothers follow suit. Once they're outside, I slide out as well.

"I'll see you back at the house," Eli says to his brothers while I straighten and close the door behind me.

They nod before starting towards their own cars. I take a step forward as well, intending to get to my bike. But before I can move any farther, Eli steps in front of me, blocking my way.

A thud echoes across the empty parking lot as he plants a hand on the driver's side door and pushes it shut as well. While his brothers start their cars and drive away, Eli moves closer, backing me up against the side of his Range Rover. He places his hands on the car on either side of me, caging me in.

My heart jerks in my chest. He is standing so close that I can almost feel the heat from his body seeping into mine, and I have to tilt my head back to meet his gaze.

"Remember what happened back at that house," he says.

How can I forget? My clit throbs at just the memory of the power and control he wielded back there.

"And remember what I told you in the car," he continues, his golden eyes boring into mine. "*That* is what I can do to you if I decide to stop playing nice."

It feels as though he's waiting for me to cower before him. For me to tremble and panic. To beg his forgiveness for what I've done to mess with him.

But I don't. I don't fear him at all. Because no matter how crazy people think *he* is, I know that I have him thoroughly outclassed in that department. He might think that he is dangerous and unhinged, but he's got nothing on me.

So I just raise my chin in a cocky gesture and give him an unimpressed look.

He takes one hand from the car and instead places it around my throat, positioning his thumb so that it's pressing under my chin and holding my head tilted back like that. A wicked smile spreads across his lips.

"So if you want to live," he begins, his voice dark and laced with threats. "You'll also bend over and take it in the ass like a little bitch."

"Metaphorically?" I match his insane smile. "Or literally?"

Surprise flickers in his eyes for a second, as if he doesn't understand why I'm not trembling like a leaf right now. But it's gone almost as quickly as it appeared.

He tightens his fingers slightly around my throat as he cocks his head. “Tread carefully.”

Reaching up, I grab the front of his shirt and pull his face down closer to mine. “Funny. I was just about to say the same thing to you.”

14

ELI

The front door rattles in its frame as I slam it shut behind me. After kicking off my boots, I stride into the hallway.

"You here?" I call.

Only silence answers me.

Grinding my teeth, I stalk into the laundry room and yank open my duffel bag before tossing my sweaty clothes and damp towel into the basket.

I had thought that two hours of grueling physical training would calm me down, but tension still coils around my body like steel vines. I normally don't sleep a lot, and I can handle the exhaustion and the feeling of constantly being high-strung that comes with it. But in the past three days, I've barely slept at all.

After our little excursion last Friday, I spotted Raina a couple of times during the weekend. But come Monday morning, she just disappeared off the face of the earth. And now, no one has seen her all week.

I can't concentrate. I can't sleep. I can't fucking breathe properly.

I'm well aware that I'm becoming dangerously obsessed with her, but I can't help it. The tension in my body bleeds away when I'm near her, and my blood-soaked soul sings when she looks at me. Never with fear. Even after what I showed her and told her last Friday, she doesn't back down. Doesn't cower. Doesn't fear me. She almost seems turned on by my threats.

It's dangerous, I know that, but my body has started to crave the way she makes me feel. As if I'm not crazy. As if there is nothing wrong with me. As if my mind didn't irrevocably snap back when I was thirteen. She makes me feel as if she can see right into my soul, and as if she doesn't care about the darkness she finds in there. It's like a fucking drug.

And then she just disappears into thin air.

Flexing my fingers, I stalk towards the stairs while reaching into my pocket. For the third time this evening, I call my brothers. None of them answer.

It takes all of my willpower not to hurl my phone through the damn window as my call goes to voice mail yet again.

Where the hell are they?

I haven't seen them since class ended this afternoon. It's not like them to disappear like that. Especially not Rico. They know that I'm one careless word away from slaughtering someone just to relieve my frustrations. And when that happens, Rico is always close by to pull me back from the edge so that I don't descend fully into madness.

So where the hell are they?

And where the fuck is Raina?

I stalk through the house, my feet thudding against the polished floorboards. It's a massive two-story building made of dark wood, and it's probably the most coveted house on the entire campus. Since I'm a Hunter, I had first pick when I started at Blackwater, so I naturally chose this house. It has a huge living room and kitchen, a study, and six bedrooms, each complete with its own private bathroom. When Rico, Kaden, and Jace enrolled, they moved in here as well.

But they're not here right now.

Moving through the hallway, I check each of their rooms, and even the two spare rooms too. But they're all deserted.

My mind is spinning and twisting, and tension crackles through my body like lightning. I know that I need sleep. I can feel my muscles protesting and my brain fraying from the lack of it, but I just can't bear the thought of lying there in my bed and staring at the ceiling yet another night. Because that's what will happen.

Striding back down the hall, I reach the door to my own bedroom and grab the handle. But then I pause. I glance towards the stairs.

Maybe I should just head back to campus instead and do another workout? That should at least help me relieve some of the restless energy still bouncing around inside me.

Yeah, that's what I should do.

I nod to myself and then push down the handle so that I can grab a new set of workout clothes from my closet.

With my mind still churning, I move across the threshold.

Then I stop dead in my tracks.

For a while, I can't process what I'm seeing, so I just stand there on the floor and stare at the scene before me.

Raina is lying on my bed.

My gaze flicks over her body again, and I amend that statement.

Raina is lying *tied* to my bed.

She's spreadeagled, her legs spread wide and rope securing her ankles to the footboard. Her arms are similarly tied. Ropes wrap around her wrists and trap her to the headboard, holding her arms pinned against the mattress above her head.

I slowly close the door behind me while my mind scrambles to catch up.

Drifting closer, I study her face.

She's wearing a blindfold, and she has a pair of noise-cancelling headphones over her ears. Her chest rises and falls with steady breaths, even though she's gagged.

I squint down at the black rubber keeping her mouth in check. If I'm not mistaken, that's a gag from Kaden's rather extensive stash. A penis gag that's probably filling her entire mouth.

My gaze drifts down over her body. She's fully clothed. I drag my gaze from her sneakers and up her bare legs to the short black skirt she's wearing. Then my eyes land on her green button-up shirt.

There's a note pinned to it.

Moving right up to the bed, I lean forward and read two words written in Kaden's neat script.

Have fun.

15

RAINA

The street around me is dark and silent. Sitting on the bench at the bus stop, I wait for the next one to arrive so that I can get back into the city and then get a cab from there back to Blackwater. I drum my fingers against the worn wood. This took longer than I expected.

Missing three days of classes would've been terrible for everyone else on campus, but since I'm not going to become a real assassin anyway, it doesn't matter. What does matter is that I have left Eli alone for three days. What if he has used that time to start messing with Connor again?

A pair of headlights appear at the end of the street. I'm about to stand up, thinking that it's the bus, when I realize that it's only a car. Remaining on the bench, I slide my gaze back to the buildings ahead instead.

Suspicion creeps over me when the car doesn't speed past. I snap my gaze to it as it instead stops right in front of me. My heart does a double beat. It's a black Range Rover.

Before I can get that realization through my brain, the

passenger's side door is opened and Kaden steps out. Jace appears from the backseat a second later.

"Hello, Raina," Kaden says.

His eyes glint in the light from the streetlamp, and a shiver rolls down my spine. There is insanity in Eli's eyes, but it's a familiar kind of madness. The cold calculation that glitters like shards of ice in Kaden's dark eyes is something else. Something crueler.

"Boys," I reply.

For a few seconds, we just watch each other. I glance past Kaden to see Rico sitting in the driver's seat. A strange sense of disappointment settles in my stomach when I realize that Eli is not with them.

"Get in the car," Kaden orders.

I was on my way back to Blackwater anyway, and this will be much faster than taking the bus, so I just shrug and stand up. "Alright."

Surprise blows across their features, as if they had expected me to refuse. With the two of them still watching me with wide eyes, I stroll past them and climb into the backseat. Since there are only four of us this time, I claim the other window seat.

Two thuds sound as Kaden and Jace get in and throw the doors shut behind them. Then Rico starts the car. After turning it around, he drives back down the street.

"Eli is not happy with you," Rico comments from the driver's seat.

"Aww, did he miss me?" I taunt, but I'm secretly kind of pleased to hear that my absence didn't go unnoticed.

"You'd better have one hell of an explanation."

"Why would I need to explain myself to him?"

"I would also suggest getting ready to grovel," Kaden adds as if I hadn't spoken. "Thoroughly."

I snort and arch an eyebrow at him. "Do I really look like someone who grovels?"

From the seat next to me, Jace flashes me a wicked grin. "Everyone grovels in the end."

Shaking my head, I roll my eyes and scoff.

Streetlights and houses turn into dark fields and forests as Rico drives us back to the area where all of Blackwater's students live. I sit up straighter as we reach the first section, where all the dorm rooms are located. But Rico just drives right past it.

"Uhm, I live over there," I say, turning in my seat and pointing towards the buildings we are quickly leaving behind.

None of them answer.

Since I'm not desperate enough to throw myself out of a moving car, I just turn back around again and shake my head at the three of them in annoyed silence.

Rico pulls up to a massive two-story building made of dark wood.

My mouth drops open. They live *here*? I thought it belonged to one of the professors or something.

As soon as we've stopped, I quickly unbuckle my seatbelt and slip out of the car while calling, "Well, thanks for the ride."

I don't even make it two steps before Jace appears in front of me, blocking my path. "Not so fast."

With a quick sidestep, I try to dodge him. But he moves like a viper. Grabbing my arm, he twists it up behind my back hard enough to make me cry out. The sound is immediately cut off as he slaps his other hand over my mouth.

I uselessly try to fight him as he starts marching me towards the front door. Jace might be the youngest of the Hunters, but he's definitely not the weakest. Pressed against him like this, I can feel his rock-hard muscles shift against my body.

Rico unlocks the front door and walks inside while speaking to Jace over his shoulder. "Get her up to Eli's room. I'm going to grab some rope."

A startled noise makes it out of my throat, but it's blocked by Jace's hand. Eli's room? Rope? What the hell are they planning to do?

I dig my heels into every step up the stairs until Jace loses patience and lifts me up and throws me over his shoulder instead. At least it gets his hand off my mouth.

"Let me go," I snarl, trying to twist my body out of Jace's arm. "Or I swear to God, I will—"

"You'll do what, exactly?" Kaden interrupts. He's following us up the stairs, and that sadistic amusement gleams in his eyes as he gives me a mocking once-over where I lie across his brother's shoulder. "You're so far out of your league here that it's almost ridiculous."

Before I can retort, Jace yanks open a door and stalks inside.

My heart lurches as I'm met by an elegant room with dark wallpaper and polished wooden floorboards. All the furniture is made of dark wood. And everything, from the grand desk by one wall to the double bed opposite it, is neat and tidy. A testament to the fact that Eli demands control over everything and everyone around him.

The room even smells like him. I can't pin down the exact scents, but it smells dark and mysterious and absolutely intoxicating.

For a moment, I'm so overwhelmed by that incredible

scent that I lose track of what I'm supposed to be doing. The next second, Jace heaves me off his shoulder and tosses me down onto the large double bed.

The mattress bounces underneath me and the dark sheets rustle as I land back first on it. I try to scramble into a sitting position, but before I can, Jace straddles me.

Air escapes my lungs in a huff as he settles his massive weight right on top of my chest. Kicking my legs and pushing against his thighs with my hands, I try to get him off me, but his muscular body remains firmly where it is.

While I'm busy cursing him to hell, Rico walks through the door carrying a bundle of thick ropes. He tosses two of them to Kaden before starting towards my legs.

My heart pounds in my chest and a throbbing starts at my core as the two of them deftly secure the ropes around my wrists and ankles and then tie me to the bedframe with efficient moves.

Once all the ropes are in place, Jace climbs off my chest. I draw in a deep breath now that his weight is no longer pressing down on my lungs. Then I try to yank my arms and legs free. My restraints remain firmly in place.

Well, they sure know their way around knots.

Narrowing my eyes, I turn to glare at the three brothers now standing by the side of the bed, watching me with amused expressions on their faces.

"Seriously?" I pull at the ropes again. "Were you all boy scouts or what?"

Jace chuckles, and Rico gives me a nonchalant shrug. But Kaden only walks over to the desk and writes something on a piece of paper. Once he's done, he returns with it and a paperclip.

My pulse thrums in my ears as he leans over the bed and

reaches towards my chest. But all he does is to secure the paper to my shirt using the paperclip. I raise my head as much as I can and read the two words written there.

Have fun.

My stomach flips.

"Have fun?" I challenge, staring at them in disbelief. "*Have fun*? Fuck, has anyone ever told you that you're a bunch of arrogant entitled assholes who don't—"

"Kaden," Jace interrupts. "Don't you have something to shut her up with?"

A wicked smile spreads across Kaden's lips. "Of course I do."

I yank furiously against the ropes again while Kaden disappears out the door. "When I get out of these restraints, I will—"

"*If* you get out of these restraints," Rico interrupts, "it will be because Eli allows it. So if I were you, I would take Kaden's advice from earlier and start practicing your groveling. Like I said, he's not happy with you right now."

"*He's* not happy? I'm the one who's..." I trail off as Kaden returns carrying three items. My eyes go wide. "What is that?"

He holds them up one at a time while saying, "Blindfold. Noise-cancelling headphones. Penis gag."

"Seriously?" Rico says, and sighs in exasperation.

"What?" Kaden replies.

"The blindfold and the noise-cancelling headphones?"

"Of course. Sensory deprivation only makes the waiting so much more... thrilling."

They continue to bicker but all I can do is stare at that penis gag. It's a black rubber ball with straps set into the sides. Except the ball isn't completely round. On one side is a thick rubber penis that looks like it will fill my entire mouth.

Before I can get my wits about me again, Kaden climbs onto the bed and forces my jaw open. Then he shoves the penis gag into my mouth. It's so big that it hits the back of my mouth when Kaden tightens the straps behind my head. I gag.

Kaden just smirks at me and gives my cheek a couple of brisk pats. "Remember what I said. Grovel."

Then he slips the blindfold over my head and places the headphones over my ears.

Everything goes dark and unnaturally silent.

I shake my head, trying to get them off, but it only makes the rubber cock hit the back of my mouth once more. I gag yet again. Yanking against the ropes, I try futilely to get free. They don't give an inch.

My heart slams against my ribs.

I have no idea if the Hunters are still in the room, watching me, or if they have already left. And I won't know when Eli returns either. But there is nothing I can do about that.

Settling back against the mattress, I place my head in a position where the gag doesn't hit my throat. And then I do the only thing I can do.

I just lie there and wait for Eli to show up.

It's impossible to tell how much time passes. Just like Kaden said, the sensory deprivation screws with my perception until time loses all meaning. Ten minutes could have passed. Or ten hours.

All I can feel is my heart thudding in my chest and the ropes pressing against my bare skin.

Soft fingers brush against my leg.

A jolt shoots through me like a lightning strike, and I jerk my head up. The move makes the rubber cock hit my throat again. I gag and then force myself to lie back down again so that it won't trigger another gag reflex. But I can't stop myself from turning my head this way and that, trying to see or hear anything. When it doesn't work, I yank against my restraints again.

Those soft fingers trail over my knee and up my thigh. And because I can't see or hear anything, my sense of touch is incredibly heightened, so every brush of his fingers makes lightning crackle across my skin. I squirm against the mattress.

The fingers disappear.

My heart pounds against my ribs.

Then the headphones are lifted off my ears, and sound rushes back to me. Suddenly, I can hear the groan of the ropes as I pull on them, the sound of my own heavy breathing, and the faint rustle of someone's clothes.

My heart stutters as those gentle fingers trace my cheekbones. Then they curl underneath the edge of the blindfold. I blink against the sudden light as the dark fabric is pulled off my head.

When my vision clears, I find myself staring up at a dangerously handsome face. A smirk plays over Eli's lips. His dark hair is slightly messy, as if he has just showered and then dragged his fingers through it. And his eyes, those eyes the color of burnt gold, stare down at me with an intensity that snatches the breath from my lungs. I run my gaze over the scar that cuts through his left eyebrow and down his cheek.

Fuck, he looks like a ruthless god come to claim his vengeance.

Heat spreads through my stomach, and my clit throbs.

He cocks his head. "Princess."

"Asshole," I reply, but he of course can't hear it through the gag.

"When I remove this gag, the first words out of your mouth had better be a satisfactory explanation detailing where you have been these past three days. Followed by a groveling apology."

Since I can't speak, I just raise my eyebrows expectantly, silently telling him to get on with it. Something flickers in his eyes. But in the end, he just climbs onto the bed.

The mattress dips underneath me as he swings a leg over my body so that he's straddling my hips. I raise my head as he leans forward and reaches for the gag. His fingers deftly undo the clasp behind my head.

I draw in a deep breath as he at last pulls the thick rubber cock out of my mouth and tosses the gag onto the nightstand. He straightens but remains straddling my hips while I work my jaw to relieve the ache in it.

When I don't say anything, he arches a dark brow at me. "Well?"

"I was finishing things up at my other school."

"What does that mean?"

"It means that I dropped out three weeks into my second year without even telling them. So I had to go back there and formally withdraw from the program and clear out my dorm room and everything."

"And you thought you could just do that without informing me?"

"Why the hell would I inform you about that? God, you're so—"

"That's right, I am your God now." He leans forward and wraps his hand around my throat. "And you do not leave this academy without my permission. Is that clear?"

My pussy aches at the unflinching command in his voice and the power pulsing from his entire being, but instead of succumbing to the heat searing through my veins, I laugh up into his face. "In your dreams, pretty boy."

His fingers tighten around my throat, and he rakes his gaze up and down my body. "Big words for someone who is tied up and helpless underneath me right now."

The throbbing in my clit intensifies.

Eli narrows his eyes, studying me with a penetrating gaze that seems to burn all the way through me. Amusement, and what looks like satisfaction, blows across his features.

"Are you turned on by this, princess?"

Clamping my jaw shut, I just stare back at him.

He releases my throat and instead leans back. I try desperately to close my legs as he moves his hand towards my pussy, but the ropes around my ankles keep my legs spread wide open.

Heat rushes into my cheeks as he brushes his knuckles over my pussy, because I know that my panties are wet.

A glittering smile spreads across Eli's lips as he locks eyes with me again. "So, being completely at my mercy makes you wet, huh?"

I shoot a pointed look down at the massive bulge in his pants. "Shouldn't you be more worried about the fact that having me tied up in your bed against my will turns *you* on?"

"Oh, I've never tried to deny that I crave, and demand, complete control over others. In bed, and all other areas of life."

I open my mouth to retort, but Eli draws his fingers along my entrance before I can, and a moan slips past my lips instead. He lets out a dark chuckle. I yank against the ropes while Eli adjusts his position so that he is kneeling between my spread legs instead.

He slowly drags hungry eyes over my body. "Look at you, just begging to be punished."

A thrill races down my spine, and my clit throbs with dark desire.

Deep down, I know that I shouldn't find this so fucking hot. That being turned on by threats and violence is wrong. But the part of me that cares about right and wrong is long gone.

The thought of my control being taken away from me, the knowledge that Eli can do whatever he wants to me right now and there is absolutely nothing that I can do to stop him, turns me on so fucking much that my body thrums with need.

As if he can read all of those forbidden feelings on my face, Eli smirks like a bloody satisfied panther. I start to retort, but I never find out what I was planning to say, because right then, he pushes aside the fabric of my panties and brushes his fingers against my bare pussy.

Lightning shoots up my spine, and I try to arch up from the bed, but the ropes keep me firmly trapped against the mattress.

I suck in a gasp as Eli circles my clit with his thumb.

The pent-up tension that has been building inside me ever since his brothers tied me to this bed roars to life. Another moan drips from my lips as Eli continues working his fingers, making the pleasure inside me grow.

"Do you want me to make you come, princess?"

Keeping my mouth firmly closed, I squeeze my eyes shut as he continues rubbing my clit with perfect precision.

He traces his other fingers right over my entrance, sending a jolt through my body. "Do you?"

My pussy aches from his sweet torture, so I force myself to press out, "Yes."

"Then you're going to have to beg me for it."

"What is it that you and your psycho brothers don't understand about this? I don't beg."

"Oh, you will."

My eyes fly open as Eli pushes two fingers inside me. Pleasure courses through my whole body, making me jerk hard against the ropes, as he starts slowly pumping his fingers in and out while simultaneously rubbing my clit with his thumb.

Incoherent noises fall from my lips, and I throw my head from side to side, as the tension inside me grows to unbearable levels.

"Beg," Eli orders.

Squeezing my eyes shut again, I clamp my jaw and instead try to shift my hips to get his hand more firmly against my pussy. He just moves it back and continues torturing me. I can feel the orgasm looming. But it never comes. His fingers are just a little too gentle. A little too slow.

A frustrated groan rips from my throat.

"Beg," Eli commands again.

I writhe against the mattress, trying to force an orgasm from sheer force of will, but it doesn't work. Eli's clever fingers stroke my clit and slide in and out of my pussy, but it's never enough. My mind threatens to shut down when he just keeps pushing me closer and closer to that sweet edge while never letting me fall over it.

"When training a new pet," Eli begins, his voice like dark silk over my skin. "I've heard that it's better to start small and work your way up." His thumb circles my clit, making a shudder rack my frame. "So I will settle for a *please* this time."

I suck in desperate breaths. It feels like my brain is going to melt. I need release. I need it more than anything right now. So I force my stubborn pride aside and press out that one word he wants to hear.

"Please," I gasp.

A dark chuckle rolls from his chest. "Good girl."

He shifts the pressure on my clit at the same time as he curls his fingers on the way out of my pussy.

Release explodes through my body.

A cry of pleasure rips from my lungs, and my legs shake with the force of the orgasm crashing through my limbs. Eli continues pumping his fingers, prolonging the sensation, while I come hard all over his hand. I yank against my restraints as pleasure crackles through my veins like electricity.

When the last of it fades out, all I can do is just to lie there and stare up into the dark wooden ceiling. My chest heaves and heat radiates from my cheeks.

Fuck, this guy knows how to use his hands.

16

ELI

My cock aches. Watching Raina's perfect body writhe on my sheets and feeling her tight little cunt flutter around my fingers was so intoxicating that I feel like I'm high. All I want to do is to just rip her panties off completely and shove my cock into her and then fuck her into the next century.

But I can't do that, because then she would know just how much she affects me. And I can't have her thinking that she has any sort of power over me.

So instead of fucking her properly and hearing those breathy screams again, I force myself to pull my fingers out of her cunt and climb off the bed. Raina just lies there, staring into the ceiling and looking completely dazed, as I stride into my bathroom and take care of my aching cock in the shower instead.

Once I'm done, I walk back into my bedroom, wearing only a pair of boxers.

Raina snaps her gaze to me the moment I come into view.

And her green eyes become a shade darker as she rakes her gaze over my half-naked body.

Smug satisfaction swirls inside me. It's followed by a brief flash of dread, but I block it out as I continue towards the bed until I know that I'm close enough for her to see all the scars that crisscross my skin. They're mostly on my chest and back, but quite a lot of them line my arms and legs too.

I can feel Raina's eyes studying them, and I brace myself, waiting for the questions. The comments. The disgust. Or worse, the pity.

None of it comes.

Instead, she draws in a shuddering breath while her eyes burn like dark flames in the way they do when she's turned on.

Stunned shock pulses through me, and I momentarily forget why I was approaching the bed. Scrambling for something to do, I instead pick up the note and all of Kaden's equipment that I placed on the nightstand earlier. While moving them over to my polished wooden desk, I try to get my head back on straight again.

"Aren't you forgetting something?" Raina says from across the room.

After putting the things down, I turn around and then lean back against the desk. Crossing my arms, I raise my eyebrows in a show of confusion. "Forgetting what?"

Raina pointedly yanks at the ropes still tying her to my bed. "What do you think, asshole?"

"Is that really how you want to start this negotiation?"

"What negotiation?"

"I'm still waiting for you to apologize for leaving campus without my permission." I flash her a wicked smile. "Since I've gotten you to say please already, I suppose a bit of light groveling will do."

"How many times do I need to tell you? I don't grovel."

I shrug. "Suit yourself."

Uncrossing my arms, I push off from the desk and stroll over to the light switch. The room is plunged into darkness as I flick it.

"Hey," Raina protests. "What the hell?"

I move back to the bed and climb onto it. The mattress sways underneath me as I scoot closer to the middle until I reach Raina. Then I roll over on my side.

A surprised sound escapes her throat as I drape my leg over hers and wrap my arm around her chest. With a possessive grip on her soft body, I hold her close.

"What am I..." Raina mutters. "A teddy bear?"

"If you grovel, I will untie you."

"Like hell."

"Then I guess you're stuck here."

"Fucking hell," she curses, but she wiggles her body against me as if trying to get comfortable.

Heaving a deep sigh, I pull her even closer to me. She smells like jasmine and warm summer days.

That's the last thought that drifts through my head before sleep pulls me under.

I draw in a deep breath, and the scent of jasmine fills my lungs. Blinking, I try to figure out what that scent is doing in my bed. But before I can process that thought fully, another realization stuns me awake.

It's light out.

I jerk upright and turn to stare at the small clock on my nightstand. It's almost eight in the morning.

For almost an entire minute, I just sit there, staring at the clock in complete and utter disbelief.

I've slept for almost ten hours.

Ten hours.

Ten hours of deep and restful sleep.

Incredulity clangs through my skull. I can't even remember the last time I slept like this.

Turning slowly, I stare down at the woman lying next to me in my bed.

Raina is still sleeping, her chest rising and falling with deep breaths.

My mind spins.

Was this her doing?

Is she somehow the reason why I have been able to sleep properly for the first time in nine years?

Panic shoots through my spine. She can't be. I can't let someone have that kind of power over me. After what happened back then, back when I was thirteen, I swore that I would never let anyone have any kind of power over me again. If Raina somehow figures out that this night with her was the only time I've really slept in nine years…

Cold sweat breaks out across my scarred skin at just the thought of it.

Shaking my head, I scramble out of bed.

The mattress bounces due to my movements, which at last wakes Raina. Keeping my back to her, I put on some clothes while I work to put my calm composure back together.

"You still haven't untied me?" she says, her tone half question, half accusation.

"You still haven't groveled."

"Which I will never do. And if you keep me tied to your bed indefinitely, I will die."

"That sounds more like a you problem."

"Ah, you'd think so. But if I die, who will you torment then?"

A soft laugh escapes my throat. Pulling the final piece of clothing on, I turn back to face Raina. She has raised her head and is arching an expectant eyebrow at me.

The sight of her tied to my bed like that just makes me want to fuck her hard enough to wipe that stubborn expression off her face. But once again, I can't let her know how much she affects me, so I click my tongue casually and instead reply, "Fair point."

I move over to the bed and deftly undo the knots.

The moment she's free, she darts off the bed, as if she's worried that I might change my mind. After brushing her hands down her clothes to straighten them, she rubs her wrists. I rake my gaze over her.

There are imprints on her skin where the ropes have been, her clothes are rumpled, and her hair is a mess. A wicked grin slides home on my lips. She really looks freshly fucked.

"Coming?" I say.

Without waiting for a reply, I open the door and walk out into the corridor beyond. For a few seconds, all I can hear is the sound of my brothers talking in the kitchen downstairs. Then Raina's footsteps come from behind me.

We descend the dark wooden staircase in silence. It takes us to the wide hallway that connects the kitchen, living room, study, and the other couple of rooms on the bottom floor.

When we're halfway down, my brothers stop talking and instead move to the hallway so that they're standing there when we get down.

Kaden flashes me a knowing smile. "Did you have fun?"

"I did." I match his grin and incline my head as I sweep my gaze over all three of them. "Thanks for the gift, guys."

"*Gift,*" Raina scoffs behind me where she walks down the final couple of steps.

"We almost thought you were going to stay home and play with her the whole day," Jace says, wiggling his eyebrows. "It's almost eight o'clock."

The moment Raina's feet have left the steps, she makes a break for the front door.

"Jace," I snap, since he's standing closest to it.

Raina makes it all the way to the door and shoves the handle down, only to find that it's locked. And before she can unlock it, Jace slams his palm against the door and leans on it. Anger flickers in Raina's green eyes as she turns to glare at me.

"You're riding with me," I say by way of explanation.

She starts to protest, but Kaden cuts her off by saying, "Then let's get going."

Our footsteps echo between the dark wood panels as we start towards the door. Rico falls in beside me.

"You sleep?" he asks casually, but his eyes tell a different story.

I hold his gaze for a second longer than necessary before admitting, "Yes."

Surprise flickers across his face. It's there and gone again so fast that I know none of the others have seen it. Then a smile, one of those genuine ones that make his eyes light up, spreads across his face.

But all he says is a neutral, "Good."

Hot September winds wash across the fields, bringing with them the scent of warm grass. I glance up at the blue sky and the bright sun climbing over the horizon. In this part of the country, fall is still a while away.

After locking the door behind us, I start towards our cars in the driveway.

Raina apparently tried to bolt again because Jace is holding her by the arm next to my car now. She glowers at me like a bloody raincloud.

"Stop being so fucking difficult and just get in the car," I say.

For a moment, it looks like she is going to fight me on it. Then she clicks her tongue and snaps, "Fine."

She tries to yank her arm out of Jace's grip. He doesn't let her. Instead, he raises his eyebrows at me in silent question. I nod.

Raina mutters something under her breath as he at last releases her and strolls over to his own car. While I round the Range Rover, she climbs into the passenger seat and slams the door shut much harder than necessary.

"Careful," I say as I slide into the driver's seat and close the door with much better care. "You break it, you buy it."

"A bit too late for that, don't you think?" she replies, giving me a mockingly sweet smile while twirling a set of keys in her hand.

Shaking my head, I start the car and drive us towards the main road.

When we pass the series of buildings where the dorm rooms are located, Raina glances towards them longingly. "Can't you just let me out here?"

"Why?"

"I need to take a shower before I head to class."

With her eyes still on the buildings, she runs a hand down

over her inner thigh. My cock pulses, and I have to grip the steering wheel hard.

"I'm still sticky from last night," she continues. Tearing her gaze from the dorms, she turns to face me again. "And it's your fault, so the least you can do is to drop me off so that I can take a shower."

"I don't remember you complaining last night. In fact, I distinctly remember you begging me to make you come."

She crosses her arms and draws her eyebrows down. "I didn't beg."

"You said *please*."

"That's not begging. That was me being uncharacteristically polite. And we're getting off topic. Are you going to stop the car and let me go in and shower, or what?"

"No."

She throws her arms out. "Why the hell not?"

Taking my hand off the steering wheel, I slide it over her bare thigh and down between her legs. She sucks in a gasp as I flick her cunt. Then I give her inner thigh a pat before returning my hand to the steering wheel again.

"Because I want you to walk around campus all day with your own dried cum on your thighs from when I made you climax on my bed." I flash her a smirk. "As a reminder of who controls your body."

17

RAINA

The gun feels all wrong in my hands. It's too clunky. Too unwieldy. I barely even know how to hold it properly, even though the instructor took pity on me and showed me the basics that everyone is already supposed to know.

Raising it, I try my best to aim at the paper target across the grass. Then I squeeze the trigger. The gun jerks in my hands, and the bullet shoots through the air and hits the wooden barrier that has been built behind the row of targets. I heave an annoyed sigh.

I truly despise performing poorly. And right now, I feel like a worldclass loser. It doesn't matter what class we have, I'm somehow always the worst one at everything we do. The only thing I know that I'm good at is chemistry, but we haven't started those classes yet. So for now, I sneak off to the chemistry lab in my spare time and work on my own, just so that I can build up my crumbling confidence again.

"I've been meaning to ask," Gabriel suddenly says. He steps up to the line, fires two perfect shots at his target, and then moves back before turning to me again. "Were those rope marks on your wrists this morning?"

Thankfully, my cheeks are already flushed from irritation at my own failures, so I don't think Gabriel notices the added heat that creeps into them. "Uhm, yeah."

A mix of amusement and confusion blows across his features. "What happened?"

My gaze drifts down the field towards where Eli is standing. For this class, we've been split up and also joined by parts of both the second year and the seniors. So that the first-years can learn from their seniors' technique, or so our instructor said anyway. Eli is here, and Kaden is among the second-years. At least Connor, Jace, and Rico were assigned to different groups today. I'm incredibly thankful for that because I don't think I would've survived if my brother, as well as all of the Hunters, had seen just how bad I am at this.

Tearing my gaze from Eli's expert shooting on the other side of the field, I shift my attention back to Gabriel. "I was, uhm… detained."

His sparkling blue eyes flick up and down my body in surprise.

Another wave of heat sears my cheeks, as if I still had dried cum on my thighs. But I skipped lunch today and instead ran back to my dorm room to shower and change clothes before I biked back to school again, so no evidence of how I spent last night remain on my body.

"That sounds like a story I need to hear," Gabriel says as he lets out a light laugh.

Chuckling, I shake my head at him. "Trust me, you really don't want to know."

Stepping up to the line again, I raise the gun once more. I'm not even sure if I understand where I'm supposed to look in order to aim, but I hope for the best as I narrow my eyes and stare at the target. Then I pull the trigger.

The bullet shoots through the warm afternoon air and slams right into the target's left knee. I scowl at the man-shaped paper.

Once I have flicked the safety back on and lowered the gun, Gabriel slaps my shoulder with the back of his hand and flashes me a brilliant grin. "Great shot! The target would be thoroughly incapacitated by now."

Glancing up at him, I scratch the back of my neck and grimace. "I was aiming for his head."

Gabriel blinks. "Oh."

I just laugh and shrug, but even I can hear that it sounds a bit self-conscious. Clearing my throat, I let my gaze drift back to Eli instead.

I really need to figure out who tampered with Connor's rifle. Even though my conversation with that senior by the name of Thomas O'Connell was cut short by Eli and his caveman behavior, I managed to get enough of a feel for what kind of person he is. Ambitious, lethal, and mostly without morals. But there was also a strong sense of honor about him. I don't think he would stoop so low as to use dirty tricks on his competitors.

A sudden thought hits me like a lightning bolt.

What if the sabotage wasn't aimed at *Connor*? What if Eli was the real target? What if someone tried to actually take him out with that tampered rifle, and Connor just happened to be the person that they chose to use as a patsy?

My stomach bottoms out.

If that's the case, if Connor was just unlucky enough to be a random scapegoat, then I've been searching in the wrong place.

I shake my head to clear it, and then drag my attention back to Gabriel. He fires three shots at his target, two in the heart and one in the head, with a confidence that I wish I had as well.

"Do the Hunters have any enemies?" I ask.

He glances at me. Then fires one more time before stepping back again. "Well, of course. All assassin families have enemies, especially among the surviving loved ones."

"No, I mean here. At Blackwater."

His eyes move towards another first-year a short distance from us. I follow his gaze. The guy he is looking at has brown hair and gray eyes and a rather forgettable face.

"You know Anton, right?" Gabriel asks.

"Not really."

"His full name is Anton Petrov. He has an older brother too. Mikhail Petrov, who is a second-year." He runs a hand through his thick blond hair and then scratches his jaw before meeting my gaze head on again. "Their family has been trying to knock the Hunters down a few pegs for a while now."

"I see." A smile spreads across my lips. "Sounds like someone I should get to know then."

Gabriel sputters protests about how getting in the middle of that conflict is a really bad idea, but I ignore him and move down the line so that I'm standing next to Anton instead.

Surprise flickers in Anton's gray eyes as I take up position next to him, but he doesn't comment. I can't just walk up and ask him if he tried to have Eli shot a couple of weeks ago, so I don't say anything at first either. I just start shooting in silence.

Gunshots echo across the vast field as we all continue practicing. Sunlight beats down on me, warming my back.

There is no wind today, and the heat of summer still hasn't broken, so a drop of sweat rolls down my spine.

I fire again. The bullet hits the wooden barrier a short distance from the target.

"You're holding it wrong," Anton says eventually.

Satisfaction bubbles up inside me. Perfect. Now, I have an excuse to start a conversation with him.

I let an embarrassed expression descend on my features as I turn my head to meet his gaze. "Yeah, I figured as much. The instructor tried to show me earlier, but after the third time, he looked like he was ready to put a bullet between my eyes instead, so I just nodded and told him that I understood even though I still don't."

Anton chuckles. "Yeah, patience isn't exactly his strong suit."

"To be fair, it's not really mine either."

He huffs out another laugh and then shoots at his target a few more times. I'm starting to think that I've lost the opportunity, but then he glances at me again. I can feel his gaze drifting over my body, lingering on my curves.

"You're that girl who started three weeks after everyone else, right?" he says.

"Yes." Shifting my gun to my left hand, I reach out with the other as I say, "Raina Smith."

He takes my hand. "Anton Petrov."

We shake hands, but he holds on to mine a little longer than strictly necessary. I give him a smile. He gives my palm one more squeeze and then releases me.

"Petrov," I say, raising my eyebrows. "As in *the* Petrov family."

I had never heard that name until a few minutes ago, but

based on what Gabriel said, it sounds like they're well-known. And flattery always works.

My assumptions are confirmed when a proud smile spreads across his face. "Yeah, one and the same."

"Then I suppose we have a common enemy too." I shoot a pointed look towards Eli.

Anton's expression darkens as he sends a glare in that direction as well. "Yeah." Turning back to meet my gaze, he flicks a quick look up and down my body. "I saw what he did to you in the canteen earlier. With the belt."

I don't even have to fake the embarrassment in my voice this time. "You saw that, huh?"

Anger brews behind his eyes. "Someone really needs to knock that family off their bloody pedestal."

"Maybe someone is already trying. I heard that someone tried to shoot Eli a few weeks ago."

My heart thunders as I wait for his response. Even if he was the one responsible, I doubt that he is just going to confess that to me after only a few minutes of knowing me. But maybe he will let something slip. Some kind of thread that I can keep pulling at until I find proof that Connor is innocent.

"Yeah." Anton huffs out a laugh. "Too bad it failed." A scheming glint creeps into his eyes as he looks down at me. "And you're not going to follow their lead and try it too. At least not with how terrible your aim is." There is a smile lurking on his lips as he jerks his chin towards the targets. "Do you want me to show you how to hold it and aim properly?"

"Oh God, yes, please."

He holsters his own gun and then raises my arms so that I'm aiming towards the target again. After adjusting my fingers, he explains what I was doing wrong with my grip and how it affects the bullet trajectory. Then he moves up behind me.

My heart lurches as he presses his muscular body against my back and then reaches around me to grab my arms again.

"Like this," he says.

But I can barely concentrate on his instructions, because every time he speaks now, his breath dances over my neck and caresses the shell of my ear.

"Raina?" he says. "Are you listening?"

"What? Yes."

"Then what did I say?"

"Uhm..."

He laughs, sending his warm breath dancing over my skin again. "I was saying that when you aim, you need to—"

The area around me goes unnaturally silent as Anton abruptly stops speaking.

Then a dark voice cuts through the air like a blade.

"Get. Your hands. Off her."

I snap my gaze towards the sound of the voice, and find Eli Hunter standing right next to us looking like the devil himself. His golden-brown eyes burn like hellfire and violence rolls off his body like dark waves.

Anton has gone stiff as a board behind me, and he slowly takes his hands from my wrists and spreads his arms wide.

That's when I notice the gun that Eli is pressing against his temple.

My stomach flips. Jesus Christ, is he going to shoot him in the head for just showing me how to hold my gun?

"What the hell do you think you're doing?" I snap as I step away from Anton and whirl around to face Eli fully.

"You do not touch her," Eli grinds out. Still holding the gun to Anton's head, he sweeps hard eyes across everyone around us. "No one touches her. She belongs to me."

"I don't belong to anyone," I snarl.

But Eli isn't listening to me. He just drags those rage-filled eyes of his back to Anton. "This is the only warning you get, Petrov. The next time you put your hands on her, I will put a bullet in your brain."

Anton clenches his jaw, and anger flickers in his eyes as well, but he says nothing.

"Got it?" Eli demands.

"Yes," he forces out.

"Then repeat it back to me."

Fury flashes across Anton's face, and he grits his teeth again, saying nothing.

Eli shoves the muzzle of his gun harder against Anton's temple, forcibly making him tilt his head to the side. "Repeat it."

"The next time I touch her, you will put a bullet in my brain," Anton presses out with what sounds like great effort.

"Good. Now apologize."

"Sorry."

"Better."

"I apologize for touching something that belongs to you."

A mocking laugh rips from Eli's throat. "Good boy."

Heat pools at my core, but it's overshadowed by the sheer amount of anger burning through me.

Every time I try to talk to someone and get information about who set Connor up, Eli shows up and ruins it. I need to figure out who really tampered with the rifle, but I can't do that if Eli keeps acting like a possessive caveman all the time.

"I don't belong to you, you fucking asshole," I growl at him. "I can talk to whoever the hell I want and—"

"One more word out of your mouth, and last night will be child's play in comparison to what I'll do to you." Eli cuts me a commanding stare before taking the gun from Anton's head and using it to motion between us instead. "If you go anywhere near him again, he'll be bleeding out on the ground. You want that on your conscience?"

I glare back at him while clenching and unclenching my jaw. Then I force out, "No."

"No," he repeats, and then jerks his chin. "Then leave while I still have some patience left."

After a very short staring contest, I'm forced to accept that I have lost this round. With an irritated snarl, I spin around and stalk towards the edge of the field.

I hand in my gun, but then swipe another one on my way out. That one has a silencer on it. I don't know how to use one of those, or if it even affects the way the gun works apart from muffling the noise, but it was the only one within reach. But it doesn't matter. It should work for what I have in mind anyway.

With revenge burning inside me, I stalk away from the field and towards the chemistry lab.

18

ELI

On instinct, I jerk my body to the side. A second later, a fist slams into the wall right where my head was supposed to be. I whip around to find Mikhail Petrov drawing his hand back for another strike. Yanking my arm up, I slam my fist into his side before he can finish swinging.

A huff rips from his throat, and he dances back a step.

I flick a quick glance up and down the concrete corridor. It's suspiciously empty. Almost as if he had it cleared beforehand.

"You put a gun to my little brother's head," Mikhail snarls, his blue eyes flashing with fury.

I shoot him a nonchalant look. "So?"

"No one threatens my family."

Before I can reply, he yanks out a knife and lunges at me. I dodge the swipe and throw a fist down on his forearm, pushing it downwards before I slam my other fist into his jaw.

Pain pulses across his face, but he recovers quickly and jabs at me with the blade again.

My mind churns with possible strategies. I don't have a weapon, which means that I need to disarm him first.

Grunts echo between the empty gray walls as I land a series of punches to Mikhail's side. He manages to get in a shallow cut on my forearm. I grit my teeth as a flicker of pain sears through my skin.

He's good. I'll give him that.

Unfortunately for him, I'm better.

At last, I manage to land a precise blow to his elbow that makes a jolt shoot through his arm. The knife flies from his grip when his muscles spasm. I follow it up with a kick to the side of his knee.

A cry of pain rips from his throat as his leg buckles and he crashes down on the floor. I slam my knee into the side of his head, sending him smacking into the ground.

Dropping down, I straddle his chest and then ram my fist into his face again and again.

Mikhail tries desperately to protect himself, but on his back with my weight across his chest, he doesn't stand a chance.

Fury roars through me like a lightning storm. I know that I should try to control myself, but those safeguards in my brain were shattered long ago.

"Uhm, did I miss something?" Rico suddenly asks.

Locking my hand around Mikhail's throat, I pause my attacks and look up to find Rico, Kaden, and Jace standing next to us. Rico just looks at me with his eyebrows raised in question while Jace cocks his head as if studying Mikhail's face and the injuries there. Next to them, Kaden watches us with a cruel smile on his lips and that customary sadistic gleam in his eyes.

"The bastard tried to knife me," I grind out between gritted teeth while trying desperately to get my rage back under control. “Because I put a gun to little Anton’s head earlier.”

“Aww, how cute,” Jace says.

I turn back to Mikhail, who is struggling to get my hand off his throat so that he can breathe again. “You want to be us, huh? You want to take our family’s place as the most feared one here? You want to be me?”

Only strained gurgling answers me.

Without taking my eyes off him, I snap my fingers at Kaden. “Knife.”

He immediately slides one out of his thigh holster and hands it to me.

I relax my grip on Mikhail’s throat, allowing him to suck in strangled breaths. Then I lift the knife and place it over his left eyebrow.

“Well, if you want to be me, then we need to start by making you look more like me.”

His blue eyes dart up to the scar running through my eyebrow and down to my cheek. But before he can say or do anything, someone else comes sprinting around the corner up ahead.

Anton Petrov skids to a halt on the concrete floor, and his eyes go wide as he stares at us. Then rage floods his features, and he charges.

“Get off him, you fucking—” he begins, but his words are quickly cut off as Rico and Jace intercept him.

Air explodes from his lungs as my brothers throw him up against the wall. He struggles like a maniac, but they keep him effortlessly trapped like a fly with his back against the wall and his arms spread wide.

I turn back to Mikhail. “Now, as I was saying, we should start by making you look more like me.” Shifting the blade, I position the tip right above his eyeball. "Though maybe I should take your eye too, so that we don't look too similar."

Dread washes over his features. But to his credit, he doesn't beg.

Someone else does, though.

"No, please," Anton calls as he struggles against Rico and Jace's hold. "Please!"

"Anton," Mikhail snaps.

But Anton ignores him and instead locks pleading eyes on me. "Please, I'm sorry. I'm sorry for what happened on the gun range this afternoon. I'm sorry for what my brother did in this corridor. Please, *please*, don't take his eye."

While holding his gaze, I let a vicious smile stretch my lips as I move the knife closer.

"No!" Anton thrashes wildly against the wall. "Please, I'm begging you. I'm *begging you*."

I stop moving the blade and arch an eyebrow at him. "Are you now?"

"Yes. Please, Hunter. I'm begging you not to take his eye. He won't come after you again. I swear it. Just please let him go."

Mikhail squeezes his eyes shut and clenches his jaw. Shame burns on his face at hearing his little brother plead so pathetically and beg us for mercy on his behalf.

And in my book, that utter humiliation is punishment enough.

With a smug grin on my mouth, I move the knife away from his eye and spin it in my hand instead. "Well, since you begged so prettily."

A gasp of relief rips from Anton's throat.

After handing the knife back to Kaden, I get to my feet again.

As soon as my weight is off his chest, Mikhail tries to push himself up too.

I plant my boot against his chest and shove him back down on the floor. "Stay down." Sliding my gaze to Anton, I lock hard eyes on him. "And you, you'd better make sure he stays that way."

His worried gray eyes flick down to Mikhail, but then he nods.

Taking my boot off Mikhail's chest, I jerk my chin at my brothers. They release Anton and then fall in beside me as we start down the hall.

The restful calm I felt this morning after sleeping for almost ten hours evaporated the moment I saw Anton put his fucking hands on Raina. And now, volatile restlessness is back again. Just waiting to explode. Beating up Mikhail helped a bit, but it's not enough.

When it comes to Raina Smith, nothing is ever fucking enough.

I drag in a deep breath to calm my churning emotions as the four of us walk out the front door and into the parking lot.

People hurry back and forth. Some heading back to their dorms and others walking towards other buildings for after-hours practice. The orange afternoon sun is slipping farther down the horizon. Its light stretches across the parking lot and reflects against the cars and the windows, making it look like part of the area is on fire.

"Well, that was fun," Jace announces, sliding his hands into his pockets, as we start towards our cars.

"I really wish you would have actually carved his eye out," Kaden says. "That would have been fun to watch."

"And also a fucking mess to clean up," Rico adds, shooting Kaden a pointed look.

He just shrugs. "It wouldn't—"

A *boom* tears through the air.

I jerk back in stunned shock as the front of my car explodes. It sends the hood flying up and slamming into the windshield with enough force to crack the glass.

People around us scream. It's probably yells of surprise rather than fear, since it wasn't that big of an explosion. After all, none of the other cars were damaged. Only mine.

Rico grabs my arm and says something, but I can't concentrate on his words. All I can do is stand there and stare in utter disbelief at the strange flames licking the engine of my car. It's not a natural color. Fire only looks like that when it's burning chemicals.

I sweep my gaze around the area, noting the faces of all the people around us.

This wasn't Mikhail's doing. If it had been, he wouldn't have tried to attack me in the corridor. He would have just waited for me to get in the car.

Only stunned faces meet me as I continue scanning the parking lot.

No one except the Petrov brothers would even consider doing something like this. So if it wasn't them, it leaves only one possible suspect.

Someone who is pissed at me for not letting her flirt with my enemies.

Someone who is just as unhinged as I am.

Raina.

19

RAINA

Uncertainty swirls through my chest. Did I miscalculate? I was so sure that Eli would understand that it was me and that he would come for revenge, but it's almost midnight now and he still hasn't shown up.

Shifting my weight, I stretch my arms out and then flex my fingers on the stolen gun. Only the faint silver light from the moon shines in through the windows and illuminates my dark dorm room. I glance towards the windows, even though I can't really see anything from my position behind the door.

Why hasn't he shown up yet? I saw his face in the parking lot when I blew up his engine. He didn't look confused. He looked determined. So he must know that it was me. Maybe I should have left a note? Then he—

A soft click comes from my door. My heart leaps into my throat, and I snap my gaze towards the lock.

Two seconds pass.

Then the handle is slowly pushed downwards.

Excitement flutters through my stomach. *He's here.*

I quickly straighten and lift the gun.

The corridor that connects all the dorm rooms is always lit, so yellow light spills across the threshold and pools on the floor as the door is pushed open. I'm standing right next to it, hidden by the door and the darkness in the room.

My heart patters in my chest as a tall and muscular man becomes partly visible.

He stops in the doorway for a moment, staring at the narrow single bed that has been pushed against the wall by the windows. I've stuffed clothes underneath the covers so that it looks like I'm lying there sleeping.

I hold my breath.

Then he steps fully into the room.

My heart does a somersault in my chest, because even in this darkness, I would recognize that lethal body anywhere.

Moving like a viper, I yank my hand up and press the gun against Eli Hunter's temple.

He stiffens in surprise. The reaction is so subtle that if I hadn't been looking for it, I would've missed it. But I did see it. And a victorious grin spreads across my lips in response.

Kicking the door shut, I use my free hand to flick the light switch next to the door.

Yellow light floods the small room, illuminating the single bed with the stuffed covers, the closet on the opposite wall, the empty desk, and the wooden chair pushed underneath it. And, of course, the dangerously hot man in front of me.

Eli slides his gaze to me, but otherwise doesn't move an inch.

I push the gun harder against his temple while flashing him a wicked smirk. "Oh you're fucked now, asshole."

Amusement and disbelief glitter in his eyes as he huffs out a laugh. "Fucked?"

"Yes, you—"

He moves so fast that my brain can't even process what's happening.

One second, I'm standing there holding the gun to his head. The next, he shoves my arm to the side, snatches the gun from my fingers, and slams me up against the wall.

My breath explodes from my lungs as my back hits the gray concrete wall hard enough to rattle my teeth. Blinking in surprise, I draw in a breath to refill my lungs.

Once my vision is clear, I find Eli standing right in front of me. He has one hand on my chest, pushing me up against the wall. In the other, he holds the stolen gun that he is now aiming at my forehead.

"Fucked?" he repeats, amusement lacing his tone. A smile that is pure villain spreads across his mouth as he rakes his gaze up and down my body. "Would you like me to show you what it means to be *fucked*?"

Insanity dances in those burnt gold eyes of his. Deep down, I know that I probably should be terrified. But I'm not. Because that madness calls to the insanity in my own soul. Like a siren song, it pulls at me, telling me to come and dance in the flames as the world burns.

The intensity in his stare is so all-consuming that I can't even formulate a response.

"Strip," he commands.

His mere presence is so dominating that my soul vibrates from the authority in that one word. There is absolutely no room for argument. This is the voice of a person who expects to be obeyed.

Dark desire washes through me.

While holding his commanding stare, I quickly strip out of my clothes and let them fall to the floor beside me. My skin prickles and my nipples harden at the exposure. I drag in a shuddering breath as I straighten again, standing before him completely naked.

With the gun still to my head, Eli removes a pair of handcuffs from his belt and tosses them to me. "Put them on. Behind your back."

Metallic rattling fills the room as I catch the handcuffs and then maneuver them into position behind me. They let out faint clicks as I snap them shut around my wrists.

As soon as they're on, Eli grabs me by the shoulder and spins me around. Then he uses his free hand to tighten the handcuffs almost to the point of pain. I grit my teeth as the metal digs into my skin.

Eli just plants his palm against my shoulder blades and gives me a shove towards the closet that has been built into the wall. I stumble forward, almost slamming into the white-painted doors.

When I've straightened, I turn around and find that Eli isn't holding the gun anymore. Instead, he's holding a small bundle of rope. My gaze darts towards the door.

"Do it," Eli says in a mocking voice. "Make a run for it. See what happens."

Sliding my gaze back to him, I lock eyes with him again but say nothing. A smug smile lurks at the corner of his lips.

There is no way that I would be able to make it to the door before he can draw the gun again. And besides, I kind of want to know where this is going.

When I make no move to run, Eli loops the rope around

my neck and then pulls it through the metal handle of the closet's top cabinet.

A thrill rushes down my spine as he flashes me a grin. Then he pulls on the rope. My heart pounds in my chest as I'm forced up onto my toes.

Once I'm standing on my toes, Eli pulls just a little bit more. The rope digs into my throat, almost choking me. *Almost*. Then he ties it in place.

Heat pools at my core as I draw in strained breaths.

With a smirk on his lips, Eli gives me a satisfied once-over. Then he slides out the gun from the back of his waistband and aims it between my eyes.

A jolt shoots through my body like electricity.

I have never been in a more vulnerable, more dangerous, position in my entire life. I'm naked, with my hands cuffed behind my back and a rope around my neck that is keeping me trapped on my toes and almost choking me, and a gun to my head. I should be terrified. But all I can feel is how hard my pussy aches with forbidden need.

Drawing the muzzle of the silencer down my cheek, Eli studies my face like he is inspecting a painting that he hasn't decided whether to buy or cut to pieces yet. My heart hammers against my ribs. He traces the very edge of the round barrel that makes up the silencer along my bottom lip.

Then his other hand shoots up.

I gasp as he pinches my nipple hard.

But because of the tight rope around my neck holding me immobile, I can't even squirm against the door as he squeezes harder, sending flashes of pain through my tit.

Then he relaxes his grip. I suck in a shuddering breath as he teases his thumb over my sensitive nipple.

A whimper spills from my lips as he grips it hard again and

pulls it towards him, stretching my tit. He presses the gun underneath my chin. I draw in strained breaths underneath the rope and try to shift my weight on my toes so that I can arch my back and relieve the pain in my tit. But I'm hopelessly trapped in place.

My clit throbs and I'm so wet that I can almost feel it dripping down my legs.

He releases my nipple. Relief washes over me. Lowering his hand, he instead draws his fingers over my pussy. Electricity flashes through me at the touch.

Raising his hand in front of his face, he inspects his fingers, and a smirk blows across his lips when he finds them wet.

A flash of embarrassment sears through me, but it's quickly replaced by another kind of heat as Eli takes the gun from my chin and instead starts drawing it down the center of my chest. The metal from the silencer is smooth and cold against my blazing hot skin.

"This, princess..." Eli begins.

My heart thunders in my chest and I suck in rapid breaths as he slides the gun over my hip and down my thigh. I can barely think straight as the muzzle scrapes against my inner thigh and then over my pussy.

My pulse thrums in my ears as he holds the round barrel of the silencer right against my entrance.

Then he pushes it inside me.

A jolt shoots through my body like a fucking lightning strike, and my eyes snap wide open.

I jerk against my restraints, but the movement only makes me choke harder on the rope. Forcing myself back up onto my toes, I thump the back of my head against the wooden door behind me and bite back a moan as Eli draws out the silencer and then shoves it back in again.

"*This,* princess," he repeats. His eyes dance with wickedness as he holds my gaze while sliding the cold metal barrel deeper inside me. "This is what it means to be fucked."

"Eli," I gasp out.

"Yes, princess?"

Lights flicker in my brain as he picks up his pace, fucking me faster with the silencer of the gun. Another whimper spills from my lips.

"Is the safety on?" I at last manage to press out in a strained voice.

"I don't know." A smirk plays over his mouth as he runs his gaze over my face, studying every emotion that blows across my features while he continues thrusting the gun into me. "*Is* the safety on?"

Something between a whimper and a moan rips from my chest, and I squeeze my eyes shut as a shudder rolls through my body. "Eli…"

He just continues mercilessly fucking me with the gun.

Every nerve inside my body is on high alert. It feels as if I have swallowed a bottle of lightning. Bolts of pure energy flicker through my veins, making me hyperaware of the tightness of the rope against my throat and the pressure of the handcuffs against my wrists and the friction of that hard metal silencer inside my pussy.

I have never felt more alive in my entire life.

Pleasure builds inside me, soaring quickly into a violent thunderstorm just waiting to be released. My chest heaves as I suck in desperate breaths.

Eli is fucking me with a gun. A fucking *gun*. If he accidentally bumps the trigger, I'm dead. Hell, he could even decide to purposely pull the trigger while that silencer is still buried inside me. And there is absolutely nothing I can do to stop him.

My life is entirely in his violent, blood-soaked hands.

And that thought alone makes my clit throb so hard that I feel like my brain is going to shatter with the lust thrumming inside me.

I love the feeling of losing control.

Or rather, I love the feeling of someone else *taking* my control away from me.

It makes me feel alive, feel free, in a way that nothing else does.

Tension builds inside me, pulsing through my body and vibrating against my bones, as Eli keeps thrusting the silencer in and out of my pussy. The friction, combined with the electrifying danger and the sheer control that Eli has over my life right now, pushes me closer and closer to the edge.

My heart pounds against my ribs.

I suck in desperate breaths that never seem to contain enough oxygen.

Then Eli shifts the angle of the gun slightly as he shoves it into me.

And release shoots through my body.

A cry rips from my lungs with enough force to make me taste blood. But the sound is immediately cut off as Eli slaps his free hand over my mouth, silencing me.

I scream and moan and whimper into his warm palm as the orgasm ricochets through my body and I come hard all over the gun still buried in my pussy.

Stars flicker before my eyes and my limbs shake violently.

The force of it makes it impossible to stay on my toes, and

I choke as the rope digs into my throat when my knees give out. But that only makes me come harder.

And through it all, those eyes like burnt gold watch me with enough intensity to steal what little breath I had left. Eli's gaze sears into me, as if he is burning this image into his memory.

When he realizes that I can no longer stand on my own, he moves his hand down from my mouth to my throat, holding me up so that I can gasp air back into my lungs again.

For a while, he just keeps me like that. Even when the orgasm has finished crashing through my body, Eli keeps me trapped against the cold closet door while he finishes studying every inch of me.

Then he at last pulls out the gun. I suck in a breath.

While still holding on to the gun, he raises his hand and then undoes the knot keeping the rope secured to the handle above my head. Then he simply releases my throat.

I don't have a single ounce of strength left in my body, so at the loss of support, I simply crash down on my knees on the floor. My hands are still shackled behind my back, so I can't even brace myself when I land. Instead, my body just bows forward over my knees.

For another few seconds, I just remain kneeling like that while I draw in deep breaths. The rope is still wrapped around my throat, but since it's not attached to anything anymore, I can now inhale fully again.

My head shifts to the side as Eli taps what feels like the butt of the gun against my temple.

"Clean it off," he orders.

After sucking in one more deep breath, I lift my head and slowly raise my gaze.

Eli is standing above me.

I look up from his black combat boots, drawing my gaze over his black pants and over the tight black t-shirt that shows off his lethal muscles. My pulse flutters erratically as I take in his dominating presence.

With the dark clothes and the scar down his face and the complete command that pulses from his powerful frame, he looks like war and death incarnate.

Kneeling naked and handcuffed at his feet, I'm acutely aware that I am still utterly at his mercy. I drop my gaze to the gun that he is holding in front of my face. The silencer is wet with the evidence of my orgasm. I know that I should be scared of what he can do to me right now. Any normal person would be. But all I can think about is how much I want him to put that gun to my head and then fuck me properly.

"Clean it off," Eli orders again.

Since my hands are shackled behind me, there is only one way for me to do that. My core throbs again as I open my mouth and lean forward until the silencer almost hits the back of my throat. Then I close my mouth before drawing my lips back down the barrel.

A faint *plop* sounds as I finish the final part of the silencer and then pull my head back.

I look up at Eli again.

Wicked satisfaction shines on his face as he smirks at me.

Shifting his grip on the gun, he glances down at it before meeting my gaze again and flashing me an amused smile. "Well, would you look at that? The safety *was* on."

I just narrow my eyes, staring back at him while he continues silently gloating about his victory for another few seconds.

Then a dangerous glint appears in his eyes as he abruptly flicks the safety off and presses the gun against my forehead.

"But if you ever put a gun to my head again, the next time I fuck you, it won't be. Understood?"

I think I manage to answer yes, but I'm not sure because my brain got stuck on the middle part of that sentence.

The next time I fuck you.

A thrill races down my spine.

20

ELI

Jace snaps his fingers in front of my eyes. "Bro? You with us?"

Yanking my hand up, I grab his annoying fingers and move them out of my face.

"He's probably thinking about Raina again," Rico teases from across the table.

"Oh come on, that was two days ago." Jace snorts. "There really—"

His words are cut off as I twist his fingers back, making him cry out in pain. Across the table, Kaden snickers while Jace tries to unsuccessfully pull his fingers back. I twist again, making him squirm in his seat and grimace.

"Okay, okay, I'm sorry," he blurts out, admitting defeat. When I just raise my eyebrows pointedly at him, he mutters curses under his breath and rolls his eyes, but then adds, "Please?"

I release his fingers.

He snatches his hand back and shakes it out while shooting me a glare. I huff out a laugh.

"Just because you have an incredibly short attention span, it doesn't mean that everyone else does too," I say.

"Exactly," Rico adds, and flashes him a grin. "We don't call you Golden for nothing, remember?"

"Shut up," Jace mutters at me before twisting to stab his finger at Rico instead. "And stop calling me that."

"You *were* thinking about Raina, though," Kaden interrupts before Rico can retort. There is a knowing look in his sharp brown eyes as he holds my gaze. "Weren't you?"

Leaning back in my seat, I rake my fingers through my hair and heave a deep sigh.

We're sitting around our massive kitchen table made of dark wood. It's Saturday night, and great portions of the student body are busy getting drunk right now, but we decided to stay in and plan our strategy for the upcoming tournament instead.

Though to be fair, that was mostly because I didn't feel like going out. Ever since I broke into Raina's dorm Thursday night, I've felt even more restless than normal.

I'm sitting in our spacious and beautiful kitchen, full of dark wooden furniture and stainless-steel appliances and marble countertops, drinking whiskey and plotting mayhem with my brothers under the golden light of the expensive chandelier above. But all I want to do is to go back to that crappy little dorm room on the other end of the compound.

Tilting my head back down again, I meet Kaden's calculating eyes and admit, "Yes."

"Why are you so obsessed with her?" There is no judgement in his tone. Just genuine curiosity.

"I don't know."

"Yes, you do."

I force out another long breath. "Look, I swear to God,

there is something wrong with that girl. She's fucking insane! And I should know. Because I'm insane too."

Rico tips his head to the side in an acknowledging nod. "Well, can't argue with that."

Jace and Kaden chuckle. Shaking my head at the three of them, I give them a half disgruntled, half amused look and then blow out another sigh.

"What exactly happened when you broke into her dorm room?" Rico asks, frowning at me. "You said you were going to get revenge, but you came back looking more stunned than ever. What did you do to her?"

"I handcuffed her, tied her up with a rope around her neck, and then fucked her with a gun."

Silence falls across the elegant kitchen as all three of them just stare back at me for a few seconds.

Then Kaden lets out a low approving whistle while Rico huffs out a laugh and shakes his head.

"Okay, that's fucking hot," Jace announces, a grin on his face.

"Yeah, it was."

"Was the safety on?" Rico asks. Always the careful one.

"Of course the safety was on. But I didn't tell her that until afterwards, so she didn't know that while I fucked her." Blood rushes to my cock at just the memory of that night, so I adjust my position slightly in my chair. Leaning back, I drag a hand through my hair again as I sweep my gaze over my brothers and then shake my head. "That's what I'm trying to tell you. I put her in such a humiliating and vulnerable position that any normal person would've been bawling their eyes out with fear. But what did she do instead? She came so fucking hard that her eyes rolled back in her head."

Grabbing the whiskey glass before me, I bring it to my lips and down the rest of the liquid in an effort to stop the sudden impulse that flashes through me. It takes all of my willpower not to lurch up from my chair and drive straight over to Raina's place.

I thrive on taking people's control away from them. Just like my control was taken away from me all those years ago. Ever since then, my soul craves the power that rushes through me when I have someone else completely at my mercy. I get off on forcing people to do what I want. Either by threats, power, or sheer physical dominance. But nothing has ever felt the way it did with Raina the other day.

My soul was feeding off her helplessness, her lack of control in the face of my power, but it was as if *her* soul was feeding off it too.

And now, it's all I can think about. I just want to corner her and torment her and do wicked, depraved things to her so that I can see just how far I can push her before she finally breaks.

Kaden lets out another low whistle and then shoots me a look full of dark anticipation. "Oh, that sounds like one hell of a plaything. You sure you don't want to share her with us?"

"No," I snap immediately.

Jealous, possessive rage burns through me at the mere thought of someone else seeing what Raina's gorgeous face looks like when stars burst behind her eyes and breathy screams rip from her throat. Even my brothers.

That sight is only for me to see.

Only ever for me.

"No," I repeat, a bit calmer this time.

Rico and Jace just shrug as if it's no big deal.

Kaden looks a bit disappointed, but then he just sucks his teeth and shrugs too, accepting my decision.

But I still add one more time, just to really drive the point home.

“No one touches her but me.”

21

RAINA

The back of my neck prickles, but I don't turn around. I already know that Eli is watching me from where he sits with his brothers higher up in the auditorium. Ignoring the way his gaze burns into the back of my head, I instead keep my attention fixed on the stage ahead where Professor Lawson has stepped up to the microphone.

"Good morning," she says in a cheerful voice. "We are now just under two weeks away from the annual tournament."

Whoops of excitement ring out from several people in the audience. Including Magda, who is sitting next to me. I steal a glance at her and then the two boys on my left. A wide grin decorates Magda's usually so serious face. On my other side, Gabriel is giving Professor Lawson his polite boy-next-door smile while Paulo just watches her with his customary unreadable expression.

Apparently, I'm the only one who is outright dreading this bloody tournament. It's easier to hide how terrible I am at everything when I'm in class. But in an actual competition, when I'm on a team with the Hunters? Everyone will see just how much I suck at everything. And I'm not looking forward to that.

"And do you know what that means?" Professor Lawson continues.

"Team training!" someone yells from the audience.

A ripple of excited laughter follows it.

"Correct." Lawson hooks her loose brown curls behind her ears and flashes us a glittering smile. "Starting today, we will begin team training. In the mornings, all the way up until lunch, you will have classes as normal. But during the afternoons, you will have time to train as a team. What you choose to spend that time on is up to you."

It takes great effort not to groan. I know that I technically want to keep Eli's attention fixed on me, but spending every afternoon for two weeks alone with him and his three psycho brothers?

I risk a quick glance over my shoulder.

My heart lurches when I find all four Hunters staring straight at me with devilish grins on their faces.

Turning back to the stage, I massage my brows. This is going to be a rough couple of weeks.

"Any questions?" Professor Lawson asks. When no one speaks up, she nods. "Excellent. Then may the odds be ever in your favor."

Everyone just looks back at her in silence.

She heaves an exasperated sigh and then snaps her fingers before pointing towards the door. "That means, get to class."

Clothes rustle and shoes thud against the ground as we all get up from our seats and start heading for the door.

My morning class is about how to stay hidden in different environments. Just like every other class, it's not something I excel at, but I know that it's at least going to be better than whatever this afternoon brings.

I follow the others out of the main campus area and towards a building that almost looks like an aircraft hangar. I've been inside it before, of course, but the sight still takes my breath away.

The massive building has been split into sections. One part is full of trees and bushes, turning it into a forest. Another part has buildings and stone streets just like a busy city. A third one has been built like a park. And so on.

We move towards the open area at the front where our instructor is waiting.

My heart stalls and I almost walk right into the person in front of me when I find Connor standing there next to our instructor. The bruises that were covering his face and body have now healed, which means that he no longer stands out in a crowd. His gray eyes linger on me for an extra second before simply moving on and scanning the rest of the people around me.

"Today, we have Connor Smith with us to help demonstrate how to efficiently move unseen through an area," our teacher begins.

I barely hear the rest of the instructions because I can't stop staring at the blank expression on Connor's face.

A stab of pain shoots through my heart. I wish I could tell him what I'm really doing here. That I'm not trying to take his place or undermine his efforts. That I'm here to help him. But if he ever finds out what Eli has done to me, he will go after him, and that would only end in more bloodshed.

Once the mandatory demonstrations are done, I move to the section as far away from Connor as possible. It's the forest part. A few other students picked that one as well, but I don't pay them any mind as I walk between the trees and breathe in air that smells like grass and dirt.

It helps ground me again, and I run through the instructions and tips we received, as well as what Connor showed. I knew that Connor is good. People tell me that all the time. But actually seeing it with my own eyes was something else. The way he moved, the way he blended in even though we all knew what to look for, was absolutely incredible. He really is going to be one of the greatest of all time. As long as I can make sure that Eli Hunter doesn't—

"You're dead."

I jerk back at the unexpected sound of that voice, *his* voice, and my spine bumps against the muzzle of a gun. Twisting my head, I look over my shoulder to find Eli standing right behind me with a gun to my back. Amusement dances in his eyes.

I scowl at him. "I hadn't even started yet."

"Too bad, princess. This profession doesn't wait for you to start. If you're not ready, you die."

Spinning around to face him, I shove his hand and the gun to the side as I glare up at him. "What are you even doing here? You're not in this class."

"I have to see where your skill level is at, so that I know what we need to work on this afternoon." A smirk lifts his lips. "As a team."

I snort.

His gaze sharpens, and he gives me a look dripping with challenge. I just raise my eyebrows expectantly. Lifting his arm, he flicks his wrist, using the gun to motion at the vegetation around us.

"Go ahead then," he says, a taunting edge to his voice. "I'm giving you two minutes to get ready and find somewhere to hide."

I don't waste a second. Darting away from him, I hurry into the trees. There are a few other students here, practicing how to move quietly across a forest floor, but they barely spare me a glance as I search for somewhere to hide.

A cluster of trees appears up ahead. Sprinting towards it, I dive in behind one of the thick trunks since I'm pretty sure that my time is up now.

The rough bark scrapes against my skin as I press myself to the tree. My heart flutters in my chest. I glance around the edge. Nothing.

One minute passes.

Two.

A smug grin threatens to break out on my face. Guess I'm not as terrible as everyone thinks.

I lean forward a little, casting another glance around the trunk.

A gun appears at my temple from the other side. "You're dead."

Since I can't move my head now, I just slide my gaze to where Eli is standing half behind me. I didn't even hear him sneak up on me.

He removes the gun from my temple and then jerks his chin. "Try again."

Branches flash past my vision as I dart away. This time, I try hiding behind a large rock instead. My heart patters in my chest as I sit there crouched behind it while scanning the forest around me. This time, I will see him coming.

I suck in a sharp breath between my teeth as the cold muzzle of a gun is pressed against the back of my head.

"You're dead," Eli repeats yet again. Then he removes it. "Go."

With frustration crackling inside me, I sprint away from the useless rock and try another hiding place.

I've only spent about a minute covered by some thick low-hanging branches before I hear, "You're dead."

I hide behind some bushes.

"Dead."

I try a massive boulder next.

"Dead."

Then I try another tree. Peeking out around it after barely a couple of minutes, I find a gun between my eyes.

"Bang." Eli smirks at me. "You're dead."

Anger ripples through me as I sprint through the trees and approach the park section instead. If he's so damn good, then let's see if he can figure out that I've switched sections entirely.

Connor is standing a short distance away, talking to our instructor. Since I don't want to get too close to them, I decide on the bushes behind one of the park benches. Crouching down behind them, I narrow my eyes as I scan the area furiously. This time, I *will* see him coming.

Hope flutters in my chest when another few minutes pass and Eli still hasn't shown up. I watch the other students practicing throughout the park. Connor helps instruct some of them. Yet again, my heart aches. He's even helping other people get better, so why the hell did someone have to put him on Eli's shit list. It's so fucking cruel and unfair.

A yelp slips past my lips as someone plants a boot between my shoulder blades and shoves me out from behind the bushes. I topple forward and barely have time to yank my hands up and brace my palms on the ground before I slam face down on the grass.

I start to push myself up, but before I can, the boot appears between my shoulder blades again, shoving me back down. I let out a huff.

Turning my face to the side, I look up and find Eli standing over me with his boot on my back and his gun pointed at my head. Vicious amusement lurks on his lethally handsome face as he tuts and shakes his head at me. "Oh Raina, this truly is pathetic." While holstering his gun, he huffs out a laugh. "Well, at least it was informative."

Before I can come up with a retort, he abruptly takes his boot off my back, spins around, and stalks away without another word.

Pushing myself up, I get to my feet while brushing blades of grass and crushed leaves off my clothes. The park around me has gone oddly silent. I look up.

Everyone is watching me. Some look confused as they glance between me and Eli's retreating back. Others look thoroughly amused. My brother, on the other hand, is looking at me with disappointment... and shame.

I swallow down the burning feeling that crawls up my throat.

Connor starts towards me.

For a moment, I can't decide what to do. I can't let people know that we're siblings, so I can't make it seem like we know each other. But he has been helping the other students too, so it shouldn't be strange for him to come over and offer some tips after watching this humiliating display of nonexistent hiding skills.

Before I can decide what to do, Connor reaches me. But to

my surprise, he doesn't stop. He keeps walking past right next to me, as if he is heading towards someone else.

However, when he is right beside me, he speaks in a low voice full of pain and embarrassment.

"You shouldn't be here."

22

ELI

Confusion creases Raina's dark brows as she steps out of my car and closes the door with a thud. She frowns up at the forest before her while my brothers park their own cars next to mine on the otherwise empty gravel patch.

"This is where we're having our team training session?" Raina asks, that dubious expression still on her features as she turns her head to look at me. "In a forest?"

"Yes," I reply.

"Doing what?"

"Seriously?" Rico's voice interrupts before I can answer. "You picked up *another* bat?"

I glance behind me to find Jace strolling towards us with a baseball bat resting on his shoulder. Next to him, Kaden is shaking his head while twirling a knife in his hand. Rico moves around his own car to meet them.

"It was just sitting there unattended," Jace replies with a grin. "I couldn't just leave it."

Rico snorts. "Of course you couldn't, Golden."

"Hey." Jace swings the bat off his shoulder and points it menacingly at Rico. "The guy without the bat should not be rude to the guy with the bat. It's Bat Etiquette 101."

"Bat etiquette?"

"Yes, bat etiquette."

"Stop saying *bat*," Kaden interrupts. "Or I swear I'm going to snatch the bloody thing out of your hands and crack both of your skulls with it."

I can see Jace about to open his loud mouth and say it, just because he feeds off chaos, but I doubt Rico's grandfather would be pleased if Kaden cracked Rico's skull open, so I speak before Jace can set those events into motion.

"Actually," I begin.

All three of them stop their bickering and turn to me. Raina does too.

"Do you have any more of those?" I finish, nodding towards the bat.

Jace's brown eyes light up like sparkling amber. "Do I have any more? Is that even a question, dear brother?"

"Yes or no?" I demand.

Changing direction, Jace heads back towards his car while jerking his chin at us. I follow. Next to me, Raina begins to move too.

I throw out my arm, blocking her path, and cut her a hard look. "Not you."

Glaring up at me, she grinds her teeth in annoyance and crosses her arms. But she remains in place while the rest of us follow Jace to the trunk of his car.

When we're all there, he pops the trunk and then sweeps his hand dramatically over it.

My eyebrows climb higher as I stare down at a pile of what has to be at least eight bats.

Rico laughs, his eyebrows raised as well, and repeats, "Seriously?"

Jace pointedly raises a finger while shooting him a serious look. "You never know when you might need a good bat."

"Well, that time is now," I say before Rico can start teasing him again.

Reaching into the pile, I pick one up and then start back towards where Raina is still standing, watching us suspiciously.

Wooden clattering from behind informs me that Kaden and Rico pick up bats too.

"You're welcome," Jace calls as he slams his trunk shut again.

I chuckle. Glancing back at them, I find Rico flipping him off over his shoulder and Kaden spinning his knife in his hand one last time before sliding it into its sheath and hefting the bat instead. Jace grumbles under his breath as he runs to catch up with them.

Warm winds whoosh across the fields and slam into the tall trees before us. Leaves rustle and branches shake as the winds whirl through the forest for another few second before everything goes silent and still again. A couple of birds caw from somewhere deeper into the woods.

Raina is standing with her back to the trees. She's wearing a short white skirt today, paired with a tight brown shirt that dips a little down her ample cleavage. Her long black hair flutters behind her as another gust, a much gentler one this time, sweeps through the air. I study the white sneakers she's wearing as I come to a halt two steps in front of her.

Why does she insist on dressing like that? This is a school for assassins, for fuck's sake. She could at least put on sensible footwear. Those shoes are going to get ruined in this forest today.

"So... what?" Raina begins in a snarky tone, her arms still crossed over her chest. "We're playing baseball in the woods?"

My brothers come to a halt as well, flanking me. For a few seconds, the four of us just stand there side by side, watching her.

"Not exactly," I answer at last.

Her gaze drifts over our muscular bodies and the bats on our shoulders. I wait for fear to flicker in her eyes. It doesn't.

Frustration wells up inside me.

What the fuck is wrong with this girl? Why is she never afraid of anything? If she had been a normal person, she would've been reduced to a trembling mess begging for permission to surrender long ago. But no matter what I do, I can't seem to get this girl to break.

"Since you're so bad at hiding, I figured we would help you train," I continue when it becomes clear that threatening silence has absolutely no effect on her.

She flashes me a mocking smile. "How sweet of you."

"We'll give you a one-minute head start." Using the bat, I point towards the forest behind her. "And then we'll hunt you."

"Sounds dreadfully boring, but okay."

"How about we sweeten the pot then? If you can manage to stay hidden, we'll leave you alone for an entire month. I won't mess with you. Nothing. For a whole month."

She cocks her head. "Huh."

"But if we catch you..." I add, donning a vicious smile. "Then I will let my brothers fuck you."

For the first time, a hint of surprise flickers in her eyes. And she raises her eyebrows as she says, "Your brother?"

I rake a deliberate glance up and down her body. "All three of them."

It's a lie, of course. I have absolutely no intention of ever letting my brothers touch her, but I'm trying to find something that will scare her. Something that will terrify her and make her finally wave the white flag of surrender. Something that will prove that she is just like everyone else, that she will break underneath the weight of my insanity and that she isn't worth all the time and energy I spend thinking about her. Proof that I shouldn't be obsessed with her.

Holding my breath, I wait for panic or fear, or anything that will give me the proof I need, to flood her eyes.

Two seconds pass.

They feel like a fucking lifetime.

Then a sly smile spreads across her lips as she flicks her gaze up and down the four of us. She licks her lips. Not nervously. Seductively. Fucking *seductively*.

"I see," she says.

I'm still so stunned by her ludicrous reaction that all I can do is to stare as she spins around and then takes off into the trees.

Branches snap underneath her white sneakers as she bolts into the forest.

Leaves rustle as another wind washes over the landscape.

I stare at the white skirt flapping around those perfect thighs of hers before she disappears from view.

"I thought you didn't want us to touch her," Kaden says. His voice is cool, neutral, but I can hear the hopeful undercurrent to his words.

"I don't," I reply simply.

A disappointed noise comes from his throat, but he doesn't argue. None of them do. They all know me well enough to understand what I'm doing. To understand that I'm trying, by any means, to break the absolute enigma that is Raina Smith.

"That's one minute," Rico observes eventually.

Shaking off the strange emotions that had settled over me, I draw in a deep breath and adjust my grip on the bat. With the confusion gone, excitement fills my chest instead.

I grin. "Then let's go hunt."

Jace lets out a whoop as he takes off straight after Raina. The rest of us exchange a glance, and then spread out so that we will be coming at her from all sides.

Afternoon sunlight filters in through the canopy above as I make my way deeper into the forest.

Raina will be able to hear Jace coming, and then she will adjust her position after that, which means that she will run straight into one of us instead.

Snapping branches and rustling leaves and thudding footsteps come from my left. I can just about see something white flapping between the tree trunks where Raina is no doubt running with Jace on her heels.

She swerves right, heading closer towards me. I match her pace, moving silently between the trees as I wait for her to come into view.

Her heavy breathing echoes through the woods.

Amusement swirls inside my chest. Well, she won't be competing in any long-distance races any time soon.

A branch sways before me.

Then Raina comes crashing through.

She screeches to a halt, and her eyes go wide with surprise as she sees me. I flash her a wicked grin.

Whipping around, she sprints in the other direction. I take off after her.

Adrenaline pumps through my veins, and I have to resist

the urge to let out a *whoop* as the thrill of the hunt washes over me, turning me almost giddy.

It takes all of my self-control to keep my pace slow so that I won't overtake her. Even with her running at full speed, I could've caught her within the first few minutes. But what would be the fun in that? After all, I'm trying to frighten her. And what could be more terrifying than being hunted through the woods by four killers?

I catch glimpses of her white skirt between the trees as she zigzags through the forest. But every time she's about to go too far, one of us steps in and forces her to change direction again. My heart pounds in excitement as we continue herding her towards the predetermined spot.

There's a section where the ground rises drastically. It's not even a slope. It's just a sheer rock face that juts up from the ground. And that's where we'll corner her.

Anticipation crackles through me as we draw closer to it. Once I can see the gray rock wall between the trees, I slow down and scan the area ahead of me. I know that Raina is here somewhere. I heard her run in here. But now, she is apparently hiding.

While lazily twirling the bat in my hand, I prowl towards the open area in front of the rock wall.

Still no sign of Raina.

Something flashes in the corner of my eye right as I'm about to break through the tree line and emerge into the open space. I yank up my bat instinctively.

A *crack* sounds as a thick tree branch slams into the bat with enough force to send chips of wood spraying through the air. If I hadn't blocked it with the bat, that strike would have knocked me to the ground.

Surprise flickers through me as I snap my gaze to the

person wielding the branch.

Raina.

I lurch towards her improvised weapon, but she knows that the element of surprise is lost now, so she quickly leaps back instead and sprints across the open area. But before she can get to the trees on the other side, Kaden appears from the woods in front of her.

She skids to a halt and spins in the other direction.

Only to find Rico walking towards her.

Snapping her gaze to the spot halfway between me and him, she moves as if to dart in that direction instead. Then her step falters as Jace saunters out from the trees there.

While still holding the thick branch before her like a weapon, she backs towards the tall rock wall as the four of us advance on her in perfect sync.

Her chest heaves, but I think it's more from the long run rather than fear because her green eyes sparkle with life as she draws the branch through the air in front of her like a sword.

My brothers spin their bats in the air in an incredibly synchronized motion. I toss mine to the ground instead as I stride towards Raina.

Once I get within striking distance, she swings at me. I duck. The branch whooshes over my head with considerable speed. For someone with such a soft-looking body, she's surprisingly good at swinging unwieldy branches at people's heads.

But when her strike doesn't land, the force of her momentum leaves her wide open. Straightening again, I throw out an arm and grab the branch before she has even finished swinging it.

She tries to yank it back, but I wrench it out of her hands

and toss it to the ground several yards behind me. I take a step forward. She takes a step back.

This wasn't even challenging.

Because she's so loud when she runs, tracking her was incredibly easy. And she has no idea how to avoid being herded. But even despite all that, I have to admit that I am a bit impressed. If she had been just a little faster, that first swing would've taken me in the side of the head. Then she could have escaped this trap we set for her.

But she didn't.

And now, it's time to pay.

23

RAINA

My chest heaves and my heart hammers against my ribs. Fuck, I'm so out of shape. This sprint through the woods has to be the longest continuous distance I've run in ages. And these four bastards have the audacity to look like this was just a leisurely stroll in the park for them. I narrow my eyes at them as they prowl closer while I drag in deep breaths to calm my heaving chest.

A taunting smirk spreads across Eli's face as he raises his eyebrows at me. "Come on, Raina, this was too easy. Did you even try?"

Of course I didn't. If I had actually managed to stay hidden, and Eli had honored his promise to leave me alone for a month, then who would he have taken out his rage on instead? My brother, that's who. So I had to make sure that I lost. Though, to be fair, I doubt that I could've escaped all four of them anyway. But I had still made more noise while running than I normally do just to be certain that they would in fact catch me.

When I don't answer, Eli narrows his eyes at me. My heart

skips a beat at the challenge that flashes in them when he stares me down.

"Or is this what you want?" He spreads his arms to indicate the others. "For me to watch while my brothers fuck you?"

I know that he doesn't mean it. Given how he reacted when Anton was teaching me how to shoot, Eli is far too territorial to ever let anyone else touch me. So I knew from the very first moment he tried to threaten me with that that he would never actually go through with it. And I know what he's trying to do. He's trying to scare me. Trying to make me see him as a monster. But what he doesn't seem to understand is that *I* am a monster too.

While letting a sly smile curl my lips, I slowly draw my gaze over his brothers. Kaden and Rico are resting their bats on their shoulders while Jace absentmindedly spins his in the air next to him.

"Well," I drawl, and nod towards Kaden. "Given that he's not even the slightest bit winded, he has much better stamina than you." I shift my attention to Rico. "And he is much prettier to look at than you." My grin widens as I slide my gaze to Jace. "And based on the rumors I've heard, your youngest brother has the biggest dick." Challenge laces my tone as I meet Eli's eyes again and finish with, "So of course I would rather have them fuck me."

Jealous, territorial rage flashes in his eyes like a lightning storm.

"I think I should probably save Jace for last," I continue with a mock contemplative voice. "Since his massive dick will otherwise kind of ruin my experience with the others. So, Kaden, how about we start? I bet you could make me scream like no one else."

"Ha!" Jace says, and then laughs while casting smug looks at the others, obviously very pleased with my comments.

Next to him, Kaden tightens his hold on the bat until he is gripping it so hard that his fingers turn white. His eyes are full of dark anticipation, and it looks like it is taking every ounce of his self-control to remain where he is.

"Shut up," Eli snaps at Jace. Then he levels a sharp look at Kaden. "My order still stands."

For a second, it's as if the moment is suspended in time.

Then Jace mutters something under his breath and shrugs while Kaden relaxes his grip on the bat, with what looks like great effort, and then flexes his fingers.

"I'll meet you back at the house," Eli says in what is clearly a dismissal.

"Alright," Rico says immediately.

Turning around, he claps Eli once on the shoulder before starting back in the direction of the cars. Kaden rakes those cold eyes up and down my body before turning around as well.

His lips lift in a half-smirk as he pauses next to Eli and says, "Don't do anything I wouldn't do."

Eli snorts, and I get the distinct feeling that there are very few things included in that particular category. After they exchange a brief knowing smile, Kaden follows Rico into the trees.

"Ugh," Jace groans as he spins around and stalks after them while muttering, "Right when things were finally starting to get fun around here."

I watch them leave. Eli doesn't. His eyes are firmly locked on mine, but I ignore his stare until Jace's white t-shirt has finally disappeared completely from view. Only then do I slide my gaze back to Eli.

A jolt shoots through me, and it takes all of my willpower to stifle a gasp, at the way he is looking at me.

"You're playing with fire, princess," he says, his voice low and dark.

"And I'm quite adept at it." My heart is thundering in my chest, and heat pools at my core, but I managed to keep a mocking expression on my features as I flash him a smirk. "Just ask your car."

Something flickers in his eyes, but it's too fast for me to read. He takes a step forward, but this time, I don't retreat. Amusement plays over his lips as he flicks a glance up and down my body. A thrill races down my spine. He is watching me as if he can't decide whether he wants to kill me slowly and very painfully or if he wants to fuck my brains out.

Since I'm kind of hoping for option two, I blurt out, "Are you ever going to fuck me for real?"

He arches an eyebrow. "I distinctly remember making you come so hard you saw stars. Twice, in fact."

"With your fingers. And then a gun. I'm asking if *you* are ever going to fuck me."

"Are you ever going to submit to me?"

"If you want my submission, then take it."

His eyebrows crease in confusion.

My heart is slamming against my ribs. I know that this is probably a terrible fucking idea. Not to mention dangerous. And sick. But I'm way past the point where I care about what other people think is acceptable or proper or normal.

"If you want to fuck me," I begin, speaking the words slowly to make sure that he understands that I truly mean what I say. "If you want my body, my submission, then take it."

Dark desire flares up in his eyes, but he keeps a guarded

expression on his features as he asks, "Do you understand what you're saying?"

"Yes." I hold his gaze. "I *want you* to fuck me. I'm going to fight back, but I want you to take me anyway."

My pulse is thrumming in my ears. For a few seconds, Eli only stares back at me in complete silence. It's so loud that I can only hear the violent pounding of my own heart.

I know that having forced sex fantasies is considered unacceptable by society at large, but it's actually a lot more common than most people think. And given that violence already turns me on, I'm not surprised that I'm one of the people who get off on being overpowered and at someone else's mercy.

"Are you sure?" Eli asks.

"Yes."

He watches me in silence for another few seconds, waiting for me to change my mind. But his eyes study my face, and he must be able to tell that I am in fact serious about this, because he at last gives me a slow nod in acknowledgement.

Then a wicked glint glitters in his golden eyes, and he flashes me a grin dripping with challenge. "Then run."

Excitement crackles through my veins. Not hesitating a second, I dart towards the tree line on my left.

After giving me a short head start, Eli moves too.

My shoes thud against the ground, crushing the thick grass underneath me as I sprint away from the rock wall behind and towards the cover of the wide forest ahead. The green leaves rustle and ripple like a curtain as a strong wind sweeps through the trees.

Footsteps sound from behind me.

Close.

Far too close.

Jesus, how fucking fast is this guy?

Before I can fully finish the thought, a massive weight slams into my body.

I haven't even made it halfway to the tree line when Eli takes my legs out from underneath me and I slam down on the ground. Blades of grass and a few crushed leaves flutter around me as I try to roll away before he can pin me completely. I'm only up on my side when Eli grabs me by the shoulder and shoves me back down on my stomach.

A huff escapes my lips.

His knees are on either side of me, caging me in. I press my palms to the thick grass, trying to use my arms to heave myself off the ground. I manage to get my chest and head up a little. Then he locks his hands around my wrists and pulls my arms to the sides.

With the loss of support, I slam down on the ground again.

Eli uses my moment of disorientation to twist my arms up behind my back. Shifting my wrists to one hand, he plants his other on the back of my neck. I kick my legs and buck my hips, trying to wiggle out from underneath him. His fingers tighten around the back of my neck, pressing my face down harder against the grass.

"Submit," he orders.

I try to yank my wrists out of his grip. "Make me."

He leans down over me until his lips brush against the shell of my ear. "I thought you'd never ask."

His warm breath dances over my skin like a gentle caress, sending a shiver through my body. It makes my brain malfunction for a few seconds, which was probably his plan all along because he uses those seconds to quickly shift his position so that he is facing the other way instead.

Right as my mind catches up, he settles his weight on my

back, trapping my hands underneath him. My heart thuds against my ribs so hard that I can almost hear it through the ground as Eli pulls my skirt up so that it's bunched around my waist instead and then slides my panties down over my ass.

Air rushes over my bare ass as he pushes the fabric down my thighs, making my skin prickle from the exposure. I kick my legs in an effort to loosen his hold on me. But he just keeps sliding my panties down.

Heat thrums through my veins.

While trying to yank my arms out from underneath him, I kick my legs again.

I gasp as a palm comes down hard on my ass. Eli slaps his hand against the other side of my ass too. Biting my lip, I swallow down a moan. My pussy throbs.

"You really do have such a spankable ass," Eli says, drawing his hand along it's curve. Then he gives it a small slap. "Now, lie still while I finish getting your panties off."

Need pulses through me as I bite back another moan. Lying there on my stomach, I wait until Eli has gotten my panties down my legs. There is no way that he will be able to get them off fully without taking his weight off my back and hands.

The moment he does, I move.

As soon as he has risen to his knees and pulled my panties over my shoes, I yank my hands out and start scrambling away.

He spins around. And before I've even made it two feet, his hand locks around my ankle. I let out a yelp as he yanks me back towards him. My shirt rides up my stomach as I slide along the grass.

Twisting around, I sit up and try to push him off me instead. But before I can, he plants a hand against my chest and shoves me back down on the grass. I hit it with a thud while he settles his weight on my hips.

His eyes dance with excitement and anticipation as he meets my gaze. My heart flips at the devilishly handsome smile on his face, and for a moment, I forget that I should be fighting him.

All I want to do is to grab the back of his neck and yank that troublesome mouth down to mine, but he's still my enemy. And I'm still his enemy. Kissing would be too intimate. It would cross that thin line we're already balancing on right now. And I still want him to fuck me hard and rough and dominantly, so I raise my arms as if to push him back.

He quickly snatches my wrists from the air and slams them back against the grass.

I squirm again, but it's no use. I'm now hopelessly trapped against the ground. My exposed pussy aches at the power pulsing from Eli as he pins me beneath him.

"Submit," he commands again.

So I flash him a grin full of challenge and repeat, "Make me."

He releases my wrists. Stunned surprise flickers through me, and before I can do anything with my newfound freedom, he locks his hand around my throat. I yank my arms up and grab his forearm, trying to push it away. He just tightens his grip on my windpipe.

"Unbuckle my belt," he orders. "You have five seconds to comply before I cut off your air completely."

Lust pulses through my body at the unflinching command in his voice. With my clit throbbing, I scramble to get my hands to his belt before his deadline has passed. Since I'm on my back, and his forearm is also blocking part of the view, it's difficult to see what I'm doing as I fumble to open his belt. But he is apparently satisfied with my speedy efforts at least, because he still allows me to breathe.

Once I've unbuckled his belt, he says, "Unzip my pants."

I undo the button before sliding the zipper down.

"Take out my cock."

Desire thrums inside me as I slip my hand beneath his black boxers and free his cock. I've seen it before, of course, but heat still rushes through me at the size of it. Once his hard length is out, I reluctantly take my hand off it and let my arms drop back down by my sides. But my eyes keep getting drawn back to his cock. Fuck, I want that inside me. And I want it now.

"Still think the rumors about Jace are true?" Eli asks, a smug glint in his eyes as he watches me stare at his cock.

There were no rumors about his little brother having the biggest dick. I only said that because I knew that it would annoy the hell out of him.

When I don't answer immediately, he gives my throat a brief squeeze. "Answer."

"No," I admit. A vicious smile tilts my lips as I lock eyes with him. "But thanks for mentioning your brother, because now I can think about him instead while my clit throbs."

Lightning flashes in Eli's eyes, and he tightens his grip on my throat as he leans closer until he's right in my face. When he speaks, his voice is like a rumbling thunderstorm. "The only face you will ever picture while your cunt does fucking *anything* is mine."

He stares me down as if trying to brand the order into my soul. Then he relaxes his grip on my throat, allowing me to breathe and speak again.

"Then fuck me already and maybe I will," I retort.

Challenge to rival my own dances in his eyes. With one

hand still around my throat, he reaches back and draws the other between my legs.

A jolt shoots through my body as his fingers brush against my wet and throbbing pussy. He keeps his eyes locked on mine as he traces his fingers over my clit before sliding them down to my entrance.

Pleasure ripples through my body, making my eyes flutter.

"Beg for it, princess."

"I don't beg."

"You will." He teases my clit again, drawing a moan from my lips, before forcing out, "*Beg.*"

"Oh, Jace," I say in my most breathless voice.

Jealous rage flashes in his eyes, and his hand tightens around my throat as he snaps, "If you ever again speak his name while *my* hands are on you, I will—"

"Fuck me properly and I'll stop imagining his face," I interrupt, holding his furious stare.

His eyes burn with challenge, but I'm not losing this round so I just continue staring right back at him.

Another few seconds pass.

Then he abruptly releases my throat. Sliding backwards, he instead grabs my thighs and forcibly spreads my legs wide. Anticipation flickers along my spine like electricity. I raise my hands, but before I can even get them halfway to his muscular chest, he grabs my wrists and slams them back down on the ground.

Then he shoves his cock into my wet pussy.

I arch up from the ground, and a gasp rips from my lips at the size of him. While pinning my hands to the grass beside me, he draws his cock out slightly and then pushes it in again. Deeper this time.

"You fucking troublesome, infuriating..." Eli grinds out

while pulling out and then thrusting inside again. "Disrespectful, insubordinate, death-courting—"

"You call this fucking? I thought I told you to take me—"

My taunt is cut off as he rams his cock all the way inside me. I gasp, my eyes going wide, at the feeling of his massive cock filling me completely. Pleasure washes through me.

With his fingers still pinning my wrists to the ground, he starts up a brutal pace that has my body jerking back and forth on the grass.

A moan tears from my throat at the incredible friction his cock creates.

I squirm underneath him, but he only fucks me harder.

Pleasure soars inside me.

I can feel the grass underneath my body, smell the woodsy scents of damp soil, hear the wind rush through the rustling canopy above, but all I can see is *him*. That lethally handsome face with that scar across his eye like a warrior god of old. That powerful body pinning me to the grass like an apex predator.

He could do whatever he wants to me. Take whatever he wants from me. And I fucking love it. The knowledge that he has me completely at his mercy sends a rush of adrenaline through me. The danger and insanity of it all makes me feel alert. Alive. Like I could breathe fire.

My heart hammers in my chest as Eli pounds into me. Fuck, he feels so damn good inside me. I want him to take more. Take everything. Make my body surrender to his until I'm gasping and trembling while my whole soul crackles with pleasure.

I stare into his eyes and see the same fire that is burning in my eyes reflected back at me in his. It's as if his craziness feeds mine, making my very soul vibrate from his dominating presence, while mine feeds his too.

Release flashes through my body as his cock hits a spot deep inside me.

I scream into the pale blue sky above as the orgasm shoots through me with enough force to make my limbs shake. Or my legs, at least, since Eli is still keeping my hands trapped and my arms motionless against the ground.

Moans drip from my lips as my inner walls tighten and flutter around his thick cock.

But Eli has stopped moving. Instead of chasing his own release, he remains perfectly still, studying every emotion in my eyes while pleasure washes through me.

Heat sears my cheeks at the intensity of his gaze, but he has me firmly pinned so I can do nothing to break his stare.

My chest heaves, and I drag in deep breaths as the final waves of pleasure die out. Then I blink. Confusion swirls in my chest as I meet Eli's gaze. I can feel his hard cock still buried deep inside me. So why isn't he chasing his own release?

"Why did you stop?" I manage to ask once my breathing has evened out again.

"Are you on birth control?" he demands.

Oh. So that's why he stopped before he could come. I have to suppress a small smile, because despite the clear command in his voice, I actually find this pretty sweet of him. But I obviously can't let him know that.

"Of course I am," I retort, which is the truth. "Do you really think that I would let you fuck me unprotected otherwise?"

"Good." A slow smile spreads across his lips as he draws his cock out and then pushes it back in again. "My turn."

I wince. My pussy is still sensitive from the previous

orgasm, so I squirm on the ground and struggle against his grip on my wrists as he pulls out and then thrusts into me again.

"Eli," I press out, as another flicker of pain courses through me.

"Yes, princess?"

But a whimper spills from my lips instead as Eli shoves his cock into me again.

"Does it hurt?" he says when I don't answer.

Another flicker of pain appears as he grinds his cock against my sensitive clit before pushing inside once more. I wiggle underneath him again before admitting, "Yes."

"Good." There's a wicked smile on his mouth as he holds my gaze. "That's what you get for daring to call out my brother's name when my fingers are on your cunt."

I bite back something between a groan and a moan.

But despite Eli's cruel words, he fucks me at a slow and almost gentle pace until the pain fades and instead turns to pleasure again. Once he sees my eyes flutter and hears a true moan from my lips, he picks up the pace. My body jerks against the grass as he thrusts into me with mind-numbing force.

Tension builds inside me and I start climbing towards another orgasm.

I yank against his grip on my wrists, suddenly desperate to run my hands through his hair and then rake my fingers down his back. But he only tightens his grip. His fingers dig into my skin so hard that I'm sure he will leave bruises to mark me as his captive, but it only makes me soar faster towards an orgasm.

Throwing my head back, I suck in desperate breaths and stare up at the sky as Eli keeps up his rough pace.

"Eyes on me," he snaps.

The sheer command in it sends a pulse of lust through my already thrumming soul. Tension builds inside me exponentially as I shift my head back and meet his gaze again. Power rolls of Eli's body like the waves of an invisible cloak. My heart lurches in my chest.

Half of his mouth tilts up in a smirk. "Good girl."

Release crackles through my veins. Breathy screams rip from my throat as another orgasm sweeps through my trembling body.

My pussy tightens around his cock, and this time, he continues fucking me through the waves of pleasure. Intensifying them. Prolonging them. But also chasing his own release.

A deep groan tears from his chest as he comes.

I study his face, noting every flicker of emotion there. Pleasure and a hint of incredulity flood his eyes. It makes a warm and incredibly smug feeling spread through my chest. He might be able to make my body surrender to his, but I sure as hell can make his surrender to mine too.

Then, as his gaze finally focuses on mine again, another feeling appears in his eyes as well.

Determination.

Intense, burning determination to force me into submission and take back complete control again. I flash him a grin full of challenge in reply.

Bring it on.

24

ELI

Standing by the window, I watch the grass field below where the first-years are forced to go through a grueling obstacle course over and over again. Soft chatter and the occasional chuckle fill the corridor as the other third-years around me comment and make bets on the outcome. We're on a short break from our own morning class, so we decided to get some entertainment. Though, I have no idea how the other first-years are doing, because my eyes have been fixed on the same person from the moment I walked up to the window.

Raina is so far behind the others that her black hair stands out like a beacon against the green grass when she runs alone towards the next obstacle. It's a smooth wooden wall with a few ropes hanging down from the top. I watch as Raina grips one of the ropes in both hands and starts trying to climb up.

Terrible restlessness and impatience flickers through my soul. She shouldn't be down there, uselessly running through an obstacle course. She should be here. With me. Trying her best to fight back while I slowly but surely grind her stubborn defiance to dust underneath my boot until she finally breaks.

Squeezing my hand into a fist, I clench my jaw and use every ounce of my self-control to stop myself from going down to that field and dragging her out of there so that I can do just that. I blow out a long breath through my nose and flex my fingers.

My obsession with Raina is becoming dangerous. I can barely concentrate on anything when she's not in the room because my mind is spinning when I don't know where she is or what she's doing. But at the same time, I can't concentrate when she's in the room either. Because when she's there, it's as if she sucks all the oxygen out of the room until all I can see is those confident green eyes and all I can hear is that utterly unapologetic voice of hers and all I can smell is that intoxicating scent of jasmine from her perfume. I can't breathe when she's not in the room but I also can't breathe when she is.

I resist the urge to rake a hand through my hair. Fuck, what is she doing to me?

Out on the field, Raina tries to pull herself up along the rope, but her arms give out before she can make it more than a foot off the ground. She drops down to the grass again.

From a couple of windows over, I notice Connor Smith abruptly turning around and stalking away. I track him with my gaze as he moves away from the window and back towards our lecture hall. I flex my fingers again. I'm itching to take out my frustrations on someone, but before I can do anything about it, my gaze is drawn back to Raina again.

I watch her grip the rope again and make another effort. Her body wiggles against the wall, and I'm reminded of the way she squirmed underneath me when I fucked her in that forest two days ago.

That experience had... not gone as expected.

I had tried to terrify her by threatening to let my brothers fuck her. I had tried to make her see me as the monster and the heartless lunatic that I am, so that she would run far away. But is that what she did? No. Instead of running from the darkness, she fucking dove headfirst right into it with me.

Telling *me*, someone who gets off on taking other people's control away from them, to act out a forced sex fantasy? It's like handing crack to an addict. Pinning her to the ground and fucking her hard until her body submitted to mine was so fucking addictive that I'm already craving my next fix.

I want her so badly that I can't think straight anymore. I sleep even less now than I usually do.

She makes me crazy. But at the same time, she makes the craziness go away. Or rather, she makes me crazy when she's not here and she makes the craziness disappear when she's with me. When she's near me, all I can see and hear and smell and feel is her, and that for some reason makes my head go completely silent.

But that also makes it hard to breathe because panic slams into me when I realize just how much power this insane girl has over me. I can't let anyone have *any* power over me. But she somehow consumes my thoughts every waking hour, and half of the already dangerously few hours I sleep too.

Exhaustion pulls at my body. I discreetly rub my fingers against my temple. I have a throbbing headache behind my left eye, and it makes me even more short-tempered and vicious than usual. I practically threw one of my classmates across the hall earlier because he was in my way when I arrived.

Every part of my body is screaming for rest, and my mind most of all. But there is no rest to be found here.

The memory of those ten hours I slept when I had Raina's body pressed against mine drifts through my brain. I would kill for another night like that right now.

Another flash of panic shoots through me.

I cannot be dependent on Raina for anything. I'm already too obsessed, too distracted, by her all-consuming presence. By the way her insanity sings to mine. I have to take back control over this.

Out by the wall, Raina loses her grip on the rope again. This time, she was almost halfway up. Her arms and legs flail around her as she plummets down and lands hard on the grass. The instructor yells at her from across the field.

Next to me, a guy laughs derisively. "What a loser. If I could get my hands on her, I would—"

I slam my fist into his stomach.

Air explodes from his lungs as he doubles over from the unexpected hit. I ram my elbow into the back of his neck, making him crumple to the floor with a dull thud.

I sweep my gaze over the other people around me, and I know that there must be absolute fury and insanity swirling in my eyes, because two of them even flinch.

"Anyone else?" I growl.

They all snap their gazes back to the field. But no one is even looking in Raina's direction now.

Rational thoughts slowly start trickling back into my mind. Didn't I just tell myself that I was going to stop letting Raina drive me crazy? And yet here I am, beating someone up just because he called her a loser.

Raking a hand through my hair, I blow out an inaudible sigh as I slide my gaze back to where Raina is completely ignoring the yells and threats from her instructor as she instead marches *around* the wall.

I shake my head.

What the hell is this girl doing to me?

25

RAINA

To say that there is tension inside our family dining room is the understatement of the decade. The very air is practically crackling with it, and the clinking of our utensils against the plates is so loud in the thick silence that it's nearly deafening.

At last, Mom's restraint snaps and she slams down her knife and fork on the table. "I still don't understand *why*!"

There is confusion, disappointment, and quite a lot of accusation in my mother's eyes as she locks them on me.

Yesterday, she finally found out that I had quit the chemistry teacher program and instead enrolled in Blackwater University. She called me and Connor immediately and demanded that we come home the next day for a family meeting. I have already spent the past hour explaining to her that yes, this was my decision, and no, I'm not changing my mind. Connor has been suspiciously silent throughout the entire dinner, but I'm pretty sure that he has already told Mom exactly how terribly I'm failing all of my classes because she has brought that up several times.

"Because I wanted to," I reply, cutting off a piece of chicken and popping it in my mouth.

"Stop with the flippant attitude, Raina," Mom says, angrily flicking back her long blond hair. "And explain why you threw away your future as a teacher to do this... this... whatever this is."

"I didn't throw away my future. If this doesn't work out, I can still re-enroll for the teacher program next year."

"I can already tell you that it won't work out. You know it. I know it. Your brother knows it. So why would you enroll at a university that you have no business being at?"

A flash of annoyance shoots up my spine, and I grip my fork harder. Since I don't trust myself to reply politely just yet, I take an extra couple of seconds before speaking as I look back at Mom.

The lines around her pale green eyes are more visible when she's angry. And she *is* angry, there is no mistake about that. But so am I. In fact, it is taking all of my willpower not to slam my fist down on the table just to hear the satisfying rattle that would fill the air when all the fine plates and dishes would jump up from the tabletop. Or to snatch up one of those crystal glasses and hurl it at the wall and watch as the red wine splashes against it and then runs down like blood, staining the stylish white wallpaper.

Drawing in a long breath through my nose, I at last grind out, "I have every right to enroll at Blackwater. I am Harvey Smith's child too, am I not?" I stab my knife in Connor's direction. "Just like he is."

Across the table, Connor is staring at a pile of broccoli with enough singular focus to make it seem like it's the most fascinating thing he has ever seen. Cutting piece after piece, he eats furiously while looking like he would rather be anywhere but here.

"Of course you are," Mom replies, her voice softening. Her eyebrows smoothen into a sympathetic look as she meets my gaze again. "But we've talked about this, Raina. You're not cut out for that line of work. Your father, God rest his soul, agreed with that too."

"Yeah, you and Dad agreed. But what about what *I* want?"

"You're making our family look bad!" she snaps, the words ricocheting through the elegant dining room like a bullet.

And there it is. The thing she has been wanting to say from the moment I walked across the threshold. My poor performance reflects badly on the family, and that will ruin our chances of recovering from this financial and social mess. Or so she thinks. If she only knew what I'm really doing.

I glance towards Connor. He is shoveling rice into his mouth as if his life depends on it. And he doesn't contradict Mom, which means that he agrees with her assessment.

Setting down my fork on the polished wooden table, I turn back to face Mom fully again. The silver candleholders on the table have been lit, and they cast flickering golden light over Mom's gorgeous face. I look so much like her. Apart from the black hair I got from Dad, I look almost like a carbon copy of her. But even while noting all of that, I've never felt less like a part of this family than I do right now.

For a second, I consider telling them what I'm really doing. That I enrolled for the sole purpose of drawing Eli's attention away from Connor so that he could finish out his senior year without any interference and then restore our family's reputation. But my rational mind shuts down the idea immediately. If Connor were to find out, he would put a stop to my plan without hesitation in order to protect me. And the plan is *working*. Eli hasn't messed with Connor since the day I keyed his car. So I do what I've been doing for weeks now. I lie and deflect.

"No one knows that I'm Con's sister," I say with a carefree shrug. "They all just think that I'm a random Smith."

"The other students might not know," Mom says. "But the teachers definitely do."

"And?"

"What do you mean, *and*?"

"And what? Who cares if the teachers know?"

"You..." she begins, but then she trails off. Pinching the bridge of her nose, she closes her eyes for a few seconds and draws in what sounds like a calming breath. When she opens her eyes and lowers her hand again, most of the anger has been replaced by pity. "Look, Raina."

A cold oily feeling snakes through my chest at the pity evident both in her eyes and in her tone.

"I'm sorry for what your father put you through when you were young," she says, holding my gaze with sad eyes. "I know that it made you a little messed-up in the head."

Hurt flashes through me, and I think I even jerk back a little. *Messed-up in the head*. I know that I'm crazy. That I don't function like normal people. That I lack some of the common restraints and emotional responses that I should probably possess. But hearing my mom say that I'm messed-up in the head still hurts more than I expected.

I think she misinterprets my reaction, though. Maybe she thinks I flinched because hearing her say that brought on flashbacks from all those times with Dad. It has to be that, because she looks at me with even more sadness.

"If I had known about it, I would've put a stop to it," she says, her green eyes searching my face. "You know that, right?"

"Yeah," I manage to press out.

She reaches across the wooden tabletop and places her hand on my forearm, giving it a little squeeze. "I wish you hadn't quit therapy, sweetheart. If you had continued going while you were still a teenager, I think maybe things would have been different. Better."

Disbelief pulses through me. Blinking, I pull my arm away from her as I sit back in my chair. "I didn't quit therapy."

"Yes, you did. When you were fifteen, remember? You were starting to make progress, but then you just suddenly stopped going."

"I didn't quit therapy," I just repeat like an idiot, because I can't believe what is coming out of her mouth.

"Sweetheart, I—"

"I stopped going because Dad had my therapist killed."

Shock crackles through the living room like a lightning strike. Even Connor looks up from his plate to stare at me with wide eyes. At the head of the table, Mom just gapes at me in stunned silence.

"I had told her that Dad was a hitman," I continue. "Since, well, it's kind of a huge part of why I went there in the first place. And Dad couldn't risk her telling anyone else and blowing his cover, so he killed her and made it look like an accident. That's why I stopped going to therapy."

The silence in the dining room is so loud that it's practically vibrating through the air. Light from the candles dances over the white walls and casts flickering shadows over Mom's and Connor's stunned faces. Since Mom and Dad were always such a perfect team, I assumed that he had told her about this. But then again, given how Mom had reacted when she found out the other secret concerning me that he had been keeping from her, I probably should have known that he hadn't dared to tell her.

"Oh," is what at last makes it out of Mom's mouth.

"Raina," Connor says. His gray eyes are so full of emotion that it sends another pang through my chest. "I didn't know."

"I know you didn't." Forcing a casual expression onto my face, I pick up my knife and fork and continue eating again, even though the chicken has now gone cold. "And the damage is already done, so don't worry about me. I'll be fine."

"No, you won't!" Mom protests, wrapping her hand around my wrist and stopping me before I can put the bite of chicken in my mouth. "This is all the more reason to stop this ridiculousness at Blackwater."

I yank my arm from her grip and raise my fork again. After holding her gaze while chewing slowly, I try to muster up all my patience for an articulate response. But I find that particular attribute nonexistent, so I just swallow and simply reply, "No."

"Raina," she groans, frustration bleeding into her voice. Leaning back in her chair, she rakes her slender fingers through her loose blond curls and stares up at the frescos in the ceiling while heaving a deep sigh. Then she at last meets my gaze again. "Please. I know that your father has messed you up in ways that can't be fixed, but *please*. This is our family's only chance to regain our previous standing before we're ruined. *Your brother* is our only chance. So please, don't screw this up for him."

Pain slashes through my chest like sharp claws.

Slumping back in my chair, I stare unseeing into the flames while those words echo through my brain.

Messed-up in the head.

Can't be fixed.

I really am broken beyond repair, aren't I?

26

ELI

My phone vibrates in my pocket. Lowering the gun, I place it on the small counter in front of me and fish out my phone. I glance down at the name visible on the display. It's a guy from my senior class. A frown creases my brow. We're not exactly friends, so why the hell is he calling me?

I slide the answer button. Since it's late on a Saturday night, the indoor firing range is empty apart from me, so I don't have to worry about other people's noise as I hold my phone to my ear.

"What?" I demand.

"Hi," he blurts out, sounding a bit stunned by my brusque reply. "I'm—"

"I know who you are. Why are you calling me?"

"I… well, I saw that girl that you're, uhm… That you're… well…"

My heart lurches in my chest. *Raina*. Shifting the phone into a better position, I listen to him stutter as he tries to define what exactly Raina is to me, and failing miserably, for another few seconds before I cut him off.

"Raina," I say.

"Yes, her," he replies, sounding relieved.

"What about her?"

"Well, I'm downtown and I just walked past that bar on High Street. Silver Saint, on the corner there, you know? And well, I saw her through the window. She's there. Alone. And as far as I could tell, she's drunk out of her mind."

The blood freezes in my veins.

"I, uhm," he continues. "I just thought you might want to know."

"Thanks."

I hang up. Leaving the gun and equipment for someone else to clean up, I run out of the building and towards the parking lot.

Fury and frustration, and a tiny bit of worry, whirl through my soul as I throw myself into my car and floor it. The car practically skids out of the parking lot, and then I'm speeding down the street and towards the city.

What the fuck is Raina doing blackout drunk in a bar downtown? She told me that she was visiting her family tonight, which is why I, against my better judgement, allowed her to leave campus. If that was a lie so that she could go out partying, I'm going to make her fucking crawl.

Since I'm connected to the Morelli family, I often get people trying to do me favors so that I'll put in a good word for them when they inevitably apply for a position there. And right now, I'm incredibly fucking thankful for that, because otherwise, that guy would never have called and I would never have known about Raina's little rebellion.

Dark fields flash past my vision until they're finally replaced by glowing streetlamps and long rows of houses. I drive all the way up to the Silver Saint and park my car right there on the side of the road. The car behind me honks loudly at my abrupt stop. But the moment I step out of the car, the other driver yanks on the steering wheel and does a U-turn before speeding out of there as if he's afraid I'm going to hunt him down. I might have. If I hadn't been so distracted by the thought of Raina stumbling around inside the bar in front of me.

Yanking the door open, I stalk across the threshold.

The bartender opens his mouth as if to call out a greeting, or maybe ask what I want, but no words make it out when his gaze lands on me. Color drains from his pinched face, and he swallows nervously.

I pay him no mind as I quickly scan the bar.

It's a crowded and dimly lit place with furniture made of dark wood. Most of the patrons are deep in their cups, and a constant murmur of voices hangs over the area.

My gaze snaps to a woman slumped on a chair close to the dartboard on the other side of the room, and for a second, I swear my heart stops beating.

Raina's eyes are open, but she's barely sitting up. Instead, she's leaning the back of her head against the wall behind her and staring up at the ceiling. There's a loopy grin on her face, as if she finds something absolutely hilarious up there in the dark ceiling.

Rage roars through me as I notice two men hovering close to her, watching her with hungry eyes. I storm towards them.

The crowd parts before me as I stalk across the floorboards until I reach Raina and the two guys. Since their attention is solely focused on her, they haven't spotted me yet. I barrel past and position myself between them and Raina.

"Touch her and I'll rearrange your fucking teeth," I warn, my voice coming out low and vicious.

They clearly don't know who I am, because the one on the left snorts and elbows his companion, who snickers.

Suddenly, I wish I had brought that gun from the range. Or one of Kaden's blades. Or Jace's bats. But I suppose I'll just have to beat them to death with my fists instead.

The one who snorted flashes me a grin full of challenge. "I'll touch whoever—"

I slam my fist into his jaw. His head snaps to the side from the force of the hit, but I don't stop to admire the sight. Instead, I ram my other fist into his companion's stomach. Air explodes from his lungs, and he drops to his knees immediately.

The first guy has recovered enough to try to swing back. I bring my hand down on his wrist, forcing his arm downwards before he can hit me. Then I smack my boot into the side of his knee.

He cries out in pain as he crashes down on the ground. I kick him in the chest, making him topple backwards and slam back first into the floor.

People around us are screaming and scrambling out of the way, but I barely hear them as I drop down so that I'm straddling the guy's chest. And then I ram my fist into the side of his face. Again. And again. Blood sprays from his mouth as his head snaps from side to side with each strike.

Two steps away, his companion has finally recovered from the hit to his stomach. Fear floods his face as he sees what I'm doing to his friend, and he starts crawling away across the floor.

Stopping my assault, I instead reach out and grab his ankle. With a firm yank, I pull him back across the floor.

"Please," the guy underneath me croaks now that I've stopped pounding his face. "Please, I'm sorry."

"Yes, yes, we're sorry," his friend blurts out while trying to yank his ankle out of my grip. "We're sorry, we're sorry."

I glance behind me to see that Raina's body is now tilting precariously to the side. A few more inches and she'll topple right out of the chair. Her unfocused eyes are still searching the ceiling.

A snarl rips from my throat. I don't have time to deal with these fucking idiots.

Leveling hard stares on both of them, I growl, "If you ever so much as look at her again, I'll carve out your eyes."

Before they can sputter out a reply, I get to my feet and spin towards Raina. The sound of rustling clothes and scuffing shoes behind my back informs me that the two guys are scrambling away from me.

In the dead silent bar, I can hear the door being shoved open as they no doubt run outside. But my eyes are focused on Raina as I stop in front of her.

However, before I can say anything, the bartender appears right next to my shoulder. Based on the way he's wringing his hands when he speaks, he apparently knows who I am at least.

"I apologize for their behavior, sir. They will never be allowed in here again. Please, what can I do to make up for this?"

"Delete the security footage for tonight," I reply without taking my eyes off Raina. "Make sure everyone in here knows that this never happened. And put two bottles of water in the Range Rover outside."

"Yes, yes, consider it done."

While he hurries away to follow my orders, I reach out and

gently grip Raina's chin. Her eyes slide in and out of focus as I tilt her head back down so that she's looking at me instead.

"Raina," I say, my voice low.

She squints at me, as if trying to figure out who I am. Then a light goes on behind her eyes. "Hey, it's Small Dick Energy."

I don't know whether to laugh or strangle her.

"You're drunk." Grabbing her wrist, I start pulling her to her feet. "Let's go."

She tries to pull her wrist out of my grip while muttering, "I'm not going anywhere. I want another shot."

"If you don't do as I say, the only shot you'll be getting is a bullet between the eyes. Now let's go."

Yanking her up from the chair, I start towing her towards the door. But she only makes it one step before her legs start wobbling and she stumbles to the side. Releasing her wrist, I whip around and grab her by the hips to stop her from toppling over.

Once she's upright again, I tentatively remove my hands from her hips and hold them a few inches from her body instead. She immediately starts swaying again.

"Jesus fucking Christ," I growl.

Bending down, I slide an arm behind her legs and one behind her back, and then lift her into my arms instead.

"Hey," she calls. Or rather, she slurs the word. Her head lolls to the side as she looks at the people we pass, and she kicks her legs weakly. "Wait…"

I stalk across the bar and shoulder open the door. The bartender is just straightening from the passenger seat after putting two bottles of water into the cupholders in the middle.

"Leave it open," I tell him as I close the final distance.

He hurries out of the way. "Again, I'm so sorry. Please accept my sincerest apologies for—"

"Accepted," I interrupt. "Now, go back inside."

Without turning to see if he follows my orders, I stop in front of the open door and lower Raina onto the passenger seat. She blinks at the car while I withdraw my arms. I grab the seatbelt and start pulling it out.

But when I begin drawing it across her body, she seems to at last realize where she is because she starts trying to swat my hands away.

"No," she says while clumsily trying to push my arms back. "No, I'm not going anywhere with you."

Ignoring her, I simply reach across her in an effort to snap the seatbelt shut. But she starts fighting harder, squirming against the seat while trying to slap my hands away from her body.

A frustrated noise tears from my chest. Releasing the seatbelt, I abruptly yank my hand up and grab her chin instead. With a firm grip on it, I force her gaze to mine.

"Keep fighting me, and I'll put you in the trunk instead," I warn.

She glares back at me. Or tries to. Because of how drunk she is, she can't keep that adorably angry expression on her features for more than a second at a time.

Then she throws up her hands and heaves a dramatic sigh. "Fine."

I release her chin and grab the seatbelt again. This time, she doesn't fight me, so I manage to snap it in place quickly. Then I slam the door shut.

After rounding the car, I slide into the driver's seat.

Snatching up one of the water bottles, I shove it into her hands. "Drink."

"I don't want water," she protests.

"You can either drink willingly, or I can force feed it to you. Your choice."

She once again tries her best to glare at me. Then she scowls down at the bottle in her hands.

"Fucking dictator," she mutters.

But she twists off the cap and starts drinking. Satisfied that she does what she's told, I start the car and then make a U-turn. Raina keeps sipping from the bottle while I drive us back to campus.

I flex my fingers on the steering wheel, trying to stop myself from brutally interrogating her on what the fuck she was doing in that bar. We've only made it halfway back to campus when my self-control is completely spent.

"What the hell were you doing in that bar?" I demand, still keeping my eyes on the dark road ahead.

"Drinking," she retorts. Her words are a bit less slurred now. "What else would I be doing?"

"You told me you were going home to your family."

"I did."

"So you'd better have one hell of an explanation for why you lied to me about that, or this is going to be a long fucking night for you."

"I didn't lie. I did go home to my family."

I glance at her when I hear the honesty in her tone. Her face shows the same sincerity. In her still half drunken state, I doubt she would be able to lie this convincingly, so I'm forced to accept that she is in fact telling the truth.

"So how did you end up wasted in a fucking bar?" I demand, sliding my gaze back to the road ahead.

She's silent for a long moment. Then she slumps back in

her seat, resting her head against the leather, and heaves a deep sigh.

"Because my mom told me that I'm messed-up in the head."

I snap my gaze back to her.

My chest constricts at the raw emotions in her eyes as she stares out at the dark night in front of the car, and it takes every ounce of my willpower not to drive back to the city and slaughter her entire family.

27

RAINA

By the time we reach Blackwater, I'm so completely drained that I don't even protest when Eli lifts me out of the passenger seat and carries me into his house. We run into Rico in the hallway, but neither of them speaks. He and Eli just hold each other's gaze for a few seconds, as if they have some kind of silent way of communicating with only their eyes, while Eli walks past and makes for the stairs.

His strong arms hold me tightly as he strides towards his bedroom. I'm still a bit drunk. Not nearly as wasted as I was back in that bar, but still drunk enough that I'm having trouble thinking straight. Or maybe that is more due to the feeling of Eli's warm muscular chest against my cheek and his intoxicating scent that fills my lungs with every breath.

After closing the door behind him, he walks across the room and then into his bathroom before setting me down on the closed toilet lid. I know that I should probably be fighting him or antagonizing him in some way, but I just can't bring myself to care about anything right now. So all I do is sit there and stare blankly at the bathroom.

It's not a massive one, but it's surprisingly elegant. Apart from the toilet I'm sitting on, there is a white marble sink with a gilded mirror above it and a spacious shower with one of those rain shower heads. Warm light from the expensive-looking lamp in the ceiling fills the room with a golden glow that seems to shimmer against the white tiles.

"I don't have a bathtub, so you're going to have to stand for a few minutes while you take a shower," he says while reaching in and turning the water on.

"I don't need to take a shower," I answer, speaking for the first time since the car ride back.

Eli cuts me a look that makes embarrassment creep into my cheeks. Running my hands over my forearms, I realize that they're sticky. I must have spilled a drink, or five, on myself at some point.

"Fine," I mutter.

My legs are still unsteady, so I sway a little as I strip out of my clothes and shoes and drop them in a heap on the otherwise spotless floor. Eli remains where he is, blocking the doorway. With his arms crossed, he watches me as I undress and then move towards the shower, as if he's making sure I'm actually following his orders.

The skin on the back of my neck prickles, and heat pools inside me, at the way he is watching me. But I turn my back on him as I step into the shower.

Water splashes down on me.

I let out a sigh.

Standing there under the warm water, I close my eyes and just let it wash over me.

"There's shower gel on the shelf," Eli says.

I ignore him. The water soaks my hair and wraps around my body like a warm blanket. It feels so good that I don't ever want to move.

"Princess," Eli pushes.

Only the splashing of water on tiles answers him. Tilting my head back, I let the water rush down over my face as if to wash away the lingering intoxication.

"Fucking hell," Eli growls after a while.

My stomach lurches as a hand lands on my shoulder and roughly spins me around. I blink against the water still clinging to my lashes.

Once my vision is clear, I find Eli standing right there.

In the shower.

Naked.

With me.

Water soaks his black hair and runs down his broad shoulders. With my mouth still slightly open from the surprise of finding him here, I run my gaze over his muscular frame.

God, he really is a fucking work of art.

With his honed body and the scars across his skin, he looks like a god of war who could make men and women drop to their knees in both fear and admiration. Lust stirs inside me as I drink in the sight of him.

While I'm distracted, he plants a hand against my collarbones and pushes me up against the wall. The tiles are cool against my heated skin, and it jolts me back to reality. But Eli has already squeezed some shower gel into his hand. After rubbing them together a few times to create a lather, he starts running his palms over my skin.

My heart leaps in my chest.

For a while, I'm so stunned by his actions that all I do is stand there while he washes my body.

He has pushed me up against the wall in the corner of the shower, and his muscular body is blocking my way out. But it's the way he is touching me that is making my heart pound in my chest and heat pool between my legs. He is running his hands over my body as if he *owns* it. His to touch, his to caress, his to bend and break and use in whatever way he sees fit. It makes my clit throb with need.

Just to test that theory, I take a step forward as if to move past him and out of the shower.

He immediately plants a hand against my chest and shoves me back against the wall. Keeping his hand there, he pauses his work and instead locks eyes with me.

Water clings to his dark lashes and hair, and drops of it run down the ridges of his powerful muscles. But we're mostly out of the still splashing water now, so there is nothing to obscure our vision as he stares me down.

I can feel the silent command pulsing from his body, can see the glint of challenge in those beautiful eyes of his, as if he is daring me to move without permission again. Since I know that I will lose this battle, I slump back against the wall again.

Satisfaction swirls in Eli's eyes.

Taking his palm off my chest, he instead draws it down along the curve of my breast. Lightning skitters across my skin in its wake. He slides his other hand up the side of my ribs.

A sigh escapes my lips. I rest the back of my head against the wall as Eli takes his time washing my chest. His hands massage my tits with slow and tantalizing motions, circling around the edge and towards the center.

I bite my lip to stop a moan as he rubs his thumbs over my

nipples. His eyes stay locked on mine, studying every expression on my face. He rolls my nipple between his thumb and forefinger. I suck in a shaky breath. My pussy throbs.

A smirk plays over Eli's lips.

Then he draws his hands down my stomach. I shift my weight to relieve the ache between my legs as he teases his fingers across the skin right above my pussy. He moves his hands down my legs. My heart pounds in my chest as he crouches down and washes my legs, starting at the ankle.

With every inch he moves upwards, the fire in my veins burns hotter. I draw in shuddering breaths as he reaches my thighs. He straightens again and locks eyes with me as he slips his hands down to my inner thighs.

My brain flickers and I brace my palm on the cold tiles behind me as Eli draws his clever fingers across my sensitive skin and up towards my pussy. The whirling tension inside me is so wild that I can barely breathe properly.

But right before he reaches that spot where I really want his fingers, he stops and pulls his hand back. I blink, disoriented, and stare up at him.

"There," he says, a sly smile full of challenge on his lips. "Now you're clean."

Only the splashing noise of the water still rushing down behind his back fills the elegant bathroom as we stare at each other in silence. My pussy aches with need. I hold Eli's smug gaze for another few seconds. Then I throw my pride and restraint to the wind.

Wrapping a hand around the back of his neck, I yank his stupid smirking mouth down to mine. Our lips clash in a violent kiss. A smug laugh rumbles from Eli's chest, so I bite his bottom lip hard. He answers by sliding an arm under my ass and lifting me up while kissing me so furiously that I forget to breathe.

Air escapes my lungs as Eli slams me up against the wall. I wrap my legs around his waist while he continues stealing what little breath I have left with his forceful kisses. His tongue tangles with mine as he claims my mouth with dominant strokes.

My head is spinning and it's all I can do to remember to breathe. This kiss is unlike anything I have ever experienced. *He* is unlike anything I have ever experienced.

His fingers dig into my skin as he holds me up and presses me hard against the wall while he kisses me like he is fighting a battle. But I have already lost that war, and I don't even care, because all I want is *more*.

Bracing my hands on his shoulders, I shift my legs around his waist so that I can get my pussy in position above his cock. He uses his grip on my ass to help move me into place. While still kissing me violently, he slides me down and then thrusts into me.

I gasp into his mouth.

He snatches my next breath from my lungs too as he pulls out slightly and then shoves his cock all the way in to the hilt. A dark groan tears from deep within his chest.

For a few seconds, we stop moving entirely. His breath caresses my wet skin as he rests his forehead against mine. I suck in deep breaths while my soul thrums from the feeling of his thick cock inside me.

Then I dig my fingers into his toned shoulders as I lift myself upwards before sliding down his shaft again. I'm rewarded by another moan from Eli at the mind-numbing friction it creates.

That breaks the spell.

With his strong arms around my ass, he shifts my body as he starts up a brutal pace of thrusting into me. I roll my hips and move in rhythm with him as he pounds into me. My back hits the cold tiles with every dominant thrust.

Shifting my position slightly, I angle my hips so that his cock grinds against my clit when he moves.

Lights flicker in my brain.

I pant, keeping my legs around his waist and bracing myself on his broad shoulders, as he fucks me hard against the wall. Pleasure builds inside me with every thrust of his hips.

Breathy screams rip from my lungs as release crackles through my veins.

My legs slip as the wave of pleasure courses through my limbs, but Eli only tightens his grip on my ass as he continues fucking me through the orgasm. His groans join mine as he comes deep inside me as well.

God, why does this feel so good? Why does *he* feel so good? His dominant hands on my body, his hard cock inside me, his violent kisses claiming my mouth, his lethal body pressed against mine… It's like my own personal drug.

When Eli at last pulls out and sets me down on the wet tiles again, I can barely stay upright. My already unstable legs wobble as I straighten, and I have to brace myself against the wall for a while before I'm confident that I won't topple over.

Eli remains standing right in front of me, running his gaze over my body like it's his property. My cheeks are already flushed from the orgasm, so I don't think he notices the heat that floods them when he's looking at me like that.

"Aw, princess," he begins, a smirk lifting his lips. "I got you dirty again."

I flick a glance down at the cum running down between my legs.

Eli uses my moment of inattention to grab me by the hips and pull me with him as he steps back into the flowing water. It washes over us as he stops there underneath the rain shower head.

After washing his cum from my skin, he turns the shower off and steps out. I'm so utterly spent now that all I can do is stand there with one hand against the wall. Water runs down my body and drips from my hair.

Eli towels himself off and then puts on a pair of fresh boxers. Then he turns back to me and arches a dark eyebrow when he finds me still standing there, naked and wet in the shower. He rolls his eyes.

While muttering under his breath, he yanks down another towel and stalks back to me. His hands are surprisingly gentle as he towels me off as well. After hanging the towel back up, he grabs a t-shirt from one of his drawers and tosses it at me. It hits my chest, and I barely manage to catch it before it can flutter down to the wet floor.

"Put it on," he orders.

Since I don't have anything else to wear, and I don't want to put my own sticky, alcohol-soaked clothes back on, I do as he says. The shirt is so big that it falls halfway down my thighs. It smells like laundry detergent and… him.

"Fucking hell, princess," Eli mutters.

That's when I realize that I'm still standing there in the shower.

Eli stalks back to me and scoops me up into his arms. I'm too exhausted to protest as he strides back into his bedroom and then puts me down on his bed.

Sleeping here is probably a really bad idea, but fuck, I'm so damn tired and this bed is so ridiculously comfortable.

Adjusting my position, I nestle deeper into the fluffy pillow. A click sounds, and then the room is plunged into darkness.

The mattress dips to my left as Eli climbs into bed as well and lies down next to me.

For a few seconds, everything is silent. My eyes start to droop as sleep begins to pull at my body.

"What happened tonight?" Eli asks, yanking me back to reality before I can tumble into the land of dreams.

"I already told you what happened," I reply, staring up at the dark ceiling. "I had dinner with my family. Then I got drunk."

"Why did you get drunk?"

"I told you that too."

"You told me half of it. Why did your mother say that you're messed-up in the head?"

"Because I am."

The bedframe groans as Eli abruptly rolls over on his side and wraps his hand around my jaw. Electricity zaps through my spine at the fire I see in his eyes when he forces me to turn my head and meet his gaze.

"Answer the fucking question, Raina," he growls.

I blink at him in surprise. He rarely calls me Raina. It's almost always *princess*. Which means that, for some reason, he considers this a serious enough matter to use my actual name.

Any remaining traces of a fight bleed out of me, and I heave a deep sigh. "Fine."

He releases my jaw, but he remains lying on his side, his eyes locked on mine. I can't handle the intensity in them, so I turn my head back and stare up into the dark ceiling again.

"My father was a hitman," I begin. Even though I have to choose my words carefully, since I can't accidentally let it slip that I'm Connor's sister, it still somehow feels like a relief to finally speak these words out loud. So I tilt my head back and meet his gaze again. "And he used to take me with him on his missions. Ever since I was a little kid, he brought me with him when he killed people."

Eli's dark brows furrow slightly. "Why?"

"Because it was the perfect cover. No one ever suspects that the nice man with the young girl next to him is an assassin."

"So you grew up… watching your dad kill people?"

"For as long as I can remember." I shrug. "My therapist says that it permanently affected my love map. Whatever that means. Or she said that, at least, before Dad had her assassinated too because I had told her that he was a hitman."

He raises his eyebrows in surprise.

I shrug again. "That's why I'm so fucked-up in the head."

Anger flickers in his eyes. "You're not fucked-up in the head."

"Yes, I am. All my life, everyone around me has been telling me that I'm crazy. And I'm pretty sure there's a reason for that."

"You're not crazy. You're insane."

A surprised laugh rips from my chest. Raising my eyebrows, I study his very serious face. "What?"

"You're not crazy. You're insane," he repeats. "There's a difference."

"There is?"

"Yes. Being crazy means that you're a nutjob who needs to be locked up. Being insane just means that you don't play by the same rules as everyone else."

My mouth drops open slightly, and I stare at him.

"And I would rather have someone insane in my corner

than some boring fucking normal person." His dark golden eyes sear into my soul. "Every fucking day of the week."

Warmth spreads through my chest. It feels like tiny bursts of sparkling fireworks. I open my mouth to say something, but I can't for the life of me figure out what.

As if suddenly realizing what he just said, Eli blinks and then gives his head a couple of quick shakes. "We should get some sleep."

"I, uhm... yeah."

The mattress shifts underneath me as he adjusts his position and reaches towards me.

Wrapping an arm over my chest, he pulls me closer until I'm lying flush against his warm half-naked body. With his arm holding me there, he drapes his leg over mine again, trapping me completely against his body.

But as I nestle deeper into his embrace, I don't think I want to escape this time.

28

ELI

I wake up with a warm, soft body against mine. For a moment, I just pull it closer to me and tighten my arms around it. Around *her*.

Then my eyes snap open. Staring over the side of Raina's head, I look at the clock on the nightstand. It's almost noon.

Noon.

Cold panic washes over me.

I've slept for eleven and a half hours.

Once is a coincidence. But now, there is no denying the fact that Raina is somehow the reason why I'm able to sleep again.

Shoving her away from me, I roll over on my other side and then quickly get out of bed. Raina mumbles and groans when my manhandling wakes her up as well.

With my heart slamming against my ribs, I stalk over to the dark wooden dresser and yank it open while I try to suck in calming breaths without Raina hearing it.

She is responsible for this. *Her* presence for some reason allows me to sleep. And that means that she has power over me. More power than *anyone*.

Fuck, fuck, fuck.

I snatch up a pair of pants and shove my legs into them before grabbing a t-shirt and yanking that over my head as well. Panic continues whirling inside me like a crackling storm.

Raina is the worst assassin-in-training at this entire fucking university. So why the hell is she still the most dangerous person I've ever met?

I can't keep doing this.

Every day, she gains more and more power over me. Every day, I grow more obsessed with her. More dependent on her. Hell, I even fucking *care* more and more about her. When I heard that she was blackout drunk in a fucking bar, I couldn't breathe because I was terrified that something might happen to her. That someone might do something to her.

It has to stop. I have to put some distance between us until I can figure out how to get my treacherous emotions under control. Until *I'm* in control. Fully. Completely.

Dragging a hand through my hair, I draw in a deep breath and then turn around to face the bed again.

"Get up," I snap, putting unflinching command into my voice.

Raina blinks and then squints at me from the bed. "Well, good morning to you too, asshole."

"You have three seconds to get out of my bed before I tie you to it and beat your ass with my belt."

Something flickers in her eyes.

"One."

She quickly scrambles out of bed.

A smug smile curves my lips.

While throwing a scowl in my direction, she brushes her hands down her shirt, *my* shirt, and then runs her fingers through her hair. As if only then realizing that the shirt isn't hers, she glances down at it again while she lets her arms drop back down by her sides. Then she looks towards where her clothes are sitting on my bathroom floor.

She starts towards them, but I'm faster.

Before she can round the bed, I move so that I'm blocking the door. Annoyance flits across her face. Planting her hands on her hips, she raises her eyebrows as she glares up at me.

"Unless you never want to see this shirt again, I suggest you step aside so that I can grab my own clothes," she declares.

The absolute authority in her voice and the cocky tilt of her chin sends a pulse through my body. And suddenly, all I want to do is to follow through on my threat and tie her to my bed, spank her bratty ass, and then fuck the insolence out of her.

But I'm supposed to be putting distance between us, not falling deeper into her all-consuming presence, so I remain firmly where I am and bring my cruelty to the surface.

"You behaved like a slut in that bar yesterday," I say, even though I don't mean it, just for the sole purpose of hurting her. "So now, you pay for that." I jerk my chin towards my bedroom door. "Time for a walk of shame."

"A slut?" She snorts and rolls her eyes. "The eighteenth century called and wanted its views on women's sexuality back. Now, get the hell out of my way so that I can grab my clothes."

"Your clothes are staying right here."

She raises her eyebrows in a pointed expression.

I flash her a cold smile. "Spoils of war."

She scoffs.

"You have two options. You either walk back to your dorm in that." I nod down at my shirt that she's wearing. "Or you walk back naked. Choose."

A knowing glint creeps into her green eyes, and a vicious smile curls her lips. "Easy."

Grabbing the hem of the shirt, she yanks it over her head and then shoves the crumpled-up fabric at my chest.

Shock clangs through me at the unexpected move, so I don't even have time to grab it before she releases it. The white fabric flutters down to the dark floorboards as she turns on her heel and marches towards my bedroom door completely naked.

Fury roars through me.

She's going to walk through the entire residential neighborhood naked? For everyone to see? Like hell.

Her fingers have barely brushed the handle when I catch up to her and slam my palm against the door. She turns around to face me. And that scheming, victorious glint in her eyes almost sends me to my fucking knees.

She knew that I would never let her walk through the neighborhood naked, so she called my bluff and obliterated my power move.

"You have two options," she begins, echoing my words, while her eyes glitter with smugness. "Either I walk back to my dorm wearing my own clothes." She nods towards the bathroom. "Or I walk back naked. Choose."

Clenching my jaw, I flex my fingers while I try to suppress the overwhelming urge to strangle the fuck out of this infuriating woman.

But she knows that she has already won, so she only looks back at me with eyebrows raised expectantly.

A low snarl rips from my throat as I stalk back to the bathroom and gather up her clothes and shoes. But I don't give them to her when I return. Instead, I shift them to one arm and use my other hand to shove the door open. Then I grab Raina by the arm and throw her out into the corridor.

She stumbles from the force of the shove, and has to brace herself against the opposite wall. Still completely naked, she straightens and levels a scathing glare at me.

"Here." I throw the bundle of garments at her. "You can get dressed out in the corridor just like all the other desperate girls I've fucked in this room over the years."

Anger pulses across her face, and she jerks back like I've slapped her.

Good. I want her to hurt. To doubt. To crumble and break. I need to destroy whatever this thing between us is before she gains too much power over me.

I haven't touched, let alone fucked, anyone else ever since I met Raina.

But I can't let her know that, so I add in a mocking voice, "Aww. Did you think that you were special? I hate to break it to you, princess…" I flick a dismissive look up and down her naked body. "But there is absolutely nothing special about you."

Emotions flash across her features. Too fast for me to decipher.

But before she can reply, I slam the door shut in her face.

29

RAINA

The sounds of fists hitting flesh echoes between the concrete walls. Sitting on a short wooden bench, I glower at Eli and his brothers as they continue sparring.

I'm not sure what exactly went wrong, but after I spent the night with Eli last weekend, he seems to have lost interest in me. He has been ignoring me all week, treating me as if I'm not there at all. When we have our team training sessions during the afternoons, the four of them are practicing together without even bothering to look in my direction. And when I complained about that, Kaden decided that it was my mission in life to fetch them water while they train. So now, that's all I do. I refill their water bottles and then I sit here and glare at them.

My pride is telling me to just leave. But I can't. I still need to keep an eye on Eli to make sure that he doesn't start messing with Connor again.

Worry snakes through my chest as I watch Eli swing at Kaden, who ducks and throws a fist back at his brother's side.

A short distance away, Jace and Rico are sparring as well. We're in a smaller, private training room instead of the massive sparring hall that we use when we have class, so we're the only ones here. At least that means that there is no risk of them running into Connor.

Another bout of worry flutters behind my ribs. If Eli truly has lost interest in tormenting me, it's only a matter of time before he sets his sights on Connor again. I can't let that happen. Resting my elbows on my knees, I stare at the gray wall on the other side of the room while I consider my options.

This week, I've tried my usual methods of messing with Eli. But it hasn't worked. I need to do something drastic. Something big. Something that will make it impossible for Eli to continue ignoring me. But what?

A shadow looms above me.

Tearing my eyes from the empty wall, I instead slide my gaze to the man standing next to me. Kaden. While holding my gaze with those cold dark eyes of his, he picks up his water bottle and pointedly shakes it in the air.

"It's empty," he announces.

I raise my eyebrows in a nonchalant gesture. "And?"

"Making sure we're hydrated is your sole purpose in life."

I snort and roll my eyes.

Kaden moves so damn fast that I don't even have time to jerk back. One second, I'm sitting there on the bench. The next, he has hauled me up by the collar and slammed me back first against the wall behind me. My breath explodes from my lungs with a huff as I hit the hard surface.

With his forearm across my collarbones, he pushes me hard against the wall while leaning closer. "Did you just roll your eyes at me?"

"Uh, yeah." Frowning, I shake my head at him to inform him that that was an incredibly stupid question. "Are you blind as well as deaf?"

Behind him to the left, Rico and Jace have stopped sparring, and both of them are watching us. Jace with a wide grin on his face, and Rico with a considering look in his brown eyes. Eli, on the other hand, only continues going through a series of punches and kicks to the air while keeping his gaze on the door.

Steel sings into the thrumming silence as Kaden unsheathes one of the knives he always keeps in his thigh holster. I study his face as he raises the blade.

I know that there is something wrong with me, and with Eli too, but I'm pretty sure that the most unhinged one of all is actually Kaden.

He doesn't look angry that I insulted him. In fact, I can't read him at all. It's as if there is this vast emptiness inside him. Looking into his eyes feels like staring into an endless void where there is no light or sound or life at all.

Light from the fluorescents above glints in the blade as Kaden spins it in his hand before positioning it in front of my face.

"I will give you one chance to apologize," he says, his voice as cold and flat as his knife.

"Yeah..." I begin, drawing out the word. "Thanks for the offer. But I'm afraid I'm going to have to decline."

Cold steel kisses my skin as Kaden lightly scrapes the point of the blade over my cheek before stopping right underneath my left eye.

"Left?" Using the blade, he taps the skin below my eye before shifting the knife to my right eye and doing the same. "Or right? Which one would you like to keep?"

"I don't really have a preference, so you can pick."

Surprise flickers in those empty eyes.

I just cock my head, watching him. Because of my experiences as a child, violence and death has never scared me. I know that logically, I should be terrified when a psychopath is holding a knife to my face and threatening to carve out my eyes. But it's as if the pathways in my brain that control those emotions were irrevocably damaged. Or maybe they were never even formed at all.

That's not to say that I don't feel fear at all. I do. I'm terrified that they will hurt my brother. But as long as they only continue threatening *me*, they will never break me.

"Does this little routine usually work on people?" I ask in a mocking voice.

Kaden pushes his forearm harder against my chest while he traces his knife down my cheek again. "I *will* find a way to put fear in your eyes. One way or another."

"Is that what you get off on?" I shoot a pointed glance down towards his cock before meeting his gaze again. "Is that what makes you hard? Fear?"

The sadistic smile that curls his lips in response sends a cold shiver down my spine. There really is something wrong with this guy.

"Kaden."

My heart does a tiny flip at the sound of the voice, and I glance towards the source of it. I had expected, or maybe hoped, that it would be Eli. But it wasn't. It was Rico.

Standing there next to Jace, he shakes his head once in a clear order to knock it off. Eli still isn't even looking in our direction.

Kaden glances towards Eli anyway, and then at last takes his forearm from my chest. I draw in a breath now that the pressure on my chest is gone, and then I brush my hands down my slightly rumpled shirt.

"Well, that was informative," I say.

Kaden, who hasn't sheathed his knife and is instead twirling it beside him, narrows his eyes at me as if wondering what that means. I just flash him a wicked grin and stroll towards the doors.

This conversation about fear gave me an idea. Now, I know exactly how to snap Eli out of his indifference and how to make sure that I will always be his target number one.

Kaden, Jace, and Rico watch me as I walk across the sparring room and towards the doors. But none of them stop me as I slip out into the corridor, and they don't follow me as I make my way through the building.

And good thing they don't, because halfway to my destination, I run into the person they can never see me with. Connor.

My brother jerks back and blinks in surprise as we almost crash into each other while rounding a corner.

"Raina," he says.

I just take a step to the side so that I can walk around him. But before I can, his hand shoots out and he grabs my elbow. I turn to face him and then shoot a pointed look down at his hand. Hesitation flits across his features, but he releases my elbow.

"Look, I'm sorry about what Mom said," he begins, his voice soft.

"It's fine."

"No, it's not." He holds my gaze, a serious expression in his gray eyes. "You're not messed-up in the head."

"Most of the world would disagree with you."

"I don't care. Because I know you're not."

A small smile tugs at my lips.

He mirrors it tentatively. Then he goes and ruins the moment by saying, "I still don't think you should be here, though. I've got things under control, so you don't need to—"

I roll my eyes and abruptly start walking again.

"Raina," he snaps.

But I only continue striding down the hall.

"You might think you're stepping up, but you're not," he calls after me. "Mom is right. You're only ruining our family name by being here and failing at everything. So just leave this to me and I promise... Raina!"

Ignoring him, I round the next corner and stalk out of sight.

Yes, I might be embarrassingly bad at everything else at this university. But there is one thing that I am good at. And it's time I start taking advantage of that.

30

ELI

Distancing myself from Raina is only partially working. I still can't concentrate properly when she's not in the room and I still sleep less than I normally do. And she still consumes all of my attention and makes my head go quiet when she's near.

After burying another two bullets in my target, I steal a covert glance at Raina.

All week, she has been trying to mess with me the way she always does. But after her confrontation with Kaden yesterday, she seems to have accepted her new role a bit better. She stalked onto the outdoor gun range this afternoon and slammed our water bottles down by our stations, and then she has been sitting on the bench behind us ever since, sulking and glowering at us while we do target practice.

It takes everything I have not to smirk. I do love messing with her. It brings me joy like few other things do. But I need to get my dangerous emotions under control before I can start fucking with her again.

After firing another couple of rounds, I set my gun down on the small table next to my station. Shots echo from where my brothers are standing in their own designated spots. There are six more targets on this range, but none of them are occupied. Most teams prefer to train separately for the tournament, so it's rare to find two teams on the same training grounds during these afternoon sessions.

I sweep my gaze across the grass before casting a glance up at the clear blue sky above. The sun is beating down on us, making a bead of sweat roll down my spine. I'm wearing black jeans and a black t-shirt, which probably wasn't the smartest choice given that the heat of summer still hasn't broken.

My gaze drifts back to Raina.

As usual, she is dressed as if she's going to the mall or something. A white blouse, a short dark green skirt, and those white sneakers she insists on wearing.

A breeze blows across the field, making the grass ripple. It snatches at Raina's short skirt. Blood pulses to my cock as the fabric flutters up, exposing more of her perfect thighs.

I just want to stalk up over there, bend her over that bench, and then fuck her so hard that she's screaming my name until her voice shatters.

Shaking my head, I discreetly adjust my cock in my pants while forcing the thought out of my mind. I need to put distance between us. *Distance.* I grab my water bottle and drink deeply from it instead.

That damn woman is so fucking dangerous.

I slam the water bottle back on the table again and drag my hand through my hair.

Maybe I should just cut all ties with her and have her… *disappear* from Blackwater. Then there would be no risk of her realizing the power she has over me. And there would be no one to distract me. But then I wouldn't be able to…

My thoughts trail off as a wave of dizziness washes over me. I blink and shake my head.

From her place on the bench, Raina studies me for a second. Then she gets up and starts towards me.

"Sit back down," I try to snap at her, but my words are coming out all slurred.

I frown and shake my head again. My tongue feels weird. As if it's swelling up. I whip my gaze towards where Rico is, and the world sways around me with the motion. I blink, trying to clear my vision.

"What's the matter?" Raina says with a taunting note in her voice. "Having trouble speaking? Moving? Breathing?"

Right as she speaks that final word, my throat starts to close up. I try to suck in a desperate breath while Raina stops before me. Crossing her arms, she watches me with a smirk on her lips.

I try to take a step towards her, but I'm losing feeling in my legs and arms, and my knee just buckles instead.

"Eli!" Rico yells from somewhere on my left as I crash down on one knee on the grass.

"You…" I begin, but my throat and tongue are so swollen that I can't press out the rest of the sentence.

Boots pound against the grass as my brothers sprint towards us while Raina leans down and wraps her hand around my jaw. I try to slap it away, but I can't lift my arms.

With that sly smile still on her lips, she tilts my chin up so that I meet her gaze. "I told you I would put you on your back and make you choke on your own lungs if you ever forced me into a car again." The smile on her mouth turns ruthless as she grins down at me. "Actions, meet consequences."

Then she's ripped away as my brothers reach us. Without her hand to hold me up, I simply tip to the side and crash down on the grass. My chest shakes violently as I try to suck air into my lungs.

Rico and Jace are immediately on their knees next to me, rolling me over on my back and opening my mouth as if to help open up my airways. It's not working.

"What the fuck did you do?" Jace growls as he whips his gaze towards Raina.

She's standing right above me while Kaden has one hand around her arm and the other holding a knife to her throat. But she isn't paying him any mind because those glittering green eyes of hers are locked solely on me as she replies.

"I poisoned him, of course."

"Jace, help me get him up," Rico orders. "We need to take him to the hospital wing."

My body spasms and gurgling noises come from my throat as I drag in rattling breaths that barely make it to my lungs. I try to sit up so that I can cough, but my body refuses to obey me. Disbelief pulses through me as I stare back at Raina from where I'm lying on the ground.

"Don't bother," she says, speaking to my brothers but keeping her eyes on me. "By the time you get there, he will already be dead."

Lightning zings through me at the way she looks right now. Even with Kaden pressing a knife to her throat, there is no mistaking that she is the one in control here.

Her long black hair flutters in the air as a gust washes over her. There is a cruel smirk playing over her luscious lips, and her green eyes are glittering with ruthlessness as she stands above me and watches me choke and spasm on the ground.

She looks like a fucking goddess of death.

My *personal* goddess of death, come to exact vengeance on me.

Fire sears through my veins.

Never in my life have I been so furious and so fucking turned on at the same time.

Jace and Rico shoot to their feet at her reply. Panic and fear flash across their faces as they whip their gazes between me and her. I know that I should probably be scared too. If her words are to be believed, I will be dead within the next few minutes. But the only emotion pulsing through me is stunned disbelief that she had the fucking balls to pull something like this. And a tiny bit of admiration too, because damn, I am impressed.

Metal glints in the bright sunlight as Jace yanks up his gun and shoves it against Raina's temple so hard that her head tilts to the side. "Give him the antidote."

"Who says there is one?" Raina replies, casting him a nonchalant look.

"You have three seconds to produce an antidote before I shoot you in the head," Jace growls in a voice so vicious that the grass around him seems to shrink back into the earth. It's a voice I have rarely heard from him.

"You have *two* seconds before I slit your throat," Kaden adds.

"Go ahead. Kill me." A smirk curls Raina's lips as she nods towards me. "But then he will also be dead."

As if on cue, my limbs jerk uncontrollably as the poison ripples through me. My throat closes up even more. A flash of primal panic, one that has been engrained into humanity since the dawn of time, flashes through my mind as I suddenly find myself unable to get any air into my lungs. Gurgling noises rip from me as I try to suck in a breath through my swollen throat and constricted lungs.

"What do you want?" Rico screams, his voice almost breaking on that final word. Desperation pulses from his entire being as he throws out his arms helplessly and stares at Raina while repeating, "What do you want?"

"I want you to beg."

Shock pulses across the field. But I'm starting to have trouble concentrating. I used to be able to smell the grass and soil that the back of my head is resting on, but now I can't smell anything anymore. My chest shakes as I try to fight a breath into my lungs. There is a terrible coldness in my unresponsive limbs.

"You want me to give him the antidote?" Raina continues. She even sounds like a goddess of death now. Cold. Cruel. Utterly untouchable. "Then get down on your knees and beg me for his life."

They don't even hesitate a second.

Kaden and Jace toss their weapons to the ground immediately, and then all three of them drop to their knees before her. They form a short line between her and my shaking body, as if they can protect me from her insanity with their own kneeling forms.

"Please, Raina," Rico says, his voice pulsing with desperation. "I'm begging you to spare his life. Please, give him the antidote."

She arches a dark eyebrow and slides her gaze to Kaden and Jace. "I said, *beg*."

"Please, we're begging you," both of them blurt out in unison.

If anyone else had been the recipient of this massive fucking powerplay that she is executing, I would have been so turned on that I would've fucked her into the next century. But unfortunately for her, *I* am the recipient. And she has made a huge fucking mistake now.

She has made *my brothers* get down on their knees and beg. Humiliated them. Made them plead for my damn life.

I'm going to fucking kill her for this.

31

RAINA

I jerk awake as hands grab me from all sides. I try to yank my arms away and kick my legs while a scream of surprise builds in my throat. But before it can erupt, duct tape is slapped across my mouth.

It's pitch black inside my dorm room since it's the middle of the night, so I can't see properly where my attackers are. My pulse thrums in my ears as I fight blindly to get free of their grip.

Pain pulses through my body as I'm thrown down on the cold stone floor. Before I can recover, someone plants a boot on the side of my head while someone else sits down on top of me and twists my arms up behind my back at the same time as a third one grabs my ankles. I struggle futilely as they tie my wrists and ankles together with rope.

Because of the boot on the side of my head, I can't see my attackers' faces. But I'm not stupid. I know exactly who they are.

After giving Eli the antidote earlier this afternoon, I left him and his brothers on that field while the cure for the poison finished working its magic. The glares that followed me when I walked away were so lethally furious that they could've set the world on fire.

I knew that the Hunters would be coming for revenge. I just hadn't expected it to be this soon. But then again, if there's one person that wouldn't need more than a few hours to recover from a near-death experience, it's Eli Hunter.

The weight on my back disappears as the person who was sitting on me stands up. But before I can do anything about it, someone bends my legs up towards my ass. My heart hammers from the adrenaline as they hogtie me.

Then they step back, and the boot at last disappears from the side of my head.

I wiggle on the floor, but the ropes keep me mercilessly trapped, so all it accomplishes is to make my sleep shirt ride up and bunch around my waist. Since I was sleeping, I'm only wearing a large t-shirt and a pair of panties.

The stone floor is cold underneath my bare thighs as I try yet again to somehow get free of the ropes. It's useless. Since there's tape over my mouth, I breathe deeply through my nose as I twist my head to look at my captors. But all I manage to see before someone blindfolds me are black boots and dark pants.

My stomach lurches as one of the Hunters lifts me off the floor and throws me over his shoulder. The hogtie is so tight that my body can barely bend, leaving my muscles straining in the awkward position. I growl a curse that the gag muffles.

The sound of doors opening and closing joins the thudding footsteps. Then cool night air washes over me. Gravel crunches underneath boots. I listen carefully as I'm carried a short distance away from the building that houses the dorm rooms.

A trunk is popped open.

If I hadn't been blindfolded, I would've rolled my eyes.

In the trunk? Seriously?

A muffled huff rips from my chest as I'm unceremoniously tossed into the trunk before it's slammed shut, locking me in. While trying to wiggle into a somewhat more comfortable position, I wait for the sound of car doors being opened and closed. To my surprise, only one is.

After what is presumably the driver's side door has been closed, the car is started. I jerk to the side as the driver does a sharp turn before speeding away.

Lying there in the trunk of a car, gagged, blindfolded, and hogtied, I can't help but feel that this is a bit overkill. I don't know what he's so upset about. It was just a little poison. Just a tiny little murder attempt. He is clearly overreacting.

At least this will make sure that Eli's attention never slips from me back to Connor. Which means that my stunt had the desired effect.

My body shifts to the side again as the driver eventually stops the car. I listen as the door is opened and then closed.

After another few seconds, the trunk is popped open. I draw in a deep breath through my nose as fresh air finally floods the space. Then I'm hauled out and thrown over a broad shoulder again. My muscles groan in protest from the restraints, and I mutter through the gag, but my abductor just continues walking.

Another huff tears from my chest as I'm dumped on what feels like a forest floor. Grass and leaves and twigs scrape against my bare skin as I wiggle on the ground.

For a few seconds, nothing happens.

Then my captor starts untying the ropes. I stop moving since I very much want these restraints off me.

Relief floods my limbs as the ropes are finally pulled off. Pushing up to my knees, I roll my shoulders and wrists before reaching for the blindfold and the gag. To my surprise, no one stops me as I pull them off and toss them to the ground.

I blink as I'm met with blinding light.

Once my eyes have adjusted, I realize that it's the headlights from the black Range Rover parked a short distance away. The light from it is the only thing breaking up the blackness in the otherwise dark forest around me.

Tilting my head back, I at last meet the gaze of my captor.

Eli Hunter is staring me down with an unyielding expression on his face.

A thrill races down my spine, and the irrational part of me that doesn't process emotions the way it should is kind of turned on by this whole situation.

"Get up," he commands, his voice dripping with authority.

I slowly climb to my feet while rubbing the tender skin around my wrists. My shirt is still half bunched around my waist, so I smooth it down so that it covers the top of my thighs again. A few crushed leaves fall from my shirt and flutter to the ground.

With that hard look still in his eyes, Eli throws a shovel at me and then jerks his chin towards something behind me. "Dig."

Since I'm not the world's most coordinated person, I barely manage to catch the metal shovel before it slams into my chest. I shoot Eli a glare as I straighten it in my hands. Then I turn to look behind me.

Surprise flickers through me.

There is a shallow grave behind me, no more than a foot deep.

With my eyebrows raised, I turn back to meet Eli's gaze. Does he actually think this will scare me?

"Dig," he orders again.

I lift the shovel.

And then swing it at his head.

He yanks up his arms, blocking the strike with his forearm and using his other hand to rip the shovel from my grip. Lightning flashes in his eyes as he locks them on me. I just grin back at him.

For a second, he almost looks a bit impressed. Then he tosses the shovel at me again and pulls a gun from the back of his waistband. I catch the shovel while he raises the gun and aims it at my head.

"Dig," he repeats yet again.

"If you want a grave, dig it yourself." I throw the shovel to the ground before his feet. "In case you didn't know, I'm not a fan of manual labor."

Something flickers briefly in his eyes again, but then he lowers his gun to his side and scoffs. "Fine, a shallow grave it is then."

Because of the cool night air, and since I'm not wearing a bra, my nipples are hard and poking at the thin fabric of my shirt, so I cross my arms over my chest as I raise my eyebrows in an exasperated gesture. "Don't you think you're overreacting a bit?"

"No."

"It was just a little poison."

"It's not about that."

"Then what's it about?"

Cold fury seeps into his eyes like ice. "You dragged my brothers into it."

I frown at him. "I didn't poison any of them."

"You *humiliated* them." The carnal rage in his voice sends a pulse through my chest. "You made them get down on their knees and beg."

Oh. So *that's* the problem. Clearing my throat, I start a sentence that I don't know how to finish. "I, uhm…"

"No one humiliates my brothers like that. No one disrespects *my family* like that."

Aw, crap. I almost heave a frustrated sigh because I know exactly where he's coming from. If someone had done that to Connor, I would have reacted in the same way. It's the entire reason why I'm here doing all of this, after all. To protect my brother.

Oh well. Too late for regrets now.

As if his words alone had summoned them, another Range Rover pulls up next to Eli's. Car doors are opened and slammed shut. Then they're walking towards us, their bodies only dark silhouettes in the light from the headlights.

"So now you're going to kill me, huh?" I say, sliding my gaze back to Eli. Flashing him a smile, I lift my shoulders in a nonchalant shrug. "Best get on with it then. Because if not, I have somewhere else to be."

"Oh, princess." A cruel smile curls Eli's lips. "I'm not going to kill you."

The words should have been comforting, but the expression on his face sends an involuntary spike of alarm up my spine and tells me that I should be very worried. I let my arms drop back down to my sides, readying myself for whatever is about to happen.

From the corner of my eye, I see his brothers arrive and flank him on both sides, but I keep my eyes on Eli because it feels like I'm going to miss something important if I blink now.

With that vicious smirk on his lips, Eli raises the gun again and points it to his right. "I'm going to kill *him*."

I snap my gaze towards where he's pointing.

My stomach bottoms out.

Dread spreads through my limbs like cold poison as I watch Kaden and Rico force a tied-up and gagged Connor to his knees next to Eli. My brother's eyes are wide with shock as he stares at me.

No, no, no. This can't be happening.

My heart thunders in my chest, but I force my voice to remain bored as I look back at Eli and let a confused expression descend on my features. "Why did you bring one of your classmates here?"

"Cut the crap, Raina." Eli cocks his head, a knowing glint in his eyes. "Did you really think I didn't know who you are? That Connor here is your brother?"

I swallow, but I remain silent because I don't know how to talk my way out of this.

"Why do you think I've been calling you *princess*?" Eli continues. "You're Harvey Smith's daughter. That makes you practically royalty at Blackwater." His mocking smile is a slash of white. "Even if you're shit at everything you do."

"I, uhm…"

"I have to admit, it was a ballsy plan. But did you really think I didn't know that you enrolled at Blackwater and keyed my car on your very first day and messed with me on purpose every chance you got just so that I would forget about your brother and come after you instead?"

My gaze darts to Connor. If I thought his eyes had been wide before, it's nothing compared to now. Utter shock and disbelief pulse across his entire face as he stares at me with eyes as wide as dinner plates. He tries to say something through the gag, but only muffled noise comes out.

"Of course I knew," Eli says, answering his own question. "But I didn't mind. Because you're much more fun to torment and..." A sly smile tugs at his lips as he rakes his gaze up and down my body. "*Fuck* with."

My heart slams so loudly against my ribs that I can almost hear it echo through the dark forest around us.

"But you crossed a line yesterday," Eli continues, his voice hardening. "When you brought my brothers into it."

Panic flashes through my chest, and I whip my gaze over the four men before me. Jace is standing on Eli's left with a wide grin on his face and a baseball bat on his shoulder. Kaden and Rico are on his right, standing on either side of Connor. Both of them keep one hand on my brother's shoulder, forcing him to stay on his knees.

Plans whirl through my skull, but none of them offer a clear solution for how I'm supposed to fix this, so all I manage to do is to shake my head and press out, "No. No."

"And now, you will pay for that," Eli finishes.

Sheer terror crashes over me as he places the gun against the side of Connor's head.

"No!" I scream.

On the ground, Connor struggles against his bonds but Kaden and Rico just tighten their grip on his shoulders.

I take a half step towards them, but Eli tuts and shakes his head at me while pushing the muzzle harder against Connor's temple.

"What do you want?" Even I can hear the desperation in my voice as I plead with the devil before me. "Do you want me to beg, Eli? Is that it? Because I will. I will do anything you want."

His eyes dance with wickedness as he holds my gaze. "No, I don't want you to beg. I want you to *grovel.* I want you to kneel and crawl and kiss our boots and grovel for our fucking mercy."

Connor shouts something and struggles hard, but I can't look at him because there is only one way out of this and we both know it.

Throwing all sense of pride to the wind, I immediately drop to my knees and crawl up to Eli's feet. Then I kiss the top of his black combat boot.

"I'm sorry." Moving my head, I kiss his left one as well. "I'm sorry." With my palms pressed against the ground, I keep my head bowed over his feet as I plead. "I should never have involved your brothers. Please, I'm sorry."

"Then beg their forgiveness as well," Eli declares.

I move so that I'm kneeling in front of Jace, and then kiss his boots as well. "I'm sorry."

"I said, *beg,*" Eli orders, echoing my own words from that gun range yesterday.

"Please, I'm begging for your forgiveness."

Above me, Jace chuckles. When he says nothing else, I take that as approval and move on to his brothers. Crawling over to Kaden and Rico, I kiss their boots and beg their forgiveness as well. Connor struggles and screams from behind his gag, but there is nothing he can do.

Once I'm done, I return to my place at Eli's feet. Leaves and twigs stick to my bare legs, but I can barely feel it.

Raising my head at last, I meet his gaze again. Smug victory glitters in his golden eyes, and a smirk stretches his lips. And if the bulge in his dark pants is any indication, he's extremely turned on by the absolute control he wields over me right now. If my brother's life hadn't been on the line, I might have been too. But with Eli's gun still against Connor's temple, all I can feel is dread and desperation.

Challenge dances in Eli's eyes as he stares me down. "Good. Now that you've apologized, I suggest groveling for mercy."

"Please, Eli, I'm begging you for mercy." I look up at him with pleading eyes. "I'll do whatever you want if you let Connor walk out of here."

He arches a dark brow. "*If* I let him walk? Do you think this is a negotiation?"

"No." I shake my head furiously. "No, I'm sorry. Please."

"You call this groveling?"

I want to scream in frustration. I know that he's doing this on purpose. That he's finding fault in everything just to make me more panicked and more desperate. But it doesn't matter, because I will do whatever he wants anyway.

Bending over, I slide my hands towards his boots and press my forehead to the ground before his feet. "I'm begging you, Eli. I'll do anything you want. Anything you say. I'll spend the entire night on my knees at your feet, licking your boots clean, if that's what you want. Just please, *please*, let my brother walk out of here unharmed."

"What are you begging for, princess? Say it. The exact word."

"Mercy. Please, mercy."

Deafening silence falls over the dark forest. I keep my forehead pressed against the ground. The scent of grass and soil and crushed leaves fills my lungs as I draw in shallow breaths. My heart slams against my ribs and my pulse pounds in my ears as I wait for Eli's judgement.

At last, he snaps his fingers. "Look at me."

I raise my head and sit back on my heels again. Dark

amusement shines in Eli's eyes as he watches me in silence for another few seconds. He must have lowered his gun at some point because he's now holding it down by his side instead. Hope and relief flutter behind my ribs.

"Better," he says eventually. Then a vicious smile spreads across his lips. "But not good enough."

In a flash, he raises his gun to Connor's head.

And pulls the trigger.

"NO!" The word tears from my lungs with enough force to almost shatter my vocal cords.

I lurch towards my brother.

But then freeze as time stops moving.

For a while, all I can do is stare while silence roars through my ears like a deafening storm.

Then reality crashes into me and time rushes to catch up again.

Two steps away, Connor has barely finished flinching. He blinks hard several times while shock pulses across his features. Then he sucks in a sharp breath through his nose.

I stare at him. No blood. No gaping hole in the side of his head. No brains splattering the forest floor.

With stunned disbelief still clanging through my whole soul, I drag my gaze back up to Eli. "You... You didn't..."

"Blow his brains out?" With efficient moves, he detaches the magazine and shows it to me. Empty. "No, I didn't." Then he smiles and draws his hand along my jaw and under my chin in an almost loving gesture. "Because you groveled so prettily."

I think I might have forgotten to breathe, because I suck in a desperate gasp.

Eli slams the magazine back in place and then presses the cold muzzle against my forehead. "But if you ever come after my family again, there will be bullets in this gun next time. Do you understand?"

With shock still ringing in my skull, I nod jerkily.

"Answer."

"I understand," I blurt out.

"Good. Now, thank me for sparing your worthless lives."

"Thank you for sparing our worthless lives."

Eli lets out a dark chuckle. He watches me for a little while longer, as if drinking in the sight of me this desperate and submissive. Then he turns on his heel and jerks his chin at his brothers.

Without another word, the four of them start back towards their cars.

Connor slumps forward the moment Kaden and Rico release his shoulders. I crawl over to him immediately and yank the duct tape from his mouth.

He gasps in a breath. "Raina."

"Are you okay?" I ask while scooting around him so that I can start untying the ropes around his wrists and ankles.

Disbelief flashes in his gray eyes as he turns his head to stare at me over his shoulder. "Am *I* okay? Are *you* okay? You're the one who…" He trails off.

Behind us, car doors slam shut. The sound of it echoes across the forest. Then two cars are started.

The light from the headlights shifts across the trees as Eli and his brothers reverse their Range Rovers.

Then the forest is plunged into darkness as they drive away.

I blink against the blackness while my fingers continue fumbling with the knots.

For a while, neither of us speaks.

"That's why you enrolled," Connor says at last. His voice

shatters the fragile silence and sends a ripple through the woods. "Not because you thought that I wasn't enough. Not because you were trying to take my place." He swallows thickly. "You did it to protect me."

Suddenly, I'm glad that I'm struggling to untie the knots because it means that I get to stay seated behind him so that I don't have to look into his eyes. Emotions well up inside me, ones that I can't handle because I'm not good with emotions, and I don't want him to see that.

"Of course I did," I reply softly. "I would never become a good hitman. I will never be able to restore our family's reputation. But if I can be a shield for you while you do it, then that's what I'll do. You have been carrying our family's burden alone for far too long."

"Raina..." There is pain in his voice.

At last, I manage to undo the knots. I gently slide the rope away from Connor's wrists and ankles, and then slowly get to my feet. But I remain behind his back while I try to compose myself. My brother doesn't let me, however, because he immediately shoots to his feet and spins around so that he is facing me.

Surprise pulses through my chest as he throws his arms around me and pulls me tightly against his firm body.

"I'm sorry," he says into my hair. "I'm so, so sorry, Raina. I'm sorry for what you've had to endure because of me. And I'm sorry for being so fucking shitty to you."

Wrapping my arms around him, I hug him back. "It's okay." Those emotions that I'm still trying to get a handle on clog up my throat. "I would do anything for you. You know that, right?"

"Yes, I do." He pulls back. Reaching up, he draws his

fingers through my hair and hooks it behind my ears. "And I for you."

I don't know how to handle the endless familial love in his eyes so all I do is swallow against the thickness in my throat.

As if Connor can sense that I'm struggling, he immediately shifts into a lighter tone as he flashes me a smile and says, "Did you really key Eli's car?"

Relief flutters through me. After the night we've had, I need some time to process all of my emotions. Connor probably does too. He almost died, for God's sake. So joking and teasing each other feels like the safer bet right now.

"Yeah," I say as I start forward. Since those bastards drove off and left us here, we'll need to walk back to campus on our own. "I carved *Small Dick Energy* into the side of it."

A genuine laugh rips from Connor's chest, and he turns to stare at me with complete bafflement in his eyes while he falls in beside me. "You did what?"

"The dude drives a Range Rover. I figured he's gotta be compensating for something."

Connor laughs again and shakes his head before throwing his arm over my shoulder. "You're crazy, sis. In the best possible way."

32

ELI

Our kitchen is unnaturally silent as I walk down the stairs. Usually, I can hear Kaden and Jace arguing about something or other while they're eating breakfast. But not today. Part of me is glad for that, because I'm still trying to come to terms with what happened last night.

I broke Raina.

To be honest, I'm a bit disappointed. I had begun to think that she might actually be indestructible. That she could take whatever I throw at her and just throw it right back at me. But apparently, she is normal after all.

And now that I hold her brother's life over her head, she is going to start acting like everyone else around me. Backing up and bowing down and being utterly fucking boring.

With a sigh, I shake my head as I round the corner and stride into the kitchen.

I trail to a halt and blink as I find the last person I ever expected to see in my kitchen today.

Raina is standing in the space between the kitchen island

and the wall, and she's boxed in on all sides by my brothers. Kaden and Rico are standing on either side of her, blocking the way out on both sides, while Jace is sitting on top of the island with his legs dangling over the side. All three of them watch her with suspicious eyes.

My gaze shifts to what looks like a pile of wrapped sandwiches next to Jace.

"What's going on?" I ask.

"Raina showed up." Jace picks up one of the sandwiches and tosses it in his hand a couple of times. "With these."

Raina flashes me a smile. "Peace offering."

"Don't eat those," I snap at Jace while I narrow my eyes at Raina. "They're probably full of poison."

"That's what I said," Rico comments.

"Yeah, I figured that out too," Jace growls. "I'm not stupid."

I keep my eyes on Raina. "Why are you here?"

"To, uhm... clear the air after last night."

I snort. "You mean you've come to make a deal."

"If you're here to beg," Kaden adds, a sadistic gleam in his eyes. "Then you really should be on your knees."

Raina cuts him a rather impressive glare before returning her attention to me. "I'm not here to beg. Or to make a deal. I'm here to make sure that we both know where we stand now."

"We'll see about that." I smirk at her before sweeping my gaze over my brothers. "Don't eat or drink anything that she brought. You..." I lock eyes with Raina and jerk my chin. "With me."

I start towards the study across the hall. Raina attempts to follow, but the path out from between the island and the wall is blocked by Kaden. He remains standing firmly in her way for a few seconds, watching her with smug amusement. Then he steps aside.

After shooting another glare his way, she stalks after me.

Hope flares to life in my chest. Maybe I haven't broken her completely after all?

The study is probably the tidiest place in the whole house since we rarely use it. But there is an elegant desk with a grand chair, and dark wooden bookshelves along the walls. I close the door once Raina has crossed the threshold as well. Then I move so that I'm standing in front of her, trapping her between my body and the wall behind her.

"So, you wanted to know where we stand?" I begin. "Exactly where we've always been. I hold your life, and your brother's life, in the palm of my hand, and I'll continue to play with you until I get bored and decide to crush you."

No fear floods her face this time when I threaten her brother. Instead, she snorts and rolls her eyes at me. I take a step closer, pressing farther into her space.

"You think I'm joking?" I demand.

"No. I just think you're delusional." A sharp glint creeps into her green eyes. "Because if you ever threaten my brother again, I will kill yours."

"Like you tried to do with those sandwiches?" I scoff and shake my head at her. "Did you really think they would be stupid enough to eat them?"

"Of course not. That's why I put the poison on the wrapping paper instead."

Coldness explodes through my chest, and deafening silence rings in my ears.

Raina flashes me a vicious smile. That smile that makes her look like a goddess of death. "Their skin absorbed the poison the moment they took those sandwiches from me."

She shrugs. "It should be making its way through their bodies as we speak."

Rage and panic and terrible fear slam into me like a lightning storm. I made her think that I was going to execute her brother yesterday, so I wouldn't put it past her to take revenge for that. And she is insane enough to actually go through with it and kill three people without batting an eye. Cold sweat trickles down my spine. If she actually follows through on this and kills my brothers, I won't be able to survive it.

My hand shoots out. Grabbing her by the throat, I slam her up against the wall and hold her there so high that her toes are barely touching the ground. "If your poison kills them, I will torture your brother to death."

She doesn't even try to fight back. Doesn't even try to get my hand away from her throat. Instead, she just looks back at me with that fucking death goddess grin on her face. "But your brothers will still be dead too."

I tighten my grip on her throat, cutting off her air completely. She doesn't panic. Only continues holding my gaze.

Fear and panic rip through my soul. All I want to do is to just snap her skinny little neck, but she's right. If I kill her, or her brother, she won't give me the antidote.

Using every ounce of willpower I possess, I release my grip on her throat and let her drop back down fully on her feet. But I don't step back.

She brushes her hands down her shirt before looking up at me again and arching an eyebrow. "So, are you finally ready to have an adult conversation?"

The fucking insolence of this girl…

I work my jaw a couple of times before managing to growl,

"Yes."

"Good. Alright then, first things first. I didn't actually put poison on the wrapping paper."

For a few seconds, I can't process her words. So I just stand there and stare at her, dumbfounded.

"Or any part of those sandwiches," she continues.

"You didn't?" I blurt out at last.

"No. So your brothers are not poisoned or hurt or dying. They're completely fine." She lifts her shoulders in a shrug. "I just wanted to make a point."

Relief crashes over me like a tidal wave. Staggering a step back, I draw in a deep breath to calm my thundering heart. Raina just stands there, watching me.

Once that terrible storm of fear and panic has drained completely from my body, other emotions take their place. Like fury, for tricking me into thinking that my brothers had been poisoned. But I'm also impressed. Really fucking impressed, actually.

Cocking my head, I study this dangerous woman before me. I have never met anyone like her. I have never met someone who challenges me the way that she does. Someone who doesn't shrink back in fear but instead steps up and hits back with equal insanity.

"And what point would that be?" I ask at last.

"That if you touch my brother, I will poison yours."

"I thought I made it very clear last night that you do not threaten my family."

"And this is me making it clear that you do not threaten mine."

Another wave of grudging admiration pulses through me, but all I say is, "Connor tried to shoot me."

"No." She holds my gaze with serious eyes. "Someone had tampered with his rifle."

I snort. "Yeah, right."

"It's true."

"Doesn't matter. Accident or not, he almost shot me. He deserves whatever I decide to do to him."

"And if you do anything to him, I will poison your brothers." She gives me a mockingly sweet smile. "In case you hadn't noticed, I'm an incredibly skilled chemist."

Despite myself, I huff out an amused breath. "I *have* noticed."

"So where does that leave us?"

"At a stalemate, I suppose."

Silence falls over the study. Morning sunlight shines in through the windows, illuminating the dark wooden furniture around us and making Raina's intelligent green eyes glitter.

The expression on her face sends a pang through my heart.

Last night, I kidnapped her from her bed, tied her up and put her in my trunk before driving her out into the forest, putting a gun to her head and tossing her a shovel, and telling her to dig a grave. Most people would be pissing their fucking pants if that happened. But what did she do? She threw the shovel back at me and told me to dig it myself.

Then I made her kiss our boots and grovel at our feet before I pretended to execute her brother just so that she would know what I will do if she ever so much as looks at me in a way I don't like. And how does she respond? Not with unconditional surrender, like any sane person would. No, she waltzes in here and threatens to kill *my* brothers if I ever touch hers again.

My whole soul aches as I watch Raina stare back at me with utter confidence on her features.

Fuck, I can't let this girl slip through my fingers. She's mine. And she has been mine since the day she carved *Small Dick Energy* into my car. She makes me crazy and not crazy and she is exactly what I need.

"But I can be persuaded to leave your brother alone," I say before I can change my mind.

She raises her eyebrows. "Oh?"

"If you sleep here."

"You want me to fuck you in exchange for my brother's life?"

The hilarious part is that she doesn't even look offended by, or opposed to, the idea. I don't know whether to laugh or punish her for that.

Shaking my head, I reply, "No. I meant exactly what I said. I want you to *sleep* here. In this house. In my room. With me."

Her brows furrow in confusion as she stares back at me, bewildered. "Why?"

Since I don't want to explain to her that she somehow helps me sleep, I just flick my wrist and start to turn around. "Fine, if you don't want my mercy then—"

"Wait!" She grabs my arm to pull me back. "Alright, alright. Fine, I'll sleep here."

Turning back around, I shoot a pointed look down at the hand she still has wrapped around my forearm, and then raise my eyebrows expectantly.

She rolls her eyes but then releases my arm. "So we have a deal?"

"You will sleep here." I hold her gaze. "Every day. Unless I say otherwise."

"And in exchange, you will leave my brother alone," she finishes.

I nod. "Deal."

"Deal."

My heart does an absolutely ridiculous backflip in my chest.

And I swear I can see a satisfied smile lurk on Raina's lips as well.

33

RAINA

Three muscular men block my path. Slowly closing the front door behind me, I stop there in the hallway and sweep my gaze over them before arching an eyebrow.

"If I had known that I would be met by such an esteemed welcome wagon, I would have prepared a more dramatic entrance," I say.

Rico, Kaden, and Jace look back at me with hard eyes. As usual, Kaden is twirling a knife in his right hand while Jace is resting a baseball bat on his shoulder. They're flanking Rico, who is standing in the middle with his arms crossed. Even though Rico is unarmed, his entire body is still pulsing with threats. Even more so than the other two.

Their entrance hall is rather wide, but so are the three of them. Especially when they're standing side by side. In their current position, they're blocking the entire hallway, leaving me stranded there in front of the door.

I adjust the duffel bag I have slung over my shoulder while I shoot them a pointed look. But right before I can spit out the snarky remark on my tongue, they at last speak up.

"If you do anything to hurt Eli," Rico begins, his voice low and dripping with threats, "and I mean *anything*, we will hunt you to the ends of the earth."

"And then you will die screaming," Jace adds, a vicious grin on his lips.

"And begging for the sweet release of death," Kaden finishes.

For a few seconds, I just look back at them in silence. Then a laugh erupts from my chest. While trying to suck in a breath between the fits of laughter, I point between the three of them. "Did you rehearse this?"

My stomach lurches as Kaden yanks my body sideways and slams me up against the dark wooden wall. I hit it hard enough to rattle one of the paintings to my right, and my breath escapes my lungs in a huff.

With his left forearm pressed against my collarbones, he raises his other hand and slowly traces his knife down the side of my face. Violence and a terrible coldness, like a merciless black sea in a storm, pulses in his eyes as he locks them on me.

"Careful with that tongue," he says, his voice seemingly devoid of all emotion. "Or someone might decide to cut it out."

"Careful with those threats." I let a smile tinted with insanity spread across my lips. "Or someone might slip poison into your coffee one morning."

A muscle ticks in his jaw, and he increases the pressure with his forearm, pushing me harder against the wall. I glare back at him. But before things can get out of hand, Rico places a hand on Kaden's shoulder and gives it a firm squeeze.

After another second of staring me down with those cold

eyes, Kaden drops his arms and steps back. I brush my hands down my shirt and adjust my bag again before starting forward.

However, before I can take so much as a single step, Jace plants the top of his bat against my chest and shoves me back against the wall.

Irritation flashes through me as I shoot them all an annoyed look. "Was there anything else?"

"If you hurt Eli—" Rico repeats.

"You'll hunt me down and torture me to death and blah, blah," I cut him off and then flick my wrist in a nonchalant gesture. "Yes, yes, I heard you the first time. Also, did he not tell you that *he* is the one who wanted me to sleep here?"

"He did," Rico admits.

"Great. Then you already know that this arrangement makes sure that both of us get what we want. So trying to hurt him now would just defeat the point of that, don't you think?"

All three of them look back at me in grudging silence, as if they know that I'm right but don't want to admit it.

"Excellent." I give Rico a brisk pat on the cheek. "But it is adorable when you all act like mother hens."

Stunned surprise pulses across their faces, probably at both my words and my actions. It gives me a second to move before they can react, and I use it well. Slipping past them, I hurry down the hallway.

"Good talk," I call over my shoulder as I start up the stairs.

I've only just placed my hand on the door to Eli's bedroom when a furious voice splits the air from downstairs.

"Raina!"

Footsteps, fast and angry, pound against the steps.

I'm about to open the door and escape into Eli's room when it's shoved open instead, forcing me to jump back to avoid being hit by it. The move makes me lose precious seconds. I glance between Eli, who is scowling at me from the door, and Kaden who has now appeared at the top of the stairs.

Murder flashes in Kaden's eyes as he stalks towards me.

"What the fuck is going on?" Eli demands, crossing his arms over his muscular chest as he watches his brother advance on me.

"I'm going to skin Raina alive," Kaden announces in a terrifyingly casual voice as he casts a glance at Eli. "Wanna watch?"

Confusion pulses across Eli's features, but he steps out into the hallway and raises his arm to block Kaden's advance. "Why?"

Kaden grinds to a halt and works his jaw, his cold rage-filled eyes locked firmly on me, before he presses out, "She stole one of my knives. Again."

Raising the blade I took from his holster when I slipped past him downstairs, I flash him a smile brimming with challenge and arch my eyebrows. "It's not my fault that you're so easy to pickpocket."

Disbelief flickers in Eli's eyes as he turns to stare at me. Then he gives his head a quick shake, as if to compose himself, before snapping his fingers and holding out a hand. I shrug and hand him the knife. Eli quickly gives it back to Kaden, who flexes his fingers on the hilt as if he is trying very hard to stop himself from gutting me with it. Which is probably the case.

"She—" Kaden begins.

"I know," Eli interrupts. "I'll deal with it."

For a few seconds, it looks like Kaden is going to barge past his brother and murder me anyway. But then he just clenches his jaw and flexes his fingers on the blade again before abruptly spinning around and stalking back down the hall.

As soon as he is gone, Eli grabs me by the arm and throws me into his bedroom before slamming the door shut behind us. I stumble a few steps before managing to right myself. While shooting him an annoyed look, I unsling the duffel bag filled with clothes and toiletries and drop it on the floor.

"What was—" I begin, but he immediately cuts me off.

"You do know that Kaden kills people who touch his blades without permission, right?"

I lift my shoulders in a nonchalant shrug. "I guessed as much."

"And still you decided that stealing one of them, *again*, was a good idea?"

"But it's so much fun seeing that cold mask on his face shatter as that beast beneath it appears." A grin lifts my lips as I wiggle my eyebrows at Eli. "Oh come on, you can't tell me you don't also love to rile him up."

Light dances in his eyes. It looks like he is trying very hard not to smile or chuckle or show any sort of approval. But I can still read it in his eyes, clear as day. He's *impressed* by my actions.

With what looks like great effort, he forces those emotions down and instead lets an imperial mask descend on his features as he jerks his chin towards the large desk by the wall. "Bend over and pull up your skirt."

I snort and raise my eyebrows. "How about no?"

"We can do this the easy way or the hard way. Your choice. But for your sake, I would suggest picking the easy way."

A wicked grin spreads across my lips. "Oh, but what would be the fun in that?"

Excitement flares up in his eyes, and a matching grin spreads across his lips as he takes a step towards me.

This is what I love about the bastard Eli Hunter. I love how he is when he's with me. He never looks at me as if I'm crazy or unstable. He just meets me with the same chaotic and thrillingly destructive energy. I have never felt so understood by anyone as I do when I'm with him.

He lunges at me, and I leap back to avoid his right arm. But as I slip towards the other side, his left hand shoots out as if he was expecting me to go that way all along. A yelp slips past my lips as his fingers lock around my forearm. I try to yank my arm out of his grip, but he just forces my hand up behind my back before yanking me towards him. My back slams against his hard chest a second before he wraps his other hand around my throat from behind.

With an iron grip on me, he marches me over to the dark wooden desk by the wall. I try to fight him as he bends me over it, but I soon find my cheek pressed against the cool wood.

"Stay down," he warns as he takes his hands off me. "Or this—"

The moment his hands are gone, I try to slip away.

I only make it half a step before I'm jerked to a halt by a brutal hand in my hair.

"Fucking hell," Eli grumbles.

With his fist buried in my hair, he drags me over to one of the drawers. I stumble along while trying to bend his fingers back and force him to release my hair.

Metal rattles from the drawer.

Then he abruptly releases my hair.

I wasn't at all ready for it, so I just blink in surprise.

Eli uses my second of stunned surprise to shove my hands

behind my back and then snap a pair of handcuffs shut around my wrists. Reality crashes back into me, but it's already too late. Eli pulls a leather belt from the drawer as well while gripping my hair with his other hand. Then he drags me back to the desk.

"Seriously?" I mutter. Since my hands are now locked behind my back, all I can do is stumble along beside him. "You just happened to have handcuffs lying around in a drawer?"

A chuckle rumbles from his chest. "You're lucky we're not in Kaden's room. He has a much more extensive collection of… equipment."

Before I can reply, we arrive at the desk. Eli uses his grip on my hair to pull me upright again. Then he loops the leather belt around my neck. I watch him through narrowed eyes. He smirks at me.

Once he's done, he plants his palm between my shoulder blades and shoves me face down over the desk again. Grabbing the end of the belt, he efficiently ties it to the table leg below the edge. It leaves me bent over the table with my hands shackled behind my back and my hips pressed against the edge.

I try to pull against the belt in order to lift my head. Since Eli slid the leather through the beltloop before placing it around my neck, all my yanking does is to tighten the belt around my throat. With a grumble, I'm forced to admit that I am firmly trapped in this position now.

Resting my cheek against the smooth tabletop, I glare at the smirking man standing next to me.

Amusement dances in Eli's eyes as he rakes them over my vulnerable body while he slowly slides his belt out of his dark jeans. I watch as he makes a show of rolling the leather belt around his fist.

"I promised Kaden I would punish you," Eli declares. "So I won't stop until you apologize for stealing his knife."

A thrill races along my spine.

With a grin on my face, I retort, "Good luck with that."

He huffs out a dark chuckle. Moving down the length of the table, he positions himself behind me instead. Because of the tight belt around my neck, I can't see him from here.

For a few seconds, nothing happens.

A jolt zaps through me when his hands suddenly appear on my bare thighs as he shoves my skirt up to my waist. Then his warm hands brush along my spine as he pushes my shirt up too, exposing my back. I wiggle against my bonds as he then curls his fingers around the edge of my panties and slides them down over my ass.

My skin prickles at the exposure as they flutter down my legs and land on the floor around my ankles instead.

"Look at this ass," Eli muses, a roughness to his dark voice, as he traces the curve of my ass with his hand. "Just begging to be punished."

A shudder of pleasure rolls through me at his gentle touch.

It's cut off halfway through as Eli quickly pulls his hand away and whips my ass with his belt instead.

I gasp and jerk instinctively against my restraints, but it only serves to restrict my breathing even more.

Eli brings the belt down on my ass again.

Pain pulses through my sensitive skin. I wiggle my ass to relieve the ache even as my thighs clench and my pussy throbs with the sensation as well.

"I love it when you squirm like that," Eli says, and I can hear the smirk in his voice.

He spanks me with the belt again.

Heat floods my core, and I fail to bite back a small moan.

Fuck, I'm so wet already. When I'm bent over a table like this, handcuffed and with a belt around my neck, Eli can do whatever he wants with me, and all I can do is to just take it. I can feel the sheer power pulsing from his entire being as his muscular body looms over me. He holds my pain, my pleasure, my very life in the palm of his hand.

Another moan rips from my throat as he brings the leather belt down on my naked ass again.

"I knew it." His smug voice vibrates through my very bones. "You're enjoying this, aren't you?"

Squeezing my eyes shut, I suck in a shuddering breath instead of answering him.

He draws his hand over my hip and then slips it down between my thighs. I squirm and shift my weight, but the restraints keep me mercilessly trapped while Eli cups my wet pussy.

"You *are*," he announces, as if I didn't already know exactly how much my depraved body is enjoying this. "Tell me, princess, were you enjoying yourself when I did this to you in the middle of the canteen too?"

Clenching my jaw, I refuse to answer.

Eli slides his fingers along my pussy before carefully circling my clit. Pleasure flickers through me, and I have to grind my teeth together to stop another moan.

"If I had put my hand between your legs that time, would I have found your cunt this soaking wet and needy that time as well?" he demands while he continues to tease my clit with expert strokes. When I still don't answer, he flicks my aching clit hard enough to make me gasp. "Answer."

"Yes," I blurt out.

A satisfied chuckle drifts through the air. With his fingers still toying with my clit, he moves up farther behind me until he's standing so close that I can feel the rough fabric of his jeans scrape against my sensitive skin. He leans over me, bracing his free hand on the table beside my hip, and grinds the bulge of his hard cock against the top of my ass.

I whimper. He rolls my clit between his fingers. I press my body harder against his forearm that he now has between my hip and the edge of the table, but he just continues torturing me with expert fingers. I force out a long breath as pleasure builds inside me.

"Apologize for stealing Kaden's knife, and I just might let you come," Eli says.

With him leaning over me like that, I can feel his warm breath against my naked back as he speaks. It sends a shiver of pleasure rolling through my body. I press my cheek harder against the cold wood.

Lightning skitters across my skin as Eli's lips brush the top of my spine.

I suck in a gasp, and desire pulses through my body.

Tension thrums inside me as Eli kisses his way down my spine while his hand continues teasing my pussy. Every touch of his lips against my heated skin sends a burst of electricity through my body. I squirm against the tabletop.

Eli swirls his thumb around my clit while he traces two fingers over my entrance.

My heart pounds so hard against my ribs that I swear I can hear it through the wooden table. I drag in unsteady breaths as the pent-up release inside me reaches terrible intensities. I need his cock inside me. I need him to fuck my brains out until all I can feel is that sweet release washing through my limbs. I need it more than I need air right now.

"Eli." His name falls from my lips like a plea. "Fuck me."

"Tell me how sorry you are for stealing that knife," he says, speaking the words directly against my skin as he kisses his way back up my spine.

"Eli." It comes out as a growl this time.

He draws his thumb over my clit while pushing one finger inside me, barely more than an inch. Then he pulls it out again. A snarl of frustration rips from me, and I stomp my foot against the floor.

"Say it," Eli commands.

The unflinching power in his voice pulses against my skin and makes my heart skip a beat. Straightening, he takes his lips from my spine and removes his left hand from the tabletop. His right continues teasing my pussy.

The sounds of a zipper being pulled down echoes into the tense silence. I draw in a shuddering breath. Eli responds by dipping a finger inside my pussy again. It's barely in before he pulls it out again.

I yank against the belt in frustration, which only makes it tighten around my throat again and heightens the feeling of utter helplessness. My clit throbs in response.

A jolt shoots through me as Eli's hard cock suddenly brushes against my ass. I try to push myself harder against him, but his free hand lands on my hip. Digging his fingers into my skin, he keeps me immobile while he tortures my clit and drags his cock down to my entrance.

Desperate moans drip from my lips. The tension pulsing inside me is so violent that I feel like I'm going to shatter if I don't get release soon.

"Say it," Eli orders, his voice brimming with absolute command and his words cutting through the air like a whip.

"I'm sorry," I blurt out. "I'm sorry for taking the knife." Another needy whimper rips from me as Eli draws his cock up and down my seam. "I'm sorry. Okay? I'm sorry. Now fuck me!"

"Good girl."

A full-body shudder racks my frame. Eli removes his fingers from my clit and pulls his arm back. Gripping my hips with both hands, he angles my ass upwards so that he can reach my pussy better.

Then he slams his cock into me.

I gasp as his thick length at last fills my pussy.

He pauses for a few seconds, allowing me to adjust to his cock, then he draws out before shoving into me again. I moan into the tabletop.

Eli lets out a dark groan as well. "It's as if you were fucking made for me."

My hips slam against the edge of the table as he starts up a brutal pace. I draw in ragged breaths as my body jerks back and forth, pulling against the belt around my neck. He digs his fingers into my hips hard enough to bruise as he holds me firmly in place while slamming into me.

Pleasure pulses through me with every savage thrust of his hips.

I fucking love the brutal dominance of it. The fact that I am handcuffed and tied to the table. That he can just take and take and take until my body shatters around his cock.

It feels as if he's claiming me. Branding his name into my body and breaking my soul so that the whole world will know that I belong only to him. And he only to me.

Release explodes through my body as his cock hits that perfect spot inside me.

I gasp as blinding pleasure ricochets through my limbs with enough force to make my legs buckle. I curl my fingers and pull against the handcuffs keeping my wrists trapped behind my back as I slide downwards, which makes the belt tighten around my throat and cut off all my air.

Eli tightens his already punishing grip on my hips, holding me up so that I can breathe again, while he continues fucking me with brutal force.

I melt into his hands as release washes through my body over and over again.

A deep moan tears from Eli's chest as he slams deep into me.

My heart pounds against my ribs and my chest heaves as I lie there bent over the table while Eli spills himself inside me.

I know that our bargain only involves actual sleeping, but in all honesty, I would have eagerly agreed to his demands even if he had meant that he wanted me to fuck him in exchange for my brother's life.

Because fucking hell, I could do this every day for the rest of my life and still never get enough.

34

ELI

My chest heaves as I lie in my bed, staring up at the dark ceiling. Raina is lying beside me, her body utterly spent as well.

After I fucked her on my desk, I claimed her against the wall as well, and then on the dresser. And then I fucked her two times on the bed after that too. But now, it appears as though we have both reached our limit. At least for tonight.

Wrapping my arm around her soft body, I pull her firmly against me and rest my hand possessively on her hip. I will burn the fucking world down before I ever let this girl go.

"Why is it that you don't sleep?"

I blink in surprise, taken completely off guard by the question. Tilting my head, I glance down at Raina. She is resting her cheek on my bicep and she has her arm draped across my chest, but her head is tilted back as she watches me with curious eyes.

"Who says I don't?" I reply.

"You. And Rico."

I arch an eyebrow at her in silent question.

"Did you really think that I didn't notice your little exchange the first time I slept here? How shocked you seemed at having slept until so late and how happy Rico's eyes were when you told him that you had slept fine." A sly smile lifts her lips. "I wasn't entirely sure at first. But then when you made it part of the bargain, I knew. You see, it's because if you—"

"Alright, alright, I get it," I grumble, interrupting her self-congratulatory explanation. "You're too smart for your own good."

"There is no such thing as being too smart."

I huff out an amused breath.

"So...?" she prompts when I don't offer any kind of explanation. "Why is it that you don't sleep?"

Heaving a deep sigh, I tear my gaze from hers and instead stare up into the dark ceiling again. Outside the windows, a strong night wind whirls around the building, creating a faint howling sound. I adjust my position, pulling the soft cover up to our waists with my free hand while I continue resting the other on Raina's hip. She wiggles closer to me but continues to study my face as if she can read the answers there.

"Because bad things happen when I'm not in complete control of everything and everyone around me," I reply at last.

"And when you're asleep, you're not aware of your surroundings anymore," she fills in.

"Yeah."

Silence falls over the dark bedroom for a while. I keep watching the ceiling until her soft voice drifts towards me again.

"What happened?" she asks.

My first instinct is to shut her down and refuse to answer. But for the first time since it happened, I feel like I actually want to tell someone about it. No, not someone. I want to tell *her* about it.

After drawing in a deep breath, I tear my gaze from the ceiling and meet her eyes again. "You remember how I told you our family is connected to the Italian mafia?"

"Yes."

"Well, being a Morelli means you have a lot of power. It also means you have a lot of enemies." I caress her hipbone with my thumb. "When I was thirteen, I was kidnapped by a rival family. I spent a week naked and shackled in a concrete basement while they tortured me."

Her eyes widen, and then her gaze drifts to the map of scars across my bare chest and arms before it returns to the scar that cuts through my eyebrow and down my cheek. Fury roars to life in Raina's green eyes. It's so fierce, and so unexpected, that I momentarily lose track of what I had been about to say.

I clear my throat in order to give myself a second to get my head back on track. Then I continue. "They filmed me. Every day. While I was naked and helpless, they filmed as they tortured me and then sent it to the Morelli family."

Dread and embarrassment crash into me unbidden. That was the worst week in my entire life. The feeling of being so completely at someone else's mercy almost broke me. After that, I swore that I would never let anyone else have even an ounce of power over me. And I started craving the feeling of taking other people's control away from them. Preferably by threat or by force.

"And the thing is…" I continue. A sigh escapes my chest. "I wasn't even the target. Rico was."

"Rico?"

"Yeah, he's…" I shake my head. That's not my secret to tell.

"It doesn't matter. Anyway, they came for Rico but I happened to be sleeping…" I hesitate while trying to figure out how to explain this without divulging that Rico is not actually my brother and blowing his cover. So as to not complicate things, I settle for simply, "In Rico's room. So when they broke in, they thought that I was Rico and took me instead. We're similar enough in appearance, and especially back when we were kids, that they never realized their mistake."

"So they tortured you in his place?"

"Yes."

"And you never told them that they had the wrong person?"

"No."

She nods, her eyes full of understanding. The expression in them makes it clear that she would have done the exact same thing for her brother. It sends a pang through my heart. It's another thing I've come to love about her. She's incredibly, almost suicidally, protective of her family. Just like me.

"Is that why Rico is so protective of you?" she asks eventually.

"We're protective of each other. But yeah. He blames himself for what happened, and for the… issues I developed as a result of it."

"They kidnapped you while you were sleeping." It's more of a statement than a question.

"Yeah. Like I said, if I'm not in control of my surroundings, bad shit happens. So after that, it's as if my body refuses to let go of control and go to sleep because I should be keeping watch in case something like that happens again."

Her eyebrows crease slightly. "But you sleep when you're with me."

"Yeah." I heave a deep sigh and caress her hip with my thumb again. "I do."

"Why?"

"Because, for some reason, when I'm with you I feel... safe."

The moment the words are out of my mouth, I regret them. I snap my gaze back to hers, waiting for her laughter.

It never comes.

Instead, her eyes fill with such warmth that my heart almost shatters.

"You do?" she asks, her voice barely more than a whisper. As if she's worried that I'll take it all back if she says it too loudly.

For a few seconds, I do actually consider taking it all back. For no other reason than the fact that saying something like that out loud gives her power over me. But I force the instinct away because, with a jolt of shock, I realize that I actually want her to know this.

"Yes," I reply, holding her gaze. "I think it's because..." Trailing off, I draw in a breath while I try to sort through the strange emotions inside me. "Because you're like me." A smile tugs at my lips. "You're absolutely insane. You don't play by any of the normal rules, and you do things few people would even consider. And I guess my soul somehow recognizes that and relaxes when you're with me, because it knows that if something happens, there are no limits to what you would do to stop the threat. So when you're here, I can sleep. Because I don't have to keep the world at bay alone anymore."

The emotions that well up in her eyes make my heart constrict. I swallow against a sudden thickness in my throat.

Raina tightens her arm around me, holding me closer as she whispers, "Did you know that you're the first person to make me feel as if there is absolutely nothing wrong with me? You're the first person who has seen all the fucked-up sides of me and still not looked at me as if I'm defective in some way. The first person to make me feel as if being insane is an asset, not a liability. To make me feel as if I don't need to be fixed."

"You *don't* need to be fixed." The words tear from my lungs with enough force to make Raina blink at me. I raise my free hand and draw it over her hair, smoothing it down and hooking a few loose strands behind her ear. "You're perfect exactly the way you are."

Her lips part slightly and her eyes shimmer with emotion.

My heart constricts again and then beats twice as hard as I hug her body tighter against mine.

I am *never* letting this girl go.

35

RAINA

There is a warm, strong body wrapped around me when I wake up. Drawing in a deep breath, I blink to clear the sleep from my eyes. Eli's dangerously handsome face meets me.

My stomach flutters.

God, he really is gorgeous.

I study the planes and angles of his face. His usually so severe expression is smoothened by sleep, his jaw relaxed and his mouth soft. He looks utterly at peace.

Reaching up a hand, I trace my fingers along his cheekbone. He stirs slightly and tightens his arms around me, pulling me closer, but he doesn't wake up.

Warmth spreads through my chest. I still can't believe that this is somehow because of me. That he can sleep this peacefully because of *me*.

What he told me last night almost broke my heart. Being kidnapped and tortured and humiliated like that when he was only thirteen…

I blow out a long breath as I let my gaze drift over the scar across his eyebrow.

No wonder he developed into someone who craves violence and control over others. I thought my unusual childhood messed with my head, but his must really have done a number on him. But thankfully, it appears as though we're at least fucked up in the same way so that we complement each other.

When I'm with you, I feel safe.

My heart constricts as Eli's words from last night echo inside my skull again.

No one has ever felt safe around me before. Even my family considers me unpredictable on the best of days and a straight up safety hazard on the worst of them. But Eli feels safe with me. Because he knows that if someone attacks him while I'm here, there is nothing I wouldn't do, no laws I wouldn't break, no lines I wouldn't cross, to protect him.

Another pang hits me straight in the heart.

God, this ruthless violent man was supposed to be my enemy. And yet, he is the one who has made me feel normal for the first time in my life. The only one who makes me feel like I'm not broken. Or crazy. Or damaged goods. But instead, makes me feel the exact opposite. As if my insanity makes me better than ordinary people. It's an intoxicating feeling, and after spending years thinking that I was defective, I don't mind getting drunk on that power. Not one bit.

"See something you like?"

I blink in surprise to find that Eli has cracked his eyes open and is watching me with a smirk playing over his lips.

"Actually," I begin, and flash him a sly smile back. "I was thinking about how much prettier Rico's face is."

His gaze sharpens as he narrows his eyes at me.

I flick a pointed look down at his cock. "And I still kind of want to find out if the rumors about Jace are true."

"Raina." My name rumbles from his chest, dark and low like a warning.

"What?" I raise my eyebrows in an innocent expression. "I'm just saying, maybe I picked the wrong brother."

Eli moves like a viper. A thrill courses through me as he rolls me over on my back and straddles me. With his weight trapping me against the mattress, he wraps one hand around my wrist and pins it next to my head while his other hand slides across my throat and up to my jaw. Lightning dances over my skin in its wake.

"Careful now," Eli warns.

I grin up at him. "I've never been careful in my entire life. Which is why I should probably try fucking Kaden as well just to see if—"

"One more word out of your mouth right now, and I will fuck that insolence out of you until you can't even remember your own name. Let alone my brothers' names. Only mine."

There is a storm brewing in his eyes as he holds my gaze, daring me to disobey him. His lethal muscles are tense, and his scars stand out even more against his skin. Every part of him pulses with power and utter command as he stares me down like a ruthless warrior god. My core throbs as he tightens his fingers slightly on my throat.

Then I let a smile full of challenge slide across my lips before I pant, "Oh, Jace."

It turns out that the bastard does indeed follow through on his threats.

Quite thoroughly too, I might add.

He fucks me mercilessly, making me beg and plead and

call his name over and over again until it's all I can hear echoing inside my skull.

By the time we've showered, gotten dressed, and are making our way down to the kitchen, my body is so utterly spent that I have to hold on to the railing when I walk down the stairs in order to stop my legs from simply giving out. Eli smirks at me over his shoulder while a very smug I-told-you-so look glitters in his dark golden eyes.

I shoot a glare back that promises revenge.

He only chuckles and turns back to the hallway ahead as we reach the floor downstairs. I wince at the soreness in… well, every part of my body, as I follow Eli into the combined kitchen and living room.

Noise blares from the TV. I flick a glance towards it and find Jace sitting on the cream-colored sofa in front of it, playing some kind of first-person-shooter game on the console there. Rico is sprawled on the cushions next to him, but he's scrolling on his phone rather than watching the video game. I slide my gaze to the dining room table, where Kaden sits, drinking a cup of coffee. His cold brown eyes lock on me the moment I step across the threshold.

"Productive night?" Kaden asks, the question clearly directed at Eli even though his eyes stay on me.

"Yeah, it was," Eli replies as he saunters over to the cabinets and pulls out a mug. While pouring coffee into it, he casts a glance at his brother from over his shoulder. "Raina has something to tell you." His gaze, suddenly dripping with command, cuts to me. "Don't you, princess?"

I raise my eyebrows at him.

He continues pouring the coffee, but he narrows his eyes threateningly. The sentiment in them is clear. Follow my orders, or we'll pick up right where we left off. Even though I wouldn't mind being fucked into oblivion by this madman again, I don't think my body could handle any more right now.

So after blowing out an annoyed sigh, I shoot him one last angry look and then turn to face Kaden again. "I'm sorry for taking your knife."

Kaden holds my gaze for a few seconds while tense silence crackles around us. Then he jerks his chin down in a nod. Apparently satisfied, he goes back to drinking his coffee.

I draw myself up on the kitchen island so that I'm sitting on it with my legs dangling over the side. There is a bowl of fruit in the middle of it, so I lean back and snatch an apple from it before sitting up straight again. Biting into it, I chew slowly while Eli moves around the island. When he's right next to me, he leans back against the edge and crosses his ankles. A smug smile tugs at his lips as he flicks a glance at me. I suppress the urge to yank that ceramic cup from his hand and use it to bash his teeth down his throat.

"I'm kind of hoping this was just a one-time punishment session," Rico begins from his place on the couch. Looking up from his phone, he arches a dark brow while amusement blows across his face. "Because if you're going to make that much noise every night, I'm gonna need to steal a pair of noise-cancelling headphones from Kaden's room."

"Touch my stash without permission, and you lose a hand," Kaden says casually, as if he were commenting on the weather and not making death threats.

Rico flashes him a grin and flips him off. "How's that for hand?"

Kaden narrows his eyes.

However, before it can escalate further, Jace pauses his video game. "I agree about the noise, but I also have a question." Turning around, he furrows his brows as he looks between me and Eli. "Did I hear *my* name earlier?"

From next to him, Rico leans over and gives his shoulder a shove. "Were you eavesdropping, Golden?"

Jace grabs the pillow next to him and slams it into Rico's side with impressive force. "Stop calling me that."

"If you were eavesdropping while I was fucking my girl, I will break every bone in your body," Eli interrupts.

My stomach flips and butterflies erupt in my chest. *My girl.* I have to put down the apple and grip the edge of the counter with both hands to stop myself from falling over.

Apparently oblivious to how my world tilted on its axis from those two words, the Hunters simply continue bickering. Jace snorts and rolls his eyes at Eli's threat, and Rico uses the opportunity to yank the pillow out of his grip.

Ignoring him, Jace turns farther around on the couch so that he's facing us head on. There's a wicked grin on his mouth as he retorts, "Good luck with that when I'm the one with the pile of bats waiting for me."

"I don't need a bat to beat you up, little brother." Eli takes a slow drink, watching Jace from over the rim of his cup. "And yes, you did hear your name earlier."

It looks like Jace was about to throw an argument back in Eli's face, but when that last sentence sinks in, he stops abruptly with his mouth still open. Raising his eyebrows, he stares at Eli with wide eyes. "Wait, what? I did?" His gaze flicks to me. "You said *my* name?"

I open my mouth to respond, but Eli beats me to it.

"Yes, she was telling me that she now knows that the rumors about you are wrong." He sets his cup down on the counter with a clink before flashing his younger brother a sharp smile. "And that there is no doubt about it that *I* have the biggest cock."

By the polished wooden table, Kaden snickers into his coffee.

"Oh fuck no," Jace snaps.

"Oh yes, *little* brother." Smugness laces Eli's voice as he stresses that one word.

With impressive agility, Jace scrambles over the backrest and leaps off the sofa. Straightening on the floor, he stabs a finger towards Eli. "You're full of shit and you know it."

"No, it's the truth." Placing a commanding hand on my knee, he gives it a firm squeeze. "Isn't that right, Raina?"

I slide my gaze to him. Yet again, power and threats swirl in his eyes. He narrows his eyes slightly, and his fingers dig harder into my skin. I know exactly what he wants me to do, and what he's going to do to me if I disobey him. But because I have absolutely no impulse control, I let a wide grin spread across my lips instead.

"I mean, I'm just working off assumptions here," I say. Shifting my attention back to Jace, I lift my shoulders in an innocent shrug. "So if you're up for a dick measuring contest, I wouldn't mind being the judge."

Jace's eyes light up with mischief as he reaches towards the top of his dark gray sweats as if to pull them down right now. But before his fingers can so much as brush the fabric, a knife flies through the air right in front of him.

It buries itself in the opposite wall with a *thwack*.

Both Jace and I whip towards Kaden in surprise. Eli and Rico only chuckle and exchange an amused look.

"Keep your fucking dick in your pants," Kaden says. "I'm eating breakfast."

"One," Jace begins, raising a finger in the air. "You're not *eating* anything. And two..." He cracks his knuckles while starting towards the table. "If you ever throw a knife at me again, I'll introduce you to my favorite bat."

Kaden snorts. "Come try it."

While they continue threatening each other, Eli pushes off from the edge and moves so that he is standing right in front of me. Placing his hands on my thighs, he forces my legs open so that he can step in between them. I arch an eyebrow at him.

Reaching up, he takes a firm grip on the collar of my shirt and uses it to pull my face closer to his. The promise of painful, wicked, and absolutely delicious vengeance dances in his eyes.

"You'll pay for that, princess." His fist tightens on my collar. Holding me in place, he leans in and slants his lips over mine. "Dearly."

I chuckle and then whisper my next words directly against his mouth. "I'm counting on it."

Eli crushes his lips against mine, claiming my mouth with a savage kiss.

My heart soars in my chest.

I feel lighter than I have in years.

I feel like I can finally breathe again.

Connor knows that I came here to protect him, so he doesn't hate me anymore. And Eli is no longer targeting Connor, so I don't have to worry about his safety. I also don't have to keep blocking out my feelings for Eli. He's no longer the enemy, so I don't have to keep pretending that he doesn't set me on fire every time he so much as looks at me. I don't have to keep ignoring the way his messed-up soul calls to mine. The way my heart pounds erratically whenever his hands are on my skin. Now, I can just feel it all. *Take* it all.

I can't go back to the teacher program. Partly because I've

already quit and would have to wait another year to reapply. But mostly because I simply don't want to be a fucking chemistry teacher. I'm done trying to hide how unhinged I am. I'm done pretending to be normal.

I have no idea what I want to do instead. I will never be a good hitman, and I'll keep failing basically all of my classes here, but I will finish out this year at Blackwater. And then, I'll take it from there.

However, even as that elated feeling sweeps through my chest, a seed of worry sprouts. There is something that I've forgotten about. Something dangerous. Something that I should have been prioritizing instead of thinking about ways to get Eli to fuck my brains out against the nearest wall.

But as Eli's lips ravage mine, the thought evaporates and I slide my fingers through his soft black hair instead as I kiss him back.

36

ELI

My gaze drifts across the canteen again. Even though I know that all first-years have been out on the fields doing training exercises all morning, which means they arrive later for lunch than the rest of us, I still can't help but look for her.

Raina Smith.

I did not see this coming. At all. When she first keyed my car and inserted herself into my life, my only plan was to play with her like a doll until she broke and then throw her aside.

But she never broke.

She saw all the violent and vicious and downright fucking monstrous parts of me, and she just grinned like a goddess of death and met me on the same level. Never flinching. Never backing down. Never allowing me even a second to purge her existence from my system like the drug it is. Instead, she just kept coming and coming. Battering at my walls and breaking them down until she is all I can see, all I can hear, all I can feel.

And yet, I have never felt more calm and in control in all my life.

After telling Raina about what happened, and after sleeping through the night with her by my side every day, I'm starting to feel like I can finally breathe again.

I never thought that someone would understand me and all the dark and fucked-up things I crave. But she does. And she not only followed me into that alluring darkness, she also carved her name all over it.

"Incoming," Rico murmurs from the chair opposite me.

His gaze glides to someone coming towards us from behind my back, but I don't turn around to look. If it had been a threat, Rico would have made that clear. Kaden, who is sitting next to me, just keeps eating as well, but Jace tracks the person with his eyes from where he's seated beside Rico.

A few seconds later, a girl with dark brown hair pulled up in a tight ponytail stops next to our table. She's wearing a tight-fitting black outfit and proper boots, and she looks like someone who can hold her own in a fight. I'm pretty sure she's a second-year, but I don't know her name.

Leaning back in my chair, I slowly turn to face her fully while flicking my gaze up and down her body nonchalantly. "Are you lost?"

"No," she replies in a surprisingly calm and steady voice.

My eyebrows shoot up as she casually pulls out the empty chair on my left and slides into it. I cast another assessing look over her. She's ballsy at least, I'll give her that.

"I don't remember inviting you over, Shelley," Rico says, his tone the epitome of lazy arrogance.

One exchanged look between us confirms that he said that for my benefit, so that I would know her name.

"I know," Shelley replies. Shifting in her seat, she turns so that she is facing me directly. "But I have a proposition that I think will benefit both you and me."

I arch an eyebrow at her. "Oh?"

"The tournament is this weekend."

"I'm aware."

"Which means that this is the last chance to make changes to any teams."

"Why would I want to make any changes?"

She gives me an incredulous look. "Because you have Raina Smith on your team. Look, I'm not a first-year, but even I know that she's the most unskilled person at this entire university. She can't shoot. She can't fight. She can't climb. She can't run. Hell, she can't even hide properly."

Rage roars through me, and my hand moves as if to grab her by the throat and snap her fucking neck. But before I can so much as lift it off the table, Kaden reaches across me and grabs the salt from the other side of my plate. The move makes his arm slide over mine, keeping it down on the table.

He pulls back and then shakes some salt onto an empty part of his plate. I flick a glance at him. He just watches me with eyes that see too much. That understand too much. He probably knows who this girl is, since he is also a second-year, and has decided that it would create too much trouble for our family if I killed her in front of a cafeteria full of witnesses.

I dip my chin a fraction in acknowledgement.

"You will never win if you have someone like that on your team," Shelley says, completely oblivious to the fact that she was one second away from dying just now. She flips her ponytail back over her shoulder and levels serious eyes on me. "My team is shit. I'm not. Kaden and Rico can attest to that."

Both of them give me a shrug as if to admit that she is indeed pretty good.

"So, here's my proposition," she continues when neither of them contradicted her. "Swap me into your team. Everyone knows that you've got sway over the instructors. Make them pull Raina from your team and put her on mine, and then put me on your team instead."

Ballsy. Very ballsy indeed.

I arch an eyebrow. "And how would that benefit me, exactly?"

"It would secure your win." Sitting forward, she moves her hand towards me while locking eyes with me. "And I know that winning is as important to you as it is to me."

Right as Shelley places her hand on my arm, Raina Smith strides across the threshold and into the canteen.

37

RAINA

I screech to a halt two steps inside the door. My stop is so sudden that the girl walking into the cafeteria behind me slams into my back. A huff escapes her throat at the impact.

"Sorry," she mutters, even though it was my fault, as she slips past me.

But I don't pay her any mind because my eyes are locked on the scene halfway across the room.

There is a girl with brown hair and tight-fitting black clothes sitting next to Eli at their usual table. She's calm, athletic, and moves like a born assassin. In short, she's everything I'm not. And she has her fucking hand on Eli's arm.

Fury roars through me as I stalk towards them.

The girl is speaking to Eli, but his eyes are firmly locked on mine as I storm towards them. I shoot a pointed look down at the hand she still has on his arm. He makes no move to push it away. Instead, he just continues watching me.

"Leave," I growl as I reach the table.

"Excuse me?" the girl says while turning towards me. When her brown eyes land on me, she flicks a dismissive glance up and down my body while contempt blows across her features. "Oh, it's you."

"You have five seconds to..." Pausing, I narrow my eyes at her and instead ask, "What's your name?"

"Shelley," she replies with a fake smile on her lips.

"Shelley, you have five seconds to take your fucking hand off his arm and get the hell out of my sight."

She laughs. It's a baffled and absolutely disbelieving sound that grates against my eardrums like iron nails. I squeeze my fingers into a fist as she flicks another dismissive glance up and down my body.

"Or what?" she retorts, clearly amused.

A vicious smile laced with utter insanity spreads across my mouth. "You really don't want to find out."

At the table, Jace is watching us with a wide grin on his face, looking like he just wishes he had brought popcorn for this show. Both Rico and Kaden glance between me and Eli. But the bastard himself only continues watching me while saying nothing.

Shelley's chair grates against the concrete floor as she pushes it back and gets to her feet. She's a good two inches taller than me, but she looks down her nose at me as if I was half her height.

"Are you threatening me?" she says, her voice cutting through the suddenly dead silent cafeteria like a blade.

"Oh, I'm sorry, I didn't realize that your ability to read between the lines was this far below the average level of the general population." I give her a mocking smile. "Allow me to spell it out for you. Yes, that was me threatening you."

Someone gasps. A few others snicker. I don't need to turn

around to know that most of the people in the massive room are watching us now.

Anger flashes in Shelley's eyes like lightning strikes. Drawing herself up to her full height, she takes a threatening step towards me. "You're going to apologize for that."

"For what? Stating facts?"

"If you think that I'm someone who lets people get away with insulting me, you're sorely mistaken.

I nod towards the empty seat two tables away that she presumably came from. "Can I suggest fucking off before things escalate?"

Another round of snickering ripples through the crowd. Kaden is one of them. That seems to be the thing that finally shatters her restraint.

Lurching forward, she grabs me by the shoulder while drawing her other hand back for a strike to my face. But before she can start swinging, she's wrenched off me and thrown several steps back.

I blink to find Mr. Hansen, our sparring instructor, standing between us. His massive frame physically blocks Shelley's path to me, but I'm pretty sure that it's his hard stare that freezes her in place once she has straightened again.

"Knock it off!" Mr. Hansen roars.

Several people around us flinch. Shelley does too.

"The one time I decided to eat in this student-infested cafeteria, there has to be two fucking children squabbling over… Over what?" Hansen snaps. "If you want to fight, you do it in the sparring ring."

"Oh, please," Shelley scoffs mockingly, apparently now having recovered from her stunned surprise. A smirk lifts her lips as she gives me a nonchalant once-over. "I would knock your pretty little teeth down your throat in the first ten seconds if I ever faced you in the sparring ring."

"You—" I begin.

"I said, enough!" Mr. Hansen stabs a hand towards the half full plate still waiting for Shelley at her table. "Sit back down and finish eating your damn lunch." His hard eyes lock on me. "And you, get something to eat. You're going to need the energy for the brutal training I'm going to put both of you through this week."

Shelley stares daggers at me from the other side of his muscular body, but Mr. Hansen doesn't move.

So in the end, she lets out a soft snarl and starts back to her seat.

"Watch your back, Raina," she tosses over her shoulder at me. "Because I'll be coming for it. So you'd better sleep with one eye open from now on."

Mr. Hansen keeps his eyes on me, as if to make sure that I won't try to follow her.

When I only slide my hand into my pocket and stand there as she walks away, he at last moves.

"Fucking children," he growls as he strides towards the doors.

I remain where I am for another ten seconds.

Shelley has already reached her table and is once more sitting there, eating using only her fork. She flashes me a threatening smile as she picks up her knife as well and twirls it in her hand.

Then she flicks a glance towards where Mr. Hansen is disappearing out the door.

Once she's certain that his back is turned, she locks eyes with me again and makes a show of drawing her knife across her throat.

A low *oooh* sweeps across the thoroughly enthralled crowd, and a few people chuckle in amusement.

I just stare back at her.

38

ELI

Raina just stands there, watching Shelley as she slowly lowers the knife after drawing it across her throat in a threatening gesture. I'm just about to shoot out of my seat and stalk over there to show Shelley exactly what I do to people who threaten my girl. But before I can, Raina starts towards her table instead. I turn in my seat so that I can see them.

The crowd around us, who had finally gone back to eating, quiets again. Everyone seems to be holding their breaths as Raina walks across the floor and then comes to a halt opposite Shelley. A grin pulsing with challenge spreads across Shelley's mouth.

"Are you that eager to get your teeth knocked out?" Shelley taunts.

Raina just stands there, her hands in her pockets, and looks back at her with an almost apologetic expression on her face. It makes me frown. Deeply.

"I'm sorry."

My eyebrows shoot up. As do Shelley's. And quite a few other people's too.

Blinking, I stare at Raina. Did she just *apologize*?

"I'm sorry," she repeats, and lifts her shoulders in an almost bashful shrug. "I overreacted. I shouldn't have insulted you like that."

It takes Shelley another couple of seconds to recover. But once she has, she leans back in her seat with a smug, victorious expression on her face. "No, you shouldn't have."

Raina leans forward over the table and holds out her hand. "Truce?"

"Truce?" she scoffs. Then the smirk on her lips turns even more vicious. "Oh, you're worried now, aren't you? That I really will slit your throat while you sleep." She shoots a disgusted glance down at Raina's hand and then jerks her chin. "Get lost."

Raina stares back at her in silence for another few seconds. Then she slowly pulls her hand back. Turning around, she starts back towards us without another word.

I flex my hand underneath the table.

To be honest, I'm a bit… disappointed.

I didn't do anything to push Shelley's hand away from my arm when Raina walked in because I wanted to see what she would do. How she would react.

If I had seen some guy put his hand on Raina's arm like that, I would have broken the motherfucker's wrist and every one of his fingers. Raina is mine. And no one touches her but me.

So I had wanted to see what she would do if the roles were reversed. I had kind of hoped that she would be equally territorial. But instead, she… apologized for overreacting?

Confusion and disappointment still swirl around inside

me as Raina reaches us. She drops into the empty chair next to Rico instead of the one that Shelley was sitting in. Without a word, she reaches across the table and grabs my tray.

I watch with raised eyebrows as she slides my plate towards her and then promptly starts eating.

All three of my brothers cast me uncertain glances.

"You okay?" I ask.

Around us, the murmur of people talking and the clinking of utensils against plates start back up again.

"Of course," Raina replies while she continues eating the rice and chicken stew from my plate. She hasn't looked me in the eye since she returned. "Though I'm a bit confused as to why you were just sitting here like a useless lump of muscle, doing absolutely nothing."

"I wanted to see what you would do," I reply truthfully. "I didn't want her at our table and I didn't want her hand on my arm, but I didn't push her off because I wanted to see how you would react."

Now, she looks up from the plate. I try to decipher the emotions in her intelligent green eyes, but the unreadable mask on her features makes it impossible to know what she's thinking.

While holding my gaze, she sets down the fork and leans back in her chair. But all she says is, "Huh."

"I have to admit," I continue. "I am a little surprised that you apologized to her."

She says nothing. Only continues watching me with those unreadable eyes. The very air between us feels charged with electricity.

"Help!" The cry splits the air like a gunshot. "Help! She can't breathe!"

Chairs scrape and clothes rustle as everyone whips

towards the sound of the voice. I turn around as well, and my eyes widen as I find Shelley clutching her throat while her face is quickly turning an alarming shade of red.

"We need to get her to medical!" the girl next to Shelley screams.

Two people immediately rush forward to help her lift Shelley up from her chair.

I turn back to Raina and raise my eyebrows.

At last, that unreadable mask cracks and a sly smile blows across her lips.

"This was you," I say. Half statement, half question.

She nods towards Jace. "Like your brother says, you never know when you might need a good bat. Except…" She lifts her hand and shows us a tiny bottle in her palm before it disappears back into her sleeve. "You never know when you might need a good vial of poison."

"Ha!" Jace calls, and points at her. "I said that!"

"Yeah, she just said…" Rico begins before heaving a sigh and shaking his head at Jace. "Never mind."

"You poisoned her?" I say, keeping my eyes on Raina.

With that smirk still playing over her lips, she lifts one shoulder in a nonchalant shrug.

A short distance from us, three people are holding Shelley up and hurrying towards the door.

"How did you even do that without anyone seeing?" Kaden asks.

Raina slides her gaze to him and flashes him a sly smile. "The same way I keep stealing your knives."

He narrows his eyes at her.

She just grins wider before shrugging again. "I've been handling dangerous chemicals since I was ten." The empty poison bottle appears between her fingers for a second before disappearing again. "I have very steady and very careful fingers."

"Will she survive?" I ask, nodding towards where Shelley is being hauled across the floor.

"Yes." Wickedness glitters in Raina's eyes. "During the next two days, while the poison slowly leaves her body, she'll just wish she hadn't."

An amused breath escapes my lungs, and I slowly shake my head at her. But in my chest, my heart is swelling.

Raina never intended to apologize to Shelley. She never had any plans to back down. Quite the opposite. She went for the kill shot before the war could even start, tricking her enemy into thinking that she had won and then pouring poison into her drink.

The commotion dies down as the small group gets Shelley out the door.

Deafening silence descends on the room instead.

For a few seconds, no one moves.

Then, as one, they all turn to stare straight at Raina.

"You should have waited and poisoned her later instead," Kaden says in a low voice from my right. His eyes are on Raina as well.

"Why?" she asks.

"Because now, everyone knows that it was you."

"I know. That was the point."

We all watch her as she picks up my glass and holds it out in front of her. The entire cafeteria stares at her in silence. A villainous smile curls her lips as she sweeps her gaze over them and raises the glass in a slow salute.

"I wanted them to know that it was me so that they would

understand..." She slides her gaze back and locks eyes with me. "That no one touches what belongs to me."

My heart flips and fire floods my veins.

Fuck, I think I love this girl.

39

RAINA

I crash into a table as Eli shoves me into the nearest empty room and slams the doors shut behind us. A click sounds as he locks it too. Straightening from his forceful push, I open my mouth to ask him what the hell he thinks he's doing. We hadn't even finished eating before he hauled me out of the cafeteria and threw me into this room. However, before that question can make it past my lips, Eli turns around to face me. And all words die on my tongue.

Desire, intensive possessive desire, burns in his eyes like wildfire. And when he drags that searing gaze over my body, I suddenly forget how to breathe. My heart spasms in my chest.

"You're so fucking hot." Eli prowls towards me like a predator while raking that fiery gaze up and down my body again. "Poisoning her in the middle of the room and then lifting your fucking glass in a nonchalant salute while everyone was staring at you…"

Shaking his head, he comes to a halt right in front of me. He's standing so close that I'm trapped between him and the edge of the table, my tits brushing against his muscled chest with every breath.

"Do you have any idea how difficult it was for me not to claim you right then and there on the fucking table?" He slides a hand along my cheek and into my hair while his eyes bore into mine. "So that everyone would know that no one touches what belongs to *me* either?"

Lightning crackles through my veins at the way he is looking at me.

Grabbing the front of his shirt, I pull his face down to mine and speak my next words directly against his lips. "Yes, well, you're not the only one who can be territorial."

"Thank fuck for that."

He crushes his lips against mine. I melt into his body as he wraps one arm around my back, pulling me harder against his toned chest, while he claims my mouth with a kiss so passionate and possessive that my toes curl.

Sliding his hand down through my hair, he wraps it around his fist until he can use it to keep my head firmly in place. While his tongue dominates mine, he rolls his hips, grinding his hard cock against me.

I moan into his mouth.

His fingers tighten in my hair and he stops assaulting my lips long enough to growl, "If you're going to make such an erotic little noise, you'd better drop your panties before I rip them off you."

A shudder ripples through me. Pushing my skirt up, I curl my fingers over the edge of my panties and immediately slide them down my thighs. Eli claims my mouth again so intensely that my brain malfunctions for a few seconds. While trying to gasp in a breath, I wiggle my hips, making my panties flutter down to the floor around my ankles. It also makes me grind myself against Eli's cock.

It grows impossibly larger, and a deep groan tears from his chest.

"Now who's making erotic noises?" I pant against his mouth.

He chuckles.

While he continues kissing me senseless, I blindly reach for his belt. My fingers fumble as Eli bites my lower lip, sending a shock through my body and making my brain flicker.

Faint metallic clinking sounds as I finally get the belt open. With deft fingers, I unbutton his jeans and yank down the zipper. Then I slide my hand into his boxers and wrap my hand around his pulsing hard length.

Heat washes through me as I pull it out of his underwear. My pussy is already soaked from just the feeling of his powerful hands on me and his dominant kisses, but now it's fucking aching for his cock.

I slide my hand up and down his shaft.

A shudder courses through Eli's body. I smile wickedly against his lips while he kisses me, and then I do the same thing again.

His body trembles once more, and another moan rips from his lungs.

Breaking the kiss, he says, "Fucking hell, princess. Are you trying to get fucked hard on top of this table before I've even started playing with your clit?"

A sly smile spreads across my lips. "Yes."

Mischief glitters in his eyes as he looks back at me. Then a smirk curves his lips too. "Well, then who am I to deny you?"

Releasing my hair, he leans forward and sweeps a hand

across the table. Equipment goes sliding off the edges, clanking and thudding as everything tumbles down on the concrete floor. Then Eli grabs my ass with both hands and lifts me up onto the tabletop.

The smooth metal is cold underneath me, and I gasp as my naked skin hits the surface.

Eli's eyes darken at the sound.

Drawing his warm hands down my hips, he grabs my thighs and then spreads my legs wide.

Anticipation ripples through me, and my skin prickles at having my pussy so fully exposed to Eli's burning stare. He fists his cock. I flick my gaze down at it. My core throbs in response.

"*That* belongs to me," I say as I lock eyes with Eli once more, and then flash him a sly smile. "So you'd better hurry the fuck up and put it inside me before I lose patience and decide to poison you too."

Lust pulses in Eli's eyes as he shifts his position and draws his cock through my wetness. A shiver rolls through me, and I push my hips forward in anticipation. But he doesn't thrust inside me. Instead, he reaches up with his other hand and wraps it around my throat.

"I love it when you threaten me." The smile on his face is pure villain. Shifting his grip on my throat, he strokes my pulse point with his thumb. "But know this, princess. You belong to me too. Every part of you belongs to me." He teases his cock over my entrance again. "Your cunt. Your body. Your mind. Your soul." His fingers tighten around my throat, abruptly cutting off my breath completely. "The very air in your lungs."

Stars flicker before my eyes as he thrusts his cock into me.

With his hand still locked tightly around my throat, he

pulls his cock out slightly and then slams all the way into the hilt. I would've gasped if I had been able to get any air to my lungs at all.

Drawing his other hand down to my hip, he grips it hard while starting up a brutal pace. I reach up and wrap my hands around his forearm in order to keep steady as he rails me with enough force to make the metal table jerk with every thrust of his hips.

My eyes flutter as he pounds into me, filling me and creating mind-numbing friction. I once more try to suck in a shuddering breath as pleasure builds inside me. But his hand remains firmly around my throat.

It's such an intoxicating feeling. My life is entirely in his bloodstained hands right now. He could deny me air for as long as he wants, or even snap my neck, and there is nothing I can do to stop him. All I can do is to take whatever he gives me.

Pleasure thrums inside me like a violent storm, heightened by the lack of air.

Eli's eyes are locked on mine as he fucks me like he owns every part of me. "This is how I feel every time you're not with me. Like there is no air left in the world. I can't fucking breathe when you're not near, Raina."

My heart pounds in my chest, and wild emotions flutter like erratic birds inside my ribcage. I try to reply, but he's still not allowing me so much as a single breath.

Everything inside me is vibrating with pent-up release, and my lungs are screaming for air. Eli just continues fucking me mercilessly while staring down at me like a brutal god who holds my life in his hands.

My body shakes from the tension pulsing inside me and

from the lack of oxygen as I soar closer and closer to the violent orgasm building inside me.

"You are my air." He slams his cock deep inside me. "And I'm yours."

He relaxes his grip on my throat.

Air floods back into my lungs right as release crashes into me with the force of a hurricane. I gasp in desperate breaths while pleasure crackles through my body like lightning strikes, making my legs shake on the cold metal table. My pussy tightens around Eli's cock as he continues railing me.

Metal grinds against stone as the table rocks backwards with every dominant thrust of his hips.

Incoherent moans mingle with my ragged breaths as I hold on to Eli's forearm for support. He still has his hand around my throat, but he's not squeezing anymore. Instead, he seems to keep it there as a reminder. A reminder that he could cut off my air again if he wants to. That my life is his to do with as he wishes.

I dig my fingers into his forearm, glad for the support while my overwhelmed body continues trembling on the table.

Eli fucks me throughout the entire orgasm and all the way to another one. Every nerve inside me is on fire and electricity flickers through my body as the second wave of pleasure crashes over me.

My inner walls flutter around Eli's cock as he rams into me.

Then he groans and his eyes shutter as he comes inside me as well.

Our chests heave.

For a while, the only thing I can hear in the ringing silence is the deafeningly loud pounding of my heart. I suck in deep breaths. Eli does the same.

Then he at last releases my throat and lets his arm drop back down by his side. I draw in another shuddering breath as he pulls his cock out. Then he moves as if to step back.

My hand shoots up and I grab the front of his shirt before he can. He blinks at me in surprise as I hold him there.

"You forgot one thing, asshole," I say, and raise my eyebrows expectantly. "You said that my cunt, my body, my mind, my soul, and the very air in my lungs belong to you."

He arches an eyebrow, and a slight smirk plays over his lips. "Are you going to try to tell me that that isn't true?"

"No. I'm telling you that there is something else that belongs to you as well." I hold his gaze. "My heart."

He blinks, and emotions pulse in his eyes, making them shimmer like pure gold. I swear even his mouth drops open a little.

Sliding his hands through my hair, he cups my head and kisses me. Deeply. Desperately. As if he truly can't breathe without me.

But deep inside, in an insecure corner of my ruthless heart, I can't help but notice that he doesn't say it back.

40

ELI

Excitement pulses across the grass like a living breathing thing. And I swear half of it is coming from Jace. Standing next to me, he's practically vibrating with anticipation. I get it, though. It's his first year and he is eager to prove himself.

And he is not alone. The crowd is buzzing all around us. Most of the first-years look to be feeling a mix of excitement and nervousness. The second-years look like they're strategizing in their heads what they should do differently this time as opposed to last year. And the third-years are watching each other, marking their targets and preparing revenge for previous years.

My gaze finds Connor Smith across the sea of people, and we lock eyes. That forgettable face of his betrays no emotions. No fear. No excitement. Nothing at all.

Even though the bastard annoys the fuck out of me sometimes, I have to admit that he is incredibly skilled and that he has more than earned his place in the top three. I was looking forward to taking on his team, or rather taking *out* his team, during this tournament, but things are more complicated now.

Because of *her*.

As if he is thinking the same thing, Connor casts a pointed look at Raina, who is standing on my left, talking to Rico. Then Connor's gray eyes lock on mine again.

The message is clear. *Take care of my sister.*

After holding his gaze for a few seconds, I give him a slow nod.

He nods back.

Truce, then. As long as his team doesn't get in my way, I won't come after them. And vice versa.

Parts of the crowd fall silent. Connor and I break eye contact and shift our attention back to the front of the gathering.

Up on the small makeshift podium, Professor Lawson approaches the microphone. Mr. Hansen is standing a few steps behind her, glaring at the students before them through narrowed eyes. When he notices that a few sections are still talking amongst themselves, he draws in a deep breath and opens his mouth.

"SHUT IT!" he bellows.

This time, Professor Lawson saw it coming and managed to tilt the microphone away from him while also covering it with her hand. It saves us from screeching electronic feedback, and Hansen's shout still accomplishes its task.

The entire field falls silent.

Soft winds rustle the grass beneath our boots and blow light gray clouds across the heavens as we all watch Professor Lawson clear her throat and throw a small smile at Mr. Hansen over her shoulder.

"Thank you," she says, looking both at us and at Hansen.

Then she turns back to face us fully. "And welcome to this year's tournament."

An excited *whoop* rises from the crowd.

"You've been getting ready for this for weeks, and now, it's finally time to showcase those skills of yours." she continues. "Each team will be driven out to their designated starting point at the edge of Blackwater Forest. All starting points are located roughly the same distance from the center of the forest, and you'll all be far enough away from each other that you won't see any of the other teams. At least not until you start moving."

She pauses, as if waiting to see if anyone has any questions. A few of the first-years look like they might be on the verge of asking something, but no one does. Probably because Mr. Hansen is glaring at them with uncompromising gray eyes.

"The objective is this," Lawson continues when no one speaks up. "Get to the dummy that we have placed at the center of the forest, and put your mark on him. Knives, guns, rope... You can even go for blow darts if the mood strikes you. It doesn't matter what tool you use, as long as you're the first one."

"As in, the first person?" a first-year calls. "Or the first team?"

"Excellent question. I know that many of you here are lone wolves and that you prefer solo assassinations, but for this exercise, you *have to* work as a team. In order to win, your entire team needs to be there when you put your killing mark on the dummy."

"So if we want to prevent other teams from winning, we could make sure that parts of their team are, uhm... *missing*."

"Now you're getting it," a third-year says while chuckling.

"Correct," Professor Lawson replies. "If you see another team on your way to the center, you can either run or engage them in any way you choose. *Except* by lethal force." Her eyes sharpen as she sweeps a hard gaze over the crowd. "Killing any of your fellow students is strictly prohibited. Understood?"

A low murmur ripples through the crowd.

"I said, is that understood?" she snaps in a commanding voice that she otherwise rarely uses.

"Yes, ma'am," everyone quickly replies.

"Good." She nods. "And while force is permitted, do try to keep any serious injuries to a minimum. We still have almost an entire school year to get through after this, and I would hate for you to miss too many of your classes."

"Yes, ma'am."

"Excellent. Any questions?"

A few first-years ask for some more clarifications of the rules, which she answers patiently. Once they're done, she scans the crowd in silence for a few seconds. Then she smiles.

"Well, then," she says. "Let this year's tournament commence. And may the odds be ever in your favor."

Excited cheers erupt from several sections. It quickly turns into chatter and murmured conversations as the crowd breaks apart and we all start towards the parking lot.

Next to me, Jace claps his hands once. "Let's go! We're gonna fucking crush this, guys."

"Alright, calm down there, Golden," Rico says, flashing him a smirk while we walk across the grass.

Jace gives him a shove. "Oh fuck you. You can't tell me you're not excited for this."

"Of course he is," Kaden interrupts. He has his customary

psychopath's smile on his face as he casually spins a knife in his right hand. "So am I. Mikhail Petrov beat me in the sparring ring by cheating last week. I plan to repay him for that now that there are no witnesses."

"By cheating," Rico snorts, and rolls his eyes. "Right."

Kaden cuts him a glare.

"Uhm," Raina begins before Kaden can stab him. "Look, there's still time for me to fake an illness."

I glance down at her. Today, I managed to convince her to actually wear a pair of pants and some sensible shoes. But she still looks thoroughly out of place in this crowd with her soft body and gentle fingers.

"And why would you do that?" I ask.

"Because I will just fuck everything up for you. You heard the professor. The whole team needs to be there to win and, well… Look, if you want someone poisoned without them realizing it, I'm your girl."

I chuckle. "Don't we know it."

A small smile tugs at her lips for a second before she charges on. "But this…" Spreading her arms, she indicates the mass of athletic hitmen around her. "This is not my scene."

"Oh you'll be fine, princess."

"No, I will slow you down. So maybe I should just pretend to be seriously sick and stay here while you—"

"Not gonna happen."

I drape an arm over her shoulders and pull her flush against my side as we continue walking towards the waiting cars. She tries to pull out of my grip, but I only tighten my hold. An adorable huff escapes her lips.

"Fight it all you want, princess," I say, smirking down at her. "But you're mine now, and I'm never going to let you go."

My heart surges at the expression that blows across her features. At the glitter in her green eyes.

I pull her more firmly against me.

Mine.

41

RAINA

My heart is pounding so loudly in my ears that I'm surprise the entire forest doesn't hear it too. Keeping my head down, I try my best to stay silent while I follow the Hunters as we make our way deeper into the woods.

They move like fucking wraiths through the trees. I didn't think it was possible for people like them to move as quietly as they are. Not only are they all tall and muscular, they also normally exude this enormous presence that can be felt from miles away. But right now, they slink across the forest floor like ghosts. Making no noise and leaving no trace.

I frantically scan the ground while I hurry after them, checking so that I'm not about to step on a twig that will give away our location.

Fuck, why did they have to drag me into this? I would've much preferred to stay in the chemistry lab, mixing some delicious poisons instead. Or even at their house, going through all of their drawers while they were occupied.

Though I have to admit that I did like the way Eli said

you're mine earlier. I might even let him get away with forcing me into this annoying tournament just because he said that.

Eli stops and holds up his hand. He does it so abruptly that I almost crash into him. His brothers, however, come to a halt swiftly and efficiently. Drawing my eyebrows down, I scowl at him as he twists his head towards us.

He makes a few hand gestures and points up ahead and to the left. Rico, Kaden, and Jace all nod as if those flicks of his fingers made perfect sense. My frown only deepens.

Then a twig snaps close by.

It takes everything in me not to start at the unexpected sound. While remaining perfectly still, I squint in the direction of the noise.

Understanding floods my mind.

Oh, so that was what Eli was saying.

Another team moves through the trees a short distance from us. Two women and three men, all with athletic bodies and careful gaits, sneak across the forest floor, but none of them appear to have spotted us yet.

Eli flashes more hand signals to his brothers, who yet again nod. Then he slides his gaze back to me. Holding up his palm, he gives me a very simple gesture.

Stay.

A hint of embarrassment flickers through my chest because I know that I am practically useless in this damn tournament. Actually, I'm worse than useless. I'm a liability. If I were to follow Eli and his brothers to ambush that other group, I would no doubt mess it up so that the entire attack fails. It makes a cold weight settle in my stomach, but I try to ignore it as I nod in acknowledgement.

For a few seconds, Eli only watches me with perceptive eyes. It looks like he wants to say something else, but then he simply nods back. Turning to his brothers, he spins a hand in the air.

Move out.

They all split up and sneak away between the trees.

I remain where I am, not moving a muscle in case that would somehow make noise, and watch as they disappear. Even though I know what I'm looking at, and *where* I'm supposed to be looking to see them, I still find it hard to spot them after a while.

Damn, they really are good at this.

The other group continues moving slightly diagonally from where I'm standing. I've lost sight of Kaden and Rico, who I assume are approaching from the other side, but I can just barely spot Eli and Jace between the trees if I strain my eyes hard.

A gentle breeze rustles the leaves above our heads. I glance up at it. The canopy this deep into the forest is so thick that barely any light makes it through. And the sky today is already gray and overcast, which makes the entire forest feel dark and gloomy. It's still warm, though. Or maybe that's just me after the fast pace we've kept through the woods. Beads of sweat trickle down my spine and temples, and I have to resist the urge to wipe them away lest I make any accidental noise.

Standing perfectly still, I watch the Hunters draw closer to their prey.

Then they stop.

For a few seconds, nothing happens.

I squint, trying to figure out what they're doing.

The other team still hasn't spotted them. They just continue moving in formation with sure steps.

More seconds pass.

I resist the urge to hold my breath.

They move.

As if on some hidden signal, all four Hunters step out of their hiding places at the exact same time. The other team doesn't even have time to whirl around before it's too late. A cry of alarm rips from one of the guys as the five of them find themselves with a gun to the back of the head. Or rather, four of them do. The fifth has a knife across the throat from behind.

My heart pounds in my chest, and a throbbing starts at my core, as I stare at the scene before me, completely transfixed.

"Tough luck," Jace says, a mocking note to his voice as he pushes the muzzle harder into the back of his captive's skull. "Hands."

The guy immediately raises his hands. As does the woman who Rico is holding a gun to. The man with the blade across his throat growls something underneath his breath, which just makes Kaden force the knife higher up under his chin, tilting his head back and exposing his throat. Only then does he reluctantly raise his hands.

I watch Eli.

Since I'm standing here completely useless, there are only four of them to the five on the opposing team. But Eli solved that by pulling two guns on the remaining couple. With one gun in each hand, he presses them against the back of their heads while he stares them down from behind. Both of them raise their hands.

Heat floods my cheeks and my pussy throbs. Fuck, he's hot when he's armed and in control.

"Kaden," Eli says.

His brother clicks his tongue and then begins walking his captive over to Rico. The guy exchanges a look with Rico's prisoner, but she shakes her head at him as if telling him not to fight.

Rico pulls out another gun and levels it at the guy's forehead. Once it's in place, Kaden removes his blade.

I watch with complete interest as Kaden then pulls rope from his pack and starts tying everyone up while the others keep their guns pointed at them. Kaden works swiftly and efficiently. One person at each tree.

They discreetly test the strength of the knots when they think no one is looking, but the ropes don't give an inch. Kaden is skilled at that. Which I know from personal experience.

When two of the five are secure, I finally release a long breath. Eli technically told me to wait, but there is no need for me to keep out of sight any longer. They already have their captives at gunpoint, so there is nothing for me to screw up.

Rolling my shoulders back, I take a step forward.

A hand is slapped across my mouth from behind.

I try to cry out, but any sound is muffled by the leather glove pressing against my mouth and holding it firmly closed.

Panic pulses through my body as a strong arm is wrapped around my middle and I'm hoisted up. I kick my legs in the air but there is nothing I can do to stop it as the unknown attacker hauls me away.

42

ELI

Anger simmers around Gregory like vibrations in the air. His brown eyes are locked on me and he grinds his teeth so hard that I think he might do permanent damage to them. But he's tied firmly to that tree, so staring daggers at me is all he can do.

"When I get out of these ropes—" he begins.

Kaden snorts. "Good luck with that."

"I will fucking—"

Jace knees him in the side of the head. "Show some fucking respect."

Gregory's head snaps to the side, and he blinks furiously against the pain. Or to clear his head. Or both. Shaking his head, he spends another few seconds blinking repeatedly.

I glance to my left where Kaden is finishing tying up the last guy. Rico stands next to him, holding a gun to the guy's head just in case.

At last, Gregory lets out a long sigh of defeat. I shift my attention back to him. Where there was fury on his face before, there is now only annoyed resignation.

Gregory is a third-year too. Though, as opposed to me, he is in the bottom half of the rankings. He isn't a threat, and he has never done anything to piss me off, so I technically don't have an issue with him. But since when do I need a reason to be a dick?

While holding my gaze, he pointedly pulls against the ropes and raises his eyebrows at me.

"Did you really have to?" he says, voice full of exasperation. "Again?"

A smirk pulls at my lips. I tied him to a tree during last year's tournament as well. And then I conveniently neglected to tell our instructors where I had left him. He was stuck there until morning the next day.

Another wicked grin blows across my mouth. Good times.

"If you didn't want to get tied up again, you shouldn't have gotten in my way," I say.

"I didn't even see you! I didn't know you were here."

Pulling one of my guns again, I close the distance between us.

The other people on his team, all first-years or second-years, tense and exchange worried looks.

I place the gun underneath Gregory's chin and tilt his head back so that he meets my gaze now that I'm looming over him. "How is that any of my problem?"

He swallows and then opens his mouth as if to say something. But he apparently can't figure out what, because he just closes it again. I chuckle.

"Tell you what…" Removing the gun, I take a step back. "If you beg me for it, I will actually tell the instructors where you are this time."

Before he can reply, Kaden abruptly stands up and says, "Done."

"Alright then, let's go," Jace replies. "I wanna take out some other teams too before we get to the target."

Rico huffs out an amused breath, but shrugs. "He's got a point."

"Well, looks like you're out of time," I tell Gregory. "Have fun here tonight."

Alarm flashes in his eyes, and he yanks desperately at the ropes again. "No, wait! Please, tell the instructors where I am."

My brothers fall in beside me as we start back towards where we left Raina.

"Please!" Gregory calls after us. "I'm begging you! Hunter!"

Ignoring his pathetic pleas, I just stride back through the trees and to the spot where Raina is waiting for us. Except, when we get there, it's empty.

Irritation flickers through me. I clearly told her to wait. Why can she never do as she's fucking told?

"Where the fuck is Raina?" Jace says as he comes to a halt next to me.

"I don't..." I trail off as I scan the ground where she was standing last time I saw her.

My blood turns to ice in my veins.

There are tracks there. Ones that don't belong to her. Or to us.

A dull ringing echoes inside my head.

Someone took her.

"Eli," Kaden says, his voice having dropped to a low and wary tone.

"I see it," I reply.

Jace squints at the ground. "Are those tracks?"

"How the hell could an entire group get this close to us without us realizing it?" Rico says.

Shaking my head, I move over to the spot behind where

Raina's footprints are still visible in the soft grass. My heart is beating erratically in my chest as I crouch down and study the ground. "Because it wasn't a team. It was just one person."

I stare at the barely visible set of prints coming this way. The ones going back the same way are more defined, which means that the motherfucker who did this was carrying Raina when he left.

Cold fury sears through my veins.

"That doesn't make any sense," Jace says. "Who would leave their team in the middle of the tournament to abduct one person? It would jeopardize their team's entire shot at victory."

Pushing to my feet, I flex my fingers on the gun and clench my jaw in an effort to stop myself from setting the whole fucking forest on fire. My brothers join me, flanking me as we all stare at the tracks leading away between the trees.

"I don't know," I reply at last. Cracking my neck, I roll my shoulders back and squeeze the gun harder. "But once I find them, I'm going to fucking kill them."

43

RAINA

Pain shoots up my elbow and ricochets through my arm as I'm thrown face first down on the hard stone floor of the cave. I barely had time to raise my arms to stop myself from smacking my head into it, which is why my elbow took the hit instead. I grit my teeth as my forearm and fingers tingle from the lingering pain of it.

I fought the entire way here, but my captor didn't budge. He kept his hand firmly across my mouth and his arm around my body as he ran through the forest until he reached this cave. I couldn't even turn my head to look at the bastard's face. But now, it appears as though we have reached our final destination. I can feel him looming over me behind my back.

Pushing myself into a sitting position, I rub my elbow in an effort to make that prickling sensation in my arm stop. With my back still to him, I try to decide how to play this. I only have a few seconds at best before my captor no doubt loses patience. So I make a snap decision.

One second, I'm sitting there rubbing my elbow. The next,

I'm whirling around, jumping to my feet, and darting in the direction we came. All at the same time.

Air explodes from my lungs as a fist crashes into my stomach.

The force of the punch is strong enough to send me flying backwards, and more pain flares through my body as I smack back first into the cave wall before crumpling to the ground. Wrapping an arm around my stomach, I curl in on myself while trying desperately to suck air back into my lungs.

A contented sigh sounds from above me. "I've been wanting to do that for weeks."

The voice is familiar. But for a second, I can't place it. After forcing a few breaths into my lungs, I blink to clear my vision from the haze of pain that is clouding it. Then I raise my head to at last face my captor.

For a few seconds, it's as if my mind can't comprehend what I'm seeing.

"Gabriel?" I blurt out.

My classmate Gabriel towers over me where I'm still lying on the ground, and he is staring at me with such hatred, such contempt, that I lose all sense of what the hell is going on.

His easy smiles are gone, and his all-American boy-next-door look has been twisted almost behind recognition by the rage now pulsing across his features.

"Raina Smith," he replies, his voice laced with venom.

"What's—"

Pain erupts in my side, cutting off my words, as Gabriel slams his boot into the side of my ribs. The kick is hard enough to make my body slide the short distance to the wall before crashing into it. I gasp again, feeling as though fire is licking my side.

"Did I give you permission to speak?" Gabriel demands above me.

Since I still haven't been able to catch my breath, I just lie there, sucking air into my lungs instead of replying. When I'm able to breathe somewhat normally again, I start pushing myself up on my knees and then climb to my feet.

My knees have barely left the ground before Gabriel rams his fist into the left side of my face. More pain pulses through my jaw and cheekbone, and my head snaps to the side as I collapse back to the ground.

"Stay on your knees," Gabriel orders.

Black spots swim in my vision. I blink hard and work my jaw for a few seconds. Then I drag furious eyes up to the bastard above me. "Would you stop hitting me and just tell me what the fuck is going on?"

In hindsight, I should probably have worded that better. Or better yet, not said it at all. But I was already running dangerously low on fucks to give before this damn asshole decided to drag me into this cave, and now I simply cannot muster a single fuck anymore.

The moment the words are out of my mouth, Gabriel's blue eyes turn colder than the arctic ocean in the middle of winter. I see the hit coming, but it doesn't matter because there is nothing I can do to stop it.

My cheek smacks into the stone as the punch to my jaw sends my entire body crashing to the ground as if I'm nothing but a puppet with my strings cut.

Then he starts up a merciless assault.

I try to disassociate from the pain as much as possible, but I can't block it all out as he continues to punch and kick me.

When Gabriel is at last satisfied, he steps back again. Agony blooms all over my body. I drag in a rattling breath.

Gabriel releases another contented sigh. "Ahh, that felt good."

Fucking asshole. I am going to poison him and watch him die screaming if it's the last thing I do.

My limbs tremble as I force myself to push my body off the ground again. But I'm not sure if my bones can handle another beating like that, so I stay on my knees this time. After drawing in a deep breath, I tilt my head back and meet Gabriel's eyes again.

The fury is still there, but he looks smug now too.

Holding my gaze, he pulls out a gun and levels it at my forehead. The muzzle is cold as the metal meets my skin.

I just continue looking back at him.

He narrows his eyes. "You should be terrified right now. Staring at me with wide eyes and begging me not to shoot you in the head." He presses the gun harder against my forehead. "Why aren't you?"

Because I'm messed-up in the head in ways that you will never understand.

But I don't tell him that. Instead, I reply, "Because the safety is on."

To my absolute shock, he actually turns the gun slightly and looks down at the safety. Which is of course off.

A genuine laugh, full of bafflement and smug satisfaction, rips from my chest. I can't believe he fell for that.

The laugh is abruptly cut off as he hits me with the butt of the gun hard enough to snap my head downwards. Blood trickles down from where the strike must have broken the skin. It runs down my forehead and slides down my temple.

Raising my head, I lock eyes with him again and flash him a mocking grin. "Worth it."

He draws back his hand as if to hit me again, but right then, noise comes from the mouth of the cave.

I turn towards it.

And dread washes through my body like ice water.

Two people walk into the cave. Or rather, a woman holds a gun to the back of a handcuffed man's head while she marches him into the cave.

"How do you think you're going to win if you waste your time abducting me like this? It makes no sense. And how did you even get my own team to betray me like that. It shouldn't even be possible if..." Connor trails off as his eyes meet mine. "Raina."

"Con," I breathe.

"Took you long enough," Gabriel says.

The woman behind my brother scoffs. I drag my stunned gaze to her.

Shelley.

It's Shelley. The girl I poisoned in the cafeteria earlier this week.

"Can someone tell me what the fuck is going on here?" I snap, all of my restraint now completely gone.

Gabriel hits me with the butt of the gun again.

"Touch her again and I'll—" Connor growls while he moves as if to take a step towards us, but he's cut off before he can complete the sentence.

"Finish that step and I *will* shoot you in the head," Shelley declares.

Connor pauses, his foot still hovering in the air. His worried gray eyes meet mine. I shake my head.

Gritting his teeth, he slowly returns his foot to the ground where it was before.

"Good," Gabriel says. And there is a vicious glint in his

eyes as he looks between me and Connor. "We'll get to the shooting part later." He locks his gaze on me. "Get up."

Before I can so much as begin to push myself up, he buries his free hand in my shirt and forcibly hauls me to my feet. Pain pulses through my battered body when I move, and I have to clench my jaw to stop a gasp from escaping my throat.

With his fist still gripping my shirt, Gabriel moves us across the cave floor until we're standing right opposite Connor and Shelley. After shifting so that he is standing behind me, he releases me and instead puts his gun firmly to the back of my head.

"Now that we're all here," Gabriel begins. "Let's get down to business, shall we?"

"What the hell is going on here?" Connor demands, his voice becoming sharper and his gray eyes hard as stone. "You're a first-year, aren't you? Do you have any idea about the consequences your actions will have?"

"Ironic. You lecturing me about consequences. And I know exactly what I'm doing. The question is, do you? Do you even know who I am?"

"Should I?"

A snarl rips from Gabriel's throat. And I have to admit, I am impressed by the utter disdain and nonchalance in Connor's voice when he said that. As if he can somehow read those thoughts in my mind, Gabriel pushes the muzzle of his gun harder against the back of my head.

"Ah, I really wish that crazy fucker Eli Hunter had tortured you to death," Gabriel says. "That would have been so entertaining to watch."

Realization crackles through my body.

It's mirrored in Connor's eyes too as he says, "You. You're the one who messed with my rifle that day."

His words are half statement, half question. But Gabriel answers anyway. "Yes. I had hoped I could get the Hunters to take care of you for me. It would've been poetic, in a way. But since you have somehow managed to get him off your back, I guess I have no choice but to get my hands dirty. If you want something done, you have to do it yourself. Isn't that what people always say?"

"Why?" I demand, completely befuddled. "Why are you doing this? I hadn't even met you until a few weeks ago. And I'm sure Connor hadn't either. What could we possibly have done to make you hate us this much?"

"You're Harvey Smith's children."

Stunned silence pulses through the cave.

I blink. In my position, I can't see Gabriel's face, but I could hear the venom that dripped from his voice when he spoke our father's name.

"What does that have to do with anything?" Connor eventually asks, sounding as confused as I feel.

"Everything!" Gabriel screams. "It has everything to do with this! Fuck, you really are his children in every way. Never caring about anyone other than you and your own fucking family." He grips the back of my neck while shoving the muzzle against my head over and over again. "Did you really think that your father's failure only affected him?"

Connor, who was staring daggers at Gabriel for how he's manhandling me, blinks in surprise. I do too.

"If this is about the inconvenience to the Morelli family," Connor begins. "I hate to break it to you, but we've already paid—"

"This is not about the fucking Morelli family," Gabriel snarls, jabbing the gun so hard into my skull that I have to bow my head forward slightly. "My father is dead because of you!"

Ringing silence descends on the cave. It's so potent that I can almost feel it pressing against my skin.

Behind me, Gabriel is breathing hard. But he has pulled back his gun a fraction, allowing me to raise my head fully again.

"My father was sent on the same mission as yours," Gabriel grinds out. "And because your dad fucked everything up, *my* father died too."

From across the cave, Connor and I stare at each other. I hadn't known that. And based on the surprise flickering in Connor's eyes, he hadn't either.

"But Harvey Smith also got himself killed," Gabriel continues. "So I can't make him pay for my father's death, which means that you have inherited his blood debt. And now, it's time to pay it."

For the first time since I was dragged into this cave, true terror pulses through my body. Not for my own life. But for Connor's. Licking my lips, I cast frantic glances around the cave in an effort to find something that can somehow get us out of this.

"What about you then?" I ask, stalling for time, as I meet Shelley's gaze. "You're not Gabriel's sister or something, are you?"

"No." A cold smile stretches her lips as she locks eyes with me. "But you made an enemy of me when you poisoned me in that cafeteria. And I always settle my scores, which is why I was more than happy to provide my assistance in this little revenge plot when Gabriel approached me about it."

Fuck. Maybe poisoning her in front of everyone like that

had been a bit too ballsy. Even for me. Oh well, too late for regrets now.

"Enough talking," Gabriel snaps before I can reply. "Give him a gun."

Confusion and disbelief wash through me as Shelley keeps her gun to Connor's head while pressing another one into his handcuffed hands. But before I can open my mouth to ask about it, Gabriel shoves a gun into my hands as well.

My first instinct is to raise it and shoot Shelley in the head. But even if my aim wasn't terrible enough that I would never hit her, even from this distance, the problem is also that she's standing right behind Connor. To hit her, I would need to shoot through my brother.

Connor flicks a glance between me, Gabriel, and the gun in his hands. And I know that he is considering the same thing. Connor has perfect aim and would definitely hit his target from this distance, but the main problem remains. Gabriel is standing right behind me, which means that my body is blocking the shot.

As if he realizes that too, Connor simply shifts the gun so that he is holding it properly, but makes no move to raise it.

"You're not going to try to shoot me?" Gabriel taunts.

"No," Connor grinds out.

"Good. Because if you shoot me, I shoot your sister." He once more pushes his gun harder against the back of my head as if to truly drive the point home. Then he tells me, "And if you try to shoot Shelley, she shoots Connor."

My brother grits his teeth. "What do you want?"

"I want you to feel what I feel." There is a savageness in Gabriel's voice that cuts through the air like a blade. "I want you to feel the pain I've felt every fucking day since that night when your dad killed my father. He was my best friend. My family."

"What. Do you. Want?" Connor forces out between gritted teeth again.

"I want you to choose who gets to live."

"What?"

My heart drops into my stomach and ice sweeps through my chest because I already know where he is going with this. Inside my skull, my mind is screaming. I don't want to hear the next words that I know will come out of his mouth. But he speaks them anyway.

"One of you will shoot your precious sibling. The one who shoots first and kills the other gets to live. If you refuse to shoot, I will kill you both."

44

ELI

My heart pounds in my chest as I run through the forest. But it's not because of any physical exertion. No, my heart is thrashing for one reason and one reason alone. Raina. If the bastard who took her has touched a single hair on her head, I'm going to fucking tear him apart. In fact, I'm going to do that regardless. Because he dared to put his filthy hands on her at all. She's mine. And no one touches what belongs to me.

"Left!" Jace suddenly screams from behind me.

I barely have time to whip my head to the left before a man crashes into me from that direction. A jolt shoots through my bones as we collide.

The speed with which he's moving, combined with mine, sends both of us toppling to the ground. Pain flashes through my shoulder as I slam down on a root with the guy on top of me. Rolling sideways, I try to shove him off me before he can get the upper hand.

He cracks an elbow into the side of my jaw, snapping my head to the right and slamming my cheek into the ground.

While blinking to clear my vision, I blindly swing at where I assume his head is. I'm rewarded by a grunt as my fist connects with his cheek.

All around us, chaos is unfolding.

From the corner of my eye, I can see my brothers fighting three other people as well.

Rage and frustration flash through me. Why the hell did we have to get attacked by another team *now*? And I didn't even see them coming. I had been so focused on those tracks before me, and on that terrible thought that someone might be hurting Raina right now, that I hadn't even noticed that another team was closing in. Hadn't even been paying attention to my surroundings. That was dangerous and stupid. But Raina has a habit of making me dangerous and stupid.

I slam my elbows down into the crook of my attacker's arms, making his hands shoot downwards instead right before he can wrap them around my throat. He lets out another grunt of pain, but doesn't falter.

Because of how we landed, he is straddling my chest and trapping my body underneath him. It also makes me unable to reach my guns. I need to get out of that vulnerable position. Fast.

Twisting my hips, I throw all of my power into a punch to the side of his ribs.

Air explodes from his lungs, and he sways to the side while pain flickers in his brown eyes. But the bastard still doesn't topple over. I draw back for another strike.

Right then, he lunges forward and locks his hands around my throat.

My breath gets stuck in my lungs as he squeezes hard.

Alarm crackles down my spine.

Fuck. He intends to choke me out. If I pass out, I will lose. And if I lose, I won't be able to get to Raina.

I ram my elbows down into the crook of his arms yet again, trying to break his grip. But he's ready for it this time. Gritting his teeth, he weathers the pain and keeps his arms straight as I pound my elbows into him. My lungs protest as he tightens his grip on my throat.

Switching tactics, I drop my arms to the ground, as if I don't have the strength to keep going. Victory sparkles in his eyes, pushing out some of the pain. With my hands on the ground, I blindly reach for the knife in my thigh holster.

In order to keep his attention on me, I blink repeatedly as if I'm fighting to stay conscious.

At last, my fingers close around the hilt of the blade.

I yank it out.

And ram it into the side of his chest.

He cries out in pain, and his hands disappear from my throat as he snaps his gaze down to his side.

I yank out the knife and then plunge it towards him again.

Panic flashes across his features.

Throwing himself sideways, he barely manages to escape the hit.

While sucking in deep breaths of air, I shoot up from the ground and roll over while raising my other hand. My attacker hasn't even gotten back to his knees when my fist connects with his temple. His eyes roll back into his head for a second, and he crashes down on the ground.

I swing my leg over his body and straddle his chest while he's busy blinking stars from his eyes. And before he can recover, I slam my fist into his jaw again.

Another grunt rips from his lungs as his face snaps

sideways. I hit him again. And again. And again. Until blood bursts from his split lip and pours from his broken nose.

He raises his hands as if to protect himself.

I ram my knife into his shoulder.

A cry tears from his chest, and his right arm drops back to the ground completely limp after I no doubt severed some important tendon.

"Stop, please," he presses out in a strained voice.

"Eli," Rico's voice suddenly comes from my left.

I blink, remembering that I'm not alone here, and turn towards him. One of the people they were fighting is lying knocked out cold by Jace's feet. The other two are on their knees while Rico holds them at gunpoint. Kaden is standing next to them, watching me with those observant eyes of his.

The rage roaring like wildfire inside me banks a little.

Dragging in a deep breath, I try to compose myself as I study the faces of the people who attacked us.

Surprise and confusion replace the fury as I realize who they are.

"This is Connor Smith's team," Kaden says, echoing my exact thoughts.

For a second, I just stare between the four people who are now at our mercy. Yes, this is indeed Connor's team. But he is not among them.

What the hell is going on here?

I turn back to the guy panting in agony beneath me. "Where is Connor Smith?"

Defiance flares in his eyes as he glares up at me.

Holding his gaze with hard eyes, I twist the knife that is still buried in his shoulder. He cries out in pain. I twist again.

"Not here!" he calls. "He's not here!"

I keep twisting. "Then where is he?"

Only screams answer me.

"Shelley has him," another voice blurts out.

I stop twisting the knife and turn towards the source of the voice. One of the people in front of Rico, a girl with loose brown curls and brown eyes, looks back at me.

"She took him in that direction." She nods towards where I know a cave is located. "Only a few minutes ago."

"Then why are you attacking us instead of going after them?" Rico asks, nudging her head with his gun.

"Because she paid us a ridiculous amount of money to betray him." Guilt flickers in her dark eyes. "And to stop anyone trying to follow her too."

Rico groans and then slides his gaze to me. "She comes from a very wealthy family."

And Raina poisoned Shelley just a few days ago. This can't be a coincidence. The tracks from the person who abducted Raina lead here, and now Shelley has taken her brother in that same direction as well. Whatever is going on cannot be good.

Fear stabs through my heart. I have to find Raina. Now.

"Where did she take him?" I grind out.

I already know about the cave because I've spent a lot of time training in these woods. But I need to know if she is going to tell me that as well or if this is some kind of elaborate ambush for us.

"There's a cave a short distance that way," she says, jerking her chin towards where the cave is located.

I yank my knife out of the guy's shoulder. He moans in pain while I use his shirt to wipe off the blood. Then I brace my hands on his chest and push to my feet while sliding the knife back into its sheath.

"If you follow, you die," I announce.

Without even bothering to check if they nod in

acknowledgement, I pull a gun from the back of my belt and start in the direction of the cave. The sound of footsteps behind me inform me that my brothers are following as well.

I don't know what the hell is going on here, or who the guy is who took Raina, but I know one thing for certain.

Whoever they are, they're going to pay in blood.

45

RAINA

The moment Gabriel has finished speaking those damning words, a strange sense of calm spreads through my body. Without a single shred of hesitation, I raise the gun. And point it at my own head.

Surprise and stunned disbelief, that are mirrored in Connor's eyes, pulse through me as we blink at each other from across the cave floor.

He has also raised his gun and pointed it at his own head.

An absolutely ridiculous urge to laugh bubbles in my chest. We're so different, in almost every way, but in this one thing we are completely the same. Apparently, both of us are willing to die for each other without hesitation.

"No," Gabriel snaps from behind me. My head jerks forward slightly as he shoves his gun harder against the back of my skull. "If you shoot yourself, I'll just shoot your brother too. Same goes for you, Connor. The only way one of you gets to walk out of here is if you kill the other. So drop your guns from your own temples before I decide to shoot you both."

I slowly lower my gun. Connor, whose wrists are still handcuffed in front of him, has to twist his hands while doing the same. With our weapons pointed at the ground, we just stare at each other in silence. I already know that I am not going to shoot him, so I make no move to do anything else. Neither does Connor.

From behind my back, Gabriel lets out a low growl. "What are you waiting for?"

We only continue watching each other. It strikes me then that I might have been wrong. I've always kind of assumed that Connor was only protective of me because he had to. Because that's what siblings do. But when I study the expression on his face and the emotions swirling in his eyes, I realize that he does actually love me just as much as I love him.

I've always thought that he found me kind of annoying since I've always been unhinged and unpredictable while he has always been stable and hardworking. That he secretly resented me because I did nothing to help restore our family's position while he spent every day pouring his blood, sweat, and tears into it.

But it looks like I was wrong. Apparently, I don't know my own brother nearly as well as I should. Unfortunately, though, it seems as if it's too late to change that now.

"You have twenty seconds," Gabriel grinds out. "Then I shoot *both* of you."

"Do it," I say, giving Connor a tired smile.

He shakes his head. "No."

"Con, we both know that *you* are the one who needs to survive. I can't restore our family's name. I can't help Mom. But you can."

"I don't care."

"Ten seconds," Gabriel says.

Terror floods my system. I flick my gaze desperately around the cave, but there is nothing there to help us. No other way out. If I can't convince my brother to shoot me in the next ten seconds, *he* is going to die too. My heart pounds so hard that it makes my ears ring. I suck in shallow breaths as fear spreads like poison through my veins.

"You have to!" I protest, my voice almost breaking.

"No."

"Con—"

"You're my little sister and I will always protect you." His gray eyes are brimming with emotions as he holds my gaze and gives me a soft smile. "Now raise that gun and shoot me in the head, or I will never forgive you."

"Five," Gabriel says.

"Connor!" I call.

"Now," he snaps. "Do it now, Raina. I love you."

"No, Connor, I—"

A gunshot tears through the air.

I gasp.

For a moment, it feels as if the entire world is suspended in time. I can't move. I can't breathe. I can't feel anything.

Then reality comes crashing back around me.

Noise and movement and color explodes around me like a violent storm. After that moment of complete stillness, it shocks me enough that I flinch.

Everything is happening all at once.

Across the cave, four men in black clothes have entered the space like a sweeping wind of pure death. Guns raised, they advance across the stone floor behind my brother's back.

Panic pulses across Shelley's face as she finds herself with four killers behind her unprotected back, one of whom has already fired a gun into the ceiling. She yanks her weapon away from Connor's head and starts to whirl around, but before she can turn, the butt of a gun cracks into the side of her head. She stumbles sideways, blood trickling down her temple.

Straightening, she finds herself face to face with Eli, Rico, Kaden, and Jace.

All color drains from her face in a flash.

With fear washing over her features, she immediately tosses her gun down on the ground and raises her hands. "Wait... Look, I—"

"Raina," Eli says, cutting her off.

Lethal fury descends on his features like a death mask when he takes in the bruises and blood on my face and the gun that Gabriel is still pressing against my skull. The expression on Eli's face could have frozen hell itself and set a glacier on fire at the same time. It's the most terrifyingly beautiful thing I have ever seen.

His dark golden eyes shift to Gabriel. "You."

Next to him, Shelley is trying to back away as Jace advances on her.

But Connor shoves his gun against the back of her head now that she has turned her back to him instead. "Keys."

Metallic clinking fills the deadly silence as she fumbles to pull out the keys to his handcuffs. Kaden snatches them from her fingers the moment she holds them out. Moving over to Connor, he takes the gun from my brother's hands and deftly unlocks the handcuffs.

"You, on your knees and face the wall," Rico orders.

Connor gives Kaden a nod while Shelley hurries to obey Rico's orders. While she's dropping to her knees in front of the wall, Kaden hands my brother his gun back.

Then all five of them turn to face us. Except for Eli, who never took his eyes from me in the first place.

I can feel the violence pulsing from his entire body, and sense the death swirling in his eyes. Blood will be spilled here today.

As if he can feel it too, Gabriel locks his hand harder around the back of my neck and uses it to hold me firmly in front of him as a shield while he declares, "Take one step closer, and I'll paint the walls of this cave with her brains."

Across the stone ground, Connor, Eli, Jace, and Rico stand side by side with guns leveled at him. Or rather, at us, since I'm standing in front of him. Kaden is holding a pair of throwing knives while his cold eyes shift over us, as if calculating angles.

"Did he put those marks on your face?" Eli asks with barely restrained anger, his eyes locked on the patchwork of bruises on my face and the dried blood caking my skin.

"One single sound out of your mouth, and I'll pull the trigger," Gabriel warns.

I slowly close my mouth again without replying.

"Yes," Shelley says from her place by the wall. Her gaze is still on the stone before her, and she stays on her knees and keeps her hands behind her head. "When I arrived with Connor, I walked in on him beating her up."

A humorless laugh threatens to spill from my lips. So, she has quickly switched sides now that she has realized what a huge fucking mistake she has made? Does she really think that anything she says or does now will save her from my wrath once this is all over? Oh, she signed her death warrant the moment she put a gun to my brother's head.

Jace and Rico glance towards her, but Eli's gaze stays on me. I dip my chin in a barely perceptible nod, confirming that what Shelley said is true.

Lightning flickers behind Eli's eyes, and a muscle ticks in his jaw as he tightens his grip on the gun.

"Here's how this is going to go," Gabriel says.

"You're trapped in a cave with four guns pointed at you," Eli interrupts in a voice that could have made mountains tremble. "Do you really think you're the one in control here?"

"It doesn't matter how many guns you have," Gabriel replies, and I can hear the vicious smirk in his voice. "As long as mine is pointed at *her*. How the fuck are you top of your class if you don't even realize that the guy with the hostage is the one in control of the situation?"

I wince as he digs his fingers even harder into the sides of my neck.

Eli's finger twitches on the trigger. "I will break every one of your fingers and rip your fucking tongue out unless you—"

"No, here's what you're going to do," Gabriel cuts him off. "All five of you are going to put your weapons on the ground. That includes those knives that your psychopath of a brother is holding. And then, all of you are going to back out of this cave. I will follow with Raina. Then you will tie each other to trees outside. And then I will leave. Once I'm safe, I will send Raina back to you."

"Like hell—"

"Or I shoot her in the head right now and take my chances. Your choice."

Connor's eyes meet mine, and we share a look that requires no words. We both know that if Gabriel leaves *with me*, I will not make it back. His plan to get us to kill each other failed, but he is still going to try to take his revenge in any way he can. If he disappears with me, he is not going to honor his word and let me go once he's safe. He's going to torture me to death for our father's crimes.

While keeping his eyes on me, Connor says something to Eli in such a quiet voice that we can't hear it from over here.

"No whispering," Gabriel barks.

He shoves his gun against my skull, forcing me to bow my head slightly, as if to make a point, before he pulls it back to its previous position. His fingers keep digging into my neck with enough force that I know they will leave bruises.

"Put your weapons on the ground and back out of here," he demands. "I won't ask you again."

Desperation flickers in Eli's eyes. My brother has no doubt told him what will happen if they let Gabriel leave with me. But they can't just shoot him either, because I'm in the way.

Right now, there are only three possible outcomes. One, Gabriel shoots me in the head and they shoot him afterwards. Two, they shoot through me to kill Gabriel. Three, they let Gabriel, who will kill me as soon as we're alone again, leave with me. Which means that there is no way out of this that doesn't involve me dying in some way.

What a fucking inconvenience.

I blink as a sudden idea hits me like a lightning bolt. It's risky and ridiculous and absolutely insane. But insanity is a dear friend of mine so it might just work.

My brother and all four of the Hunters notice the sudden expression on my face. But they thankfully keep their features blank so as to not give anything away. While Rico takes it upon himself to distract Gabriel by asking questions about how this retreat he's demanding should work, I lock eyes with

Eli. He's the best shot out of all of them, and I trust him to get this right.

While holding his gaze, I tap my finger against the side of the gun I'm still holding. It's pointed down at the ground, so Gabriel hasn't deemed it a threat. Once I'm certain that Eli has seen the discreet gesture, I covertly tap my foot a few times. His expression doesn't change, but I'm sure he understands. He has to.

Then I use my other hand that I have been holding pressed over my aching ribs to tap one finger against my body and then point to the right. Since Gabriel is standing behind me, he can't see what my fingers are doing. And besides, Rico is keeping him busy with questions about the retreat.

Eli's chin lowers in a nod so shallow it's barely a movement at all.

My heart leaps into my throat. He understood. And we need to do this now, because Rico is running out of excuses to keep him talking.

With my pulse thrumming in my ears, I shift my right hand discreetly. The gun is still pointed at the ground, but now it's in a slightly different position from before.

I feel like I'm going to throw up. I'm not a good shot. But even I can't miss from two feet away. Right?

If I miss, this is going to turn into a blood bath. I don't fear my own looming death, but I'm not the only one who would die here if bullets start flying.

Swallowing, I try to push down the flare of nervousness rippling through me.

Rico casts me a look.

We're out of time.

I resist the urge to close my eyes.

Instead, I clench my jaw.

And fire.

The sound of the gunshot is so loud inside the cave that it seems to tear the very air apart.

One moment, Gabriel is telling Rico to shut up and put their fucking weapons down. The next, my bullet slams into his right foot.

A cry rips from his lungs, and he loosens his grip on my neck just enough for me to yank my head to the right.

It takes Gabriel a second to realize what I have just done. But it's a second too much.

Another bang echoes between the stone walls as Eli pulls the trigger.

Gabriel's head snaps back as the bullet hits him straight in the forehead.

I rip myself from his grip and scramble to the side. Every bone in my body aches from the beating I took, but I can't even feel it anymore because there is so much adrenaline thrumming through my veins right now.

Eli rushes forward while Gabriel's body hits the ground with a dull thud. The gun in his hand clatters as it falls from his fingers and bounces across the stone.

Then Eli's arms are around me.

"You're okay," he presses out. And I swear I can feel his heart pounding against his ribs and all the way into my own chest as he holds me tightly. "You're okay. You're okay." Then he draws back and locks wild eyes on me. "Are you okay?"

I draw my fingers down his cheek as I smile up at him. "Yes."

I'm sure my body will be aching all over tomorrow, but right now I feel fucking invincible. Like I could breathe fire or toss a mountain across a chasm. It's probably because of all the adrenaline pumping through me, but I love the feeling nonetheless.

An insane laugh bubbles from my throat, and I wiggle my eyebrows at Eli. "Good shot."

Eli lets out a whooshing breath and shakes his head at me. "Fuck, that plan was insane."

Before I can reply, Connor appears next to me. His gray eyes search my face. They don't possess the same wild intensity as Eli's, but I can still read the emotions swirling in them clear as day.

"Are you really okay?" he asks.

"Yes." I flash both of them a grin. Then I narrow my eyes as I turn towards the woman still kneeling by the wall. She has hunched forward a little after those shots were fired. "And I'm going to feel even better after I kill *her*."

Shelley whips her head around.

Smug satisfaction blows through my soul when I notice the fear in her eyes as she looks at me.

Eli lets out a dark chuckle and sweeps his hand towards Shelley. "Knock yourself out."

"No, wait!" Panic flashes across her face as she scrambles around so that she's facing us instead. Still on her knees, she holds up her hands while the six of us stalk forward and form a semi-circle before her, cornering her against the wall. "Look, things got out of hand and—"

"Shut up," I snap as I come to a halt in front of her. "You put a gun to my brother's head."

Eli and Connor flank me, with Kaden on Connor's other side and Rico and Jace on Eli's.

"Do you have any idea what I do to people who threaten my family?" I demand.

Shelley opens and closes her mouth a couple of times, but

no sound makes it out. Her desperate eyes flick back and forth across all six of us.

With a cruel smile on my lips, I pull out a small vial from one of my pockets. "When you swallow this, you're going to *wish* that you had died from the first poison I gave you." With my eyes locked on her panicked ones, I jerk my chin. "Hold her."

"No, wait!" she blurts out. "Please, I'm begging you. I can help. I can tell the instructors what happened here. That you killed him in self-defense."

"Give me one reason to care."

"Killing someone is strictly against the rules. You'll get expelled for it."

"Again, why should I care about that?" I take a step towards her.

Panic crackles across her features again, and she drops down, pressing her forehead to the ground. "Please, please, I'm begging you."

"She has a point," Connor says.

Stopping my advance, I glance at him and arch an eyebrow in silent question.

He shrugs. "The Hunters will be fine because they're, well… them. But you and I play by different rules. If we can't convince the university that this was in fact self-defense, we will likely be expelled."

The words hang in the air between us, filling in the parts that Connor doesn't speak out loud. If he gets expelled for this, he won't be able to restore our family name.

I blow out a breath.

"Fine." I slide the vial of poison back into my pocket and drag a hand through my hair. "You get to live so that you can tell everyone that this was self-defense."

Shelley snaps her head up. Relief floods her eyes as she nods frantically. "I will. I will."

"Good." I flash her such a savage smile that she actually flinches.

And in that moment, when she is kneeling before me like that and looking up at me with that delicious fear in her eyes, I realize that I quite like playing God.

46

ELI

"How long is Jace going to sulk?"

Amusement pulls at my lips, and I glance down at Raina. "Probably only for another week or so."

"A week?" She raises her eyebrows at me. "This morning, I swear I could hear him lamenting all the woes of the world from halfway across the house. You sure a week is all it takes?"

"Yeah." I chuckle. "He has a very short attention span."

After we killed Gabriel and finished threatening Shelley, we made our way towards the edge of the forest where most of the instructors were waiting. We had to report Gabriel's death, and hand Shelley over to the university staff, as soon as possible. And get Raina to the hospital wing.

My blood boils every time I look at Raina's face. Bruises cover her skin like a gruesome patchwork of red and purple. That fucker Gabriel didn't deserve the quick and painless death he got. He deserved to be taken to a secluded location and then tortured for weeks on end until he was begging me for death.

But with his gun to Raina's head like that, there hadn't been a lot I could do without putting her life at risk. I'm still trembling just thinking about that absolutely insane plan Raina came up with in the cave. One mistake, and it could have ended in disaster. Though I have to admit, it did make my heart swell knowing that she trusts me so completely that she's willing to let me shoot a bullet mere inches from her head.

Sun beats down on the stone steps where we stand watching the parking lot. A gentle breeze pulls at Raina's long black hair, making it flutter slightly around her face. I once more study the bruises marring her skin and the now stitched-up wound from where Gabriel hit her with his gun.

Another wave of fury roars through me, and I once again curse the fact that he got such a clean death. Though I suppose it would have been difficult to explain it to our instructors otherwise.

When we showed up at the edge of the woods with a beaten-up Raina and a terrified Shelley, we told them what had happened and that Gabriel was now lying dead in a cave. Because of the death, the instructors decided to cancel the tournament. Which is why Jace is currently sulking like a toddler.

He had been looking forward to his first tournament for weeks and doesn't understand why one person's death would change anything. We're all hitmen, after all. And to be honest, I agree with him. If Raina hadn't been hurt, I would've felt the same way. But when she was standing next to me with blood and bruises on her face, all I wanted to do was to throw her into the car and race her to the hospital wing. Which is exactly what I did. Fortunately, nothing was broken. But the bruises, that it turns out she has all over her body too, are bad enough.

"At least she kept her word," Raina comments, and nods towards a figure crossing the parking lot.

I follow her gaze and find Shelley hurrying across the pavement while throwing nervous looks over her shoulder. When she sees us, her steps falter, and she almost stumbles into the car she was sneaking past. Snapping her head back around, she picks up the pace.

"Yeah, at least she did," I reply.

Shelley kept her promise and spilled everything to the instructors. She told them about how Gabriel had planned to kill both Raina and Connor as revenge for the role Harvey Smith had played in his father's death, and how he had recruited her to help. Then she had explained exactly what happened in the cave and that shooting Gabriel had been the only option.

All six of us had been called in to give our statements too, but since everything lined up, there were no repercussions for Gabriel's death. Rather the opposite, in fact.

Since Blackwater has a strict no killing policy, Gabriel's surviving family members were forced to pay a steep fee for his crimes. And Shelley was expelled because of her involvement.

A smirk blows across my lips when I think about the look on her face when she heard the news. Or even better, the look on her face once she received a phone call from her father.

Because he didn't want to fall out of favor with our family, and by extension the Morelli family, he apparently decided to take preemptive action and disown Shelley. As far as I know, he has three other kids, so cutting Shelley off was apparently not too difficult for him. It made my fucking day, though.

As did watching Raina threaten her in that cave.

Tearing my eyes from the fleeing Shelley, I look down at Raina while a sly smile plays over my lips. "Did I tell you just how fucking hot you looked back in that cave?"

She snorts and glances up at me before raising her eyebrow in a dubious expression. "When I had a gun to my head?"

"No." I give her shoulder a soft shove before pulling her back to my side again so that I can lean down and kiss her temple. "When you were threatening to kill Shelley."

A smug expression spreads across her features, and she grins at me. "You thought that was hot, huh?"

"Very."

Her green eyes glitter with mischief. "If you want to see it again, I could always try it on you."

I place my fingers on her jaw, tipping her head back, as I lean down and whisper against her lips, "Careful now, princess."

She chuckles against my mouth, her warm breath dancing over my skin. I steal a gentle kiss from her lips and then draw back again.

When I meet her gaze, there is such a serious expression in her eyes that my stomach flips. She studies me as if she is trying to read answers behind my eyes.

"Earlier, I told you that my heart belongs to you," she begins.

Dread floods my chest. Fuck, is she going to take it back? Because I couldn't protect her from Gabriel? Because I failed to do the one thing that I should have—

"But you never said it back," she finishes.

Stunned surprise flutters through me, and for a moment, I can't get my mind to work properly. I told her that I can't breathe without her. Is she seriously unsure of whether I love her or not?

"So I just wanted to know where we stand." She shrugs, as if it's no big deal. But I can practically feel the tension in her body. "Does your heart belong to me as well?"

"No."

Hurt flickers in her eyes, and she starts to turn her head away. I quickly grab her chin and turn it back to me.

"My heart does not *belong* to you." I hold her gaze with a steady expression. "You *are* my heart."

Her mouth drops open slightly, and emotions flood her eyes. It makes my own chest tighten too. Leaning down, I kiss her deeply. Her body melts into mine.

Then I draw back.

And she punches me in the chest instead.

Her small fist doesn't actually manage to cause any pain, though. In fact, she shakes out her hand as if she felt that punch more than I did.

"Bastard," she snaps. "That's for making me worry." She glares up at me. "I actually believed you when you said no at first."

I trail my fingers from her jaw and down her throat. "Then I guess I will have to spend the rest of my life teaching you even more thoroughly just how much every single part of me belongs to you. Because know this, princess..." I wrap my hand possessively around her throat and then bend down to speak my next words directly against her lips. "I am never letting you out of my sight again."

"Good. Now, are you going to kiss me or—"

An explosion tears through the air.

I shove Raina behind me, shielding her with my body as fire erupts from halfway down the parking lot. Flames lick the air and smoke billows up from a red sportscar, making hellish light dance over the other cars around it. Even from this distance, I can see Shelley's already dead body lie slumped in the driver's seat.

Stunned shock pulses through me as I stare at the scene before me.

A smug chuckle comes from beside me.

With my eyebrows raised, I turn to face Raina again. Light from the flames dance in her eyes and a villainous grin decorates her lips as she watches the fire consume both the car and the now dead woman inside it.

"Was this you?" I ask, surprise still clanging through my skull.

Raina's grin widens. Then she looks up at me with a mock innocent expression. "It really is fascinating what a few chemicals can do."

A baffled laugh tears from my chest. Cupping her cheeks, I lean down and kiss her wicked mouth while the flames from the explosion dance in front of us. My entire chest is pulsing with incredulity and crazy fucking love for this absolutely unhinged woman.

Pulling back, I drape my arm over her shoulders instead. And then we stand there, watching the fire burn like the devils we are.

Raina Smith is insane.

But she is my insanity.

And my salvation.

EPILOGUE

ONE YEAR LATER

My hands are steady as I use a small brush to spread poison across the synthetic skin that covers Eli's palms. He leans his hip against the white marble counter beside the sink, his eyes fixed on the door to the small private bathroom we're currently occupying. Light from the golden lamp in the ceiling casts his face in a warm glow and makes him look even more handsome in his sharp black suit.

I'm just about to dip the tiny brush into the vial of poison again when a buzzing sound interrupts. Raising my eyebrows, I glance down at the phone in Eli's pocket.

He sighs. Tearing his eyes from the door, he looks down at his hands, which he can't use right now, and then back up at me.

"Want me to check it?" I ask.

"Yeah. It might be the Morellis. If they're calling off the hit, it would be good to know that before we kill him."

I chuckle. "Agreed."

After carefully setting down the brush on the small lid to the poison bottle, I slide my hand into Eli's pocket. And just because I'm a wicked little bitch, I brush my hand over his cock on the way. A shudder rolls through his body.

Narrowing his eyes, he fixes me with a pointed stare. "Careful now, princess. Just because I can't touch you right now doesn't mean that I can't still fuck your brains out right here in this bathroom."

I snicker and wiggle my eyebrows in challenge. But before either of us can do anything about it, I pull out the phone and look down at the name visible on the screen.

Worry blows across Eli's face. "It's Rico."

"Want me to answer it?"

"Yeah. Kaden told me that, with me having graduated and the new first-years who have arrived, the Petrov family apparently outnumbers our family back at Blackwater this year. And those crazy Russian fuckers have apparently been coming at them hard. Something might have happened."

Sliding my finger across the screen, I answer the call and then put it on speaker so that Eli can hear it too.

"Hey, Rico," he says. "You're on speaker because Raina is currently spreading poison across my hands."

"Eli, I..." Rico begins but then trails off. "Wait, what? Poison? Do you need help? Is she trying to kill you?"

"I heard that," I mutter.

Eli chuckles. "No, it's for a hit. We're out of state for another stealth mission since Connor and that forgettable face of his is still stuck in New York for that other high-profile job." He smiles at me, knowing how relieved I am that our family's reputation has now been restored. But then worry etches his face again as he focuses on the phone. "What's going on? Is it the Petrovs?"

"What?" Rico replies, sounding very distracted. "Oh, the Petrovs. No, we'll handle those morons. Don't worry."

"Then what is it?"

"I found her."

Eli's eyes widen. "*Her* as in...?"

"Yeah. The girl who saved my life that night." Even through the phone, I can hear the stunned incredulity in his voice. "She's here. At Blackwater."

"Do you want me to come back? To help you... do something? Anything?"

"No. No, I, uhm... I just wanted to tell you because—" He stops and instead lets out an exasperated groan. "Aw, fuck. The Petrovs are here. I'll call you back."

Before Eli can answer, Rico ends the call.

I raise my eyebrow in silent question, but Eli just shakes his head. "He'll call back later. And besides, we have a man to kill."

"True."

After slipping the phone back into his pocket, I finish coating the synthetic flesh with a thin layer of poison. It's the kind of fake skin that actors use, so it will hold up well enough for our plan.

"Alright, done," I say while screwing the lid back on the small bottle. "As soon as you brush your hand over some part of his skin, the poison will start to take effect. I recommend the back of his hand, since you can get away with bumping into that without raising suspicion, but any part of his body works. After the poison begins seeping into his skin, the clock starts ticking. He'll be dead after about three hours, give or take."

"By which time, we will be long gone."

"Exactly." I smirk back at him. "Aren't you glad I dropped out of Blackwater to be your partner in crime?"

"You're my partner in *everything*, not just crime."

"Aww, aren't you sweet."

Mischief glitters in his golden eyes. "And besides, you sucked at everything back at Blackwater and failed every class, so they practically begged me to take you off their hands."

"Watch it, asshole." I narrow my eyes at him, but can barely suppress the amusement in my voice. "Don't forget I'm the one with the poison."

He holds up his hands and flashes me a sly smile. "Except now, I have it too." Before I can retort, he chuckles and then jerks his chin. "When we get back to the hotel, I will be showing you exactly how glad I am that you dropped out of Blackwater to be my partner in crime. But for now, get your ass up on that counter."

I raise my eyebrows at him. "Why?"

"Because we need a plausible excuse for why we've been in this bathroom for so long. So I want you to look freshly fucked when we walk back into that gala."

Heat ripples through my stomach at his words and at the look in his eyes.

After putting the poison and the rest of my equipment back into my small purse, I brace my palms on the white marble counter and lift myself up so that I'm sitting on it with my legs dangling over the edge.

"Pull your dress up, princess," Eli orders.

I curl my fingers in the smooth green silk and slowly slide the skirt of my dress up my legs until it's bunched around my waist.

Desire flares to life in Eli's eyes as his gaze travels up my bare legs. Then something flickers across his face as he reaches my pussy. "No panties."

His words are both question and statement and accusation all rolled into one.

I just grin back at him in challenge.

"How am I supposed to concentrate on my mission now that I know you're walking around next to me with no fucking panties on?" Eli demands, his voice a low growl.

My grin widens. "I don't see how that's any of my problem. My part of this mission is already done."

"Oh, the things I will do to you when we're back at the hotel."

A thrill races down my spine.

"Spread your legs," Eli commands.

Adjusting my position on the counter, I lean back on my elbows and spread my legs wide for him. His eyes darken. My heart skips a beat at the sight.

Even after an entire year, Eli's feelings for me still haven't dimmed in the slightest. In fact, they seem to grow stronger every day. Every time he looks at me, his breath catches a little and his eyes pulse with both insatiable lust and unending love. It's an incredible sight.

I suck in a gasp as Eli drops to his knees and draws his tongue over my pussy. He chuckles, making his warm breath caress my sensitive skin. A shudder rolls through my body as Eli swirls his tongue around my clit before taking it into his mouth.

Pleasure washes through me, and I let out a moan.

Leaning back, I rest the back of my head against the mirror behind me. The pleasure inside me grows as Eli rolls my clit between his lips and then slides his tongue down to my entrance.

A whimper spills from my mouth, and I curl my fingers on the cold marble as he pushes his tongue inside me.

Closing my eyes, I breathe deeply through my nose as he licks and sucks and nips at my clit and my throbbing pussy until I feel as though my brain is going to explode. Tension thrums inside me, begging to be released.

"Oh, fuck," I gasp out, my thighs clenching and my pussy aching with need. "Eli."

He swirls his tongue around my clit again.

I suck in shallow breaths as I soar towards that orgasm.

One more second. One more stroke. One more—

He stops.

Pulling back, he gets to his feet.

I blink, feeling completely disoriented by the loss of his lips and the release that never came.

When I raise my eyes, I find Eli smirking down at me like the fucking villain he is.

"Eli..." I say, my voice low and full of warning.

"Yes, princess?"

"Finish what you started."

"I might. Back at the hotel room." His eyes glint and the devilish smile on his lips grow. "If you beg me for it." Chuckling, he jerks his chin towards the door. "Now, come on, princess. We have a mark to kill."

With my eyes narrowed, I glare at him while I slide off the counter and smoothen my dress down over my legs again. Turning around, I face the mirror. My cheeks are flushed and my hair is slightly messy from where I leaned against the mirror. I do actually look freshly fucked.

Huffing out a half amused, half disgruntled breath, I pick up my purse and start towards the door. Eli follows since he can't touch anything right now.

"I hate you," I announce as I reach for the lock. "Bringing

me to the edge like that and then not letting me come is cruel, you know."

"Yes, well, you should've thought about that before you decided to torture me by not wearing panties tonight." He flashes me a wicked smile. "And you know you love me."

A soft laugh escapes me. Shaking my head, I unlock the door and pull it open. After moving across the threshold, I hold it open for Eli as well so that he won't have to touch it. The people outside take one look at my flushed face and exchange knowing smiles.

"Yes, unfortunately I do," I reply as Eli falls in beside me and we start back into the glittering ballroom. A smirk tugs at my lips as I glance up at him. "But not as much as you love me."

Eli matches the sly smile on my face, but his eyes are pulsing with deep emotions as he brushes a kiss against my temple. "That's right."

Joy sparkles in my chest as we turn back to the elegant ballroom before us. People wearing shimmering dresses and expensive suits fill the entire space. We drift through the room for a while before we spot our target.

After exchanging a look, we start towards the man we're about to kill.

From the outside, we look like any other couple in this room. But we're not normal. And we never will be.

A ruthless hitman and an unhinged chemist.

We are a match made in hell.

But thankfully, hell is our kingdom.

And we love it here.

BONUS SCENE

Do you want to know how Eli rewards, and punishes, Raina when they get back to the hotel room after that assassination? Then scan the QR code to download the exclusive spicy bonus scene:

Made in United States
Orlando, FL
03 July 2025

62633086R00215